ANGEL
IN MY
POCKET

ANGEL
IN MY
POCKET

ILENE COOPER

FEIWEL AND FRIENDS

NEW YORK

A Feiwel and Friends Book
An Imprint of Macmillan

ANGEL IN MY POCKET. Copyright © 2010 by Ilene Cooper.
All rights reserved. Printed in December 2010 in the United States of America by
R. R. Donnelley & Sons Company, Harrisonburg, Virginia.
For information, address Feiwel and Friends,
175 Fifth Avenue, New York, N.Y. 10010.

Library of Congress Cataloging-in-Publication Data

Cooper, Ilene.
Angel in my pocket / Ilene Cooper. — 1st ed.
p. cm.
Summary: When seventh-grader Bette finds an angel coin she puts it in her
pocket and forgets it but soon the mysterious and kind Gabby moves into her
building and helps her face her major losses, and then the coin connects her with
three classmates who all find new ways to believe in themselves.
ISBN: 978-0-312-37014-5
[1. Talismans—Fiction.   2. Interpersonal relations—Fiction.
3. Self-actualization (Psychology)—Fiction.   4. Loss (Psychology)—
Fiction.   5. Schools—Fiction.   6. Chicago (Ill.)—Fiction.]
I. Title.   PZ7.C7856Amm 2011
[Fic]—dc22   2010034756

Book design by Susan Walsh

Feiwel and Friends logo designed by Filomena Tuosto

First Edition: 2011

10 9 8 7 6 5 4 3 2 1

www.feiwelandfriends.com

For all my angels in the here and the hereafter

ANGEL
IN MY
POCKET

I

There was a pile of money on Bette Miller's kitchen table. It was mostly change, but Bette spotted crumpled dollar bills, even a couple of fives and tens, hidden among the quarters and nickels.

Before getting down to the serious work of counting, she picked up handfuls of silver and let them fall through her fingers, enjoying the satisfying clinks as the coins touched the rest of the change. It made her feel rich.

Barbra, Bette's older sister, had collected the money in a canister for a campus charity, standing in the street and knocking on car windows to get donations. Now Barbra slid into the seat across the table and commanded, "Don't do that, Bette. Money is dirty. Full of germs."

Bette sighed. Since their mother died, Barbra had become a fountain of clichés that she spouted frequently. "Be careful on the Internet, perverts are lurking there." "Don't go out with wet hair, you'll catch a cold." "Never forget to wash your hands after you touch raw chicken."

"Why would I be touching raw chicken?" Bette had asked in horror the first time Barbra had offered that particular dictum.

"Well," Barbra had replied with resignation, "we'll probably have to cook for Dad. And he loves chicken."

And, in fact, in the last couple of years, Bette had touched more slimy, slippery raw chicken than she cared to remember.

But don't touch the money, it's dirty? What was next? Look both ways when crossing the street?

"How can I count the money without touching it?" Bette asked crossly.

"We're not supposed to count it. The machine at the bank will do that. I'm just supposed to separate the bills from the coins and pick out all the funny stuff."

"Funny stuff?"

"Canadian coins. Pieces of paper, lint. Stuff that will clog the machine." Barbra pulled a white orb from the money. "A Necco Wafer."

Bette made a face. "Who would throw candy into a charity can?"

Then something caught Bette's eye. She thought it was a quarter at first, but an oddly shaped one. She looked at it, puzzled. And then she looked at it again. It wasn't a real coin after all. Embossed on one side of the pewter-colored token was an angel in profile, wings unfurled, hands clasped in prayer, its long gown sweeping the bottom of the talisman.

She held it for a moment, and the angel seemed to grow larger, slightly rising from its hammered background.

"What's that?" Barbra asked.

Bette was loath to give it over, but there was no way to avoid her sister's outstretched hand.

"Oh, cute," Barbra said, handing it back.

"I can keep it?" Bette asked, her heart beating a little faster.

"Sure, why not?" Barbra asked curiously. "It's just a good luck charm. You've seen them in stores. Sometimes they're in a little basket up by the cash register."

Had she seen a token like this before? Bette wasn't sure.

Maybe she had seen ones with four-leaf clovers, but she didn't think she had seen one with an angel on it.

Barbra began sweeping the money into a cloth bag. "Well, I guess I'd better take this over to the bank. Then I have to get back to campus."

Bette got up and took their glasses to the sink. She still wasn't used to Barbra going to Northwestern University and living in Evanston. Of course, Evanston was only an El ride away from Chicago. Well, two, really, since you had to change from the Red Line to the Purple Line. Not that she had visited Northwestern since she and her dad had dropped off Barbra and a considerable amount of stuff at her dorm at the end of August. When would she have the chance anyway? Barbra had been home every Saturday or Sunday for the last six weeks.

"I'll walk with you," Bette said, grabbing a jacket.

"Don't you have anything better to do?" Barbra asked, putting the sack of money into her backpack.

Bette scowled. Don't *you* have anything better to do, Miss College Freshman, than make sure that the refrigerator is stocked with enough frozen hamburgers for the next week? But that wouldn't be very nice, because Bette knew that Barbra did have better things to do, or should anyway, like studying or rushing a sorority or trying to find a boyfriend, and the reason that she came back on weekends was to make sure that her sister and father were all right.

What really made Bette angry was that the honest answer to Barbra's offhand question was, No, I don't have one thing better to do than to walk you to the bank.

When they got outside, Barbra looked around and said happily, "I love October. It's the most gorgeous month."

"It's getting cold," Bette said, zipping her jacket.

"But, Bette, look at the sky," Barbra said, standing still for a moment. "It's the color of those Popsicles Mom used to buy. And the leaves. They're amazing. Scarlet, orange, even purple."

"Don't you know why leaves change color? It's because they're not making any more chlorophyll. That's what keeps them green and healthy. The colors mean they're getting old and dead."

Barbra looked at her sister strangely. "Bette, do you realize a lot of what you come up with relates to death?"

Bette snorted. "I wonder why?" If anyone ought to be able to understand why Bette's thoughts drifted to death as easily as leaves slid across the sidewalk, it should be her sister. Barbra had experienced the shock of their mother's death just as she had.

First had come the phone call from the hospital. A car accident on a rain-slicked road. Then the rush to the hospital. The call to their father's cell phone went directly to voice mail, so the girls had taken a cab to an unfamiliar neighborhood close to where the accident occurred.

Pessimist that she was, Bette assumed that she would have plenty of bad moments in her life, but if she lived to be 110, she couldn't believe that there could be any worse than those desperate minutes that had ticked by during that taxi ride to the hospital. It had been endless yet surprisingly quick, a time out of time.

She and Barbra had sat silently clutching hands. But even as she was conscious of the dirty ashtray smell of the cab, the collected tones of the NPR reporter coming from the radio, what was most real were the images that pelted her, as incessant and random as the raindrops hitting the taxi's windshield.

Her mother in a hospital bed. Was she scarred? Were her bones broken? In pain? Bette knew her mother was alive because at least the person at the hospital had told her that. But

Bette could tell from the urgency in the woman's voice that might not soon be the case.

Once they had arrived at the hospital, everything had been confusion. Barbra had taken over with Bette standing mutely beside her. At first no one could tell them their mother's whereabouts. When they finally located her in the emergency room, the hospital personnel didn't want them to see her. After Barbra demanded they be taken to her cubicle, a nurse had tried to prepare them.

The nurse's quiet words about internal bleeding and contusions on Mrs. Miller's face, and the effects of the pain medication, hadn't been enough. *Who is that woman?* Bette had thought, when she saw her mother, looking small and frail and years older; hooked up to so many blinking, beeping machines they seemed to be more a part of her than her arms and legs. Only her golden red curls spread out against the white cotton pillow—the same curls Barbra had been lucky enough to inherit—were familiar.

Looking back, Bette was eternally grateful her mother had lived long enough for her to say good-bye. Bette could not, *could not* have stood it if they had arrived at the hospital only to find their mother gone. It would have been like falling into a vortex with nothing to hold on to.

Even with the chance to whisper "I love you" in her mother's ear and feel the squeeze of her hand, it was bad enough. Bette walked through the funeral and, for a good many of the days afterward, behaved as if she were an actress in a play titled *The Grieving Daughter*. She knew she was supposed to feel terrible, and some part of her, maybe the part that was crying hysterically, did feel terrible. But most of the time, she felt like she was floating on the ceiling, staring down indifferently at Bette sobbing and Barbra trying to take care of everyone and her shell-shocked father looking as if he had been the one in a car accident.

And there had been times when she'd experienced the weirdest emotions. Like the stab of excitement before the funeral when she wondered if Peter Waugh, the best-looking boy in her class, would attend and maybe give her a sympathetic hug. So many people had come to the funeral, she didn't know if he came or not, and by the time the eulogy was over, she had completely forgotten about the hug.

Although it had been nearly two years since her mother had died, Bette sometimes felt as if she were still just playing a part, that of her now-almost-thirteen-year-old self. Other times her life seemed all too real. How could it not, when it was filled with such mundane things like making dinners, straightening up, washing clothes, and watching television. Lots and lots of television.

"Bette," Barbra said, breaking into her sister's thoughts, "do you know what's happening with the apartment?"

Bette turned to look back at their two-flat greystone. Their near-north Chicago neighborhood was full of dwellings that looked similar to theirs, but Bette had always known that her two-flat was special, and that was because of the hearts. Some anonymous mason, perhaps artistic, perhaps just bored, had carved a series of small decorative hearts into the smooth, fog-colored stone, and they circled the width between the upstairs and downstairs apartments. Bette had been so proud of those hearts when she was a little girl. Her mother told her lots of different stories about the hearts, but they all ended the same way: "And then the hearts looked for the happiest house in Chicago, and when they found it, they pressed themselves into the stones!"

Bette walked alongside Barbra toward the bank. "It hasn't been empty that long. Just a couple of months."

"Bette." Barbra had the you're-not-five-years-old-anymore tone in her voice. "Dad's probably losing a thousand dollars a month by having the apartment empty."

"We have plenty of money," Bette replied defensively. And it was true. Her mother, a very efficient accountant, had made sure she had lots of insurance. What the family had lost with their mother gone, ironically, had been replaced with more money than the family had ever had before. Not the kind of money you could run your fingers through, though. The kind you put away for college educations. And in the case of her father, enough money to give up his law practice and buy part interest in a jazz club.

"Well," Barbra continued with a frown, "I don't like you living in the building with an empty apartment right below you. It's not safe."

Bette wanted to tell her sister she was used to being by herself, that she didn't get scared at night at all anymore. Well, not much anyway. But she knew that anything she said would just make Barbra feel guilty all over again about not living at home while she went to college. Barbra's guilt spilled over everything enough as it was. Bette felt plenty guilty herself because she knew that if it wasn't for her, Barbra would have felt free to go to college in Claremont, California, or to Duke in North Carolina, two of the other schools that had accepted Barbra.

"Has he even put an ad in the paper?" Barbra asked as they walked toward busy Chicago Avenue.

"I don't know," Bette replied.

"Well, I'll ask him about it the next time I talk to him."

"Whenever that is," Bette muttered.

Barbra didn't say anything for a moment. Then she asked, "Isn't he getting home any earlier? He promised he would try."

If getting home early meant before midnight instead of an hour or so after, then Bette guessed he was trying. But she didn't want her sister to worry. "Yeah, he's getting home earlier."

"I wish he'd never bought into that jazz club," Barbra fretted.

This was an old conversation. Both sisters had been shocked when several months after their mother's death, their father had told them he was going to put law aside for a while and buy part interest in a jazz club located in a hot area, the city's South Loop.

"But I thought you liked being a lawyer," Bette had said at the time.

"I do. I did. But your mom's passing, well, that made me realize I shouldn't waste time doing something I just *like*. I want to do something I *love*. And I love jazz."

Bette hated when her father referred to her mother's death as her "passing." The word made it sound as if she had somehow just been passing through their lives instead of being the most important part of it.

"Besides," her father said, "I'll be working mostly at night. That way I can be around in the daytime for you."

It hadn't worked out that way, and sometimes Bette had her suspicions that her father had known that when he had started his glorious undertaking. First the club needed to be renovated, and her father had to be there to oversee the contractors who were enlarging it and installing the sound system. Then he had to learn how to book the talent, and after that he had to hire and train the staff. It added up to a father who wasn't around much during the day or night.

"Do you want to come in with me while I make the

deposit?" Barbra asked as they came to the bank on the corner. "Then you can walk me to the subway."

Bette's day may have been empty, but trying to fill a little of it by waiting in a bank so she could take a two-block trip to a dark, dank subway station seemed pathetic even to her.

"No. I have to stop at the bookstore," Bette said, gesturing vaguely in the direction of the used bookshop across the street.

"Okay, then," Barbra said, giving Bette's bushy, brown hair, so unlike her own, a pat. "I'll call you tomorrow."

After Barbra disappeared inside the bank, Bette thought for a moment about actually going into the bookstore. If her father wasn't generous with his time, he was certainly generous with money, and Bette always had enough to buy whatever she wanted, and usually that was books.

But her sister was right, it was a beautiful day, and Bette felt like being out in the sunshine rather than under the glow of fluorescent lights. Taking the long way home, she first strolled down Clark Street, peeking into shop windows. Bette wished she liked clothes more. There were such cute things to buy, but when you were thin and plain, it didn't seem like clothes would help much.

She pushed by several shops catering to urban babies and was tempted to go into one of the ubiquitous coffee shops that vied for customers, but she didn't really want to sit by herself. When she got closer to home, she passed one of her favorite landmarks in the neighborhood, the Church of the Holy Comforter. When she was little she thought the name was so funny, because she had a comforter on her bed with several holes in it, one in particular that she liked to make bigger by poking her finger into it.

It took her mother several tries to explain that the Holy

Comforter was really the Holy Ghost, and then she had to go into a whole long, rather unwieldy explanation of who that was, since the Miller family was spectacularly unreligious. Which made things rather uncomfortable after her mother's death. Mr. Miller was so lost in his own grief, Bette didn't think she could go to him with her questions, so she had gone to Barbra.

"Where do you think Mom is?" Bette had asked.

Barbra was startled by the question. "What do you mean?"

"Well," Bette began uncomfortably, "do you think she's in heaven?"

"Heaven?"

"Yes," Bette repeated. "In heaven with God. And the angels."

"I don't know, Bette. I'm not sure I believe in heaven. Do you?"

How was she supposed to know? She was only ten. And she had only the vaguest idea about heaven. Just what she had picked up in books. She tried hard to remember if her mother had ever talked about heaven, but nothing came to mind. Bette hated the idea that her mother was just lying in the cold ground, but she couldn't conjure up that better place that people talked about. With no immediate answers forthcoming, Bette had tried to bury the questions along with her mom.

But she did go inside the Church of the Holy Comforter sometimes. The church, made of the same gray stone as her house, was imposing from the outside, but inside it was dark and warm with stained glass windows that glowed when the sun shone through them. When she was inside, she felt peaceful.

Bette paused in front of the church. She stuck her hands in her jeans' pocket, and she felt the angel token nestled there. It was much warmer than her hands. Hesitating a few seconds longer, Bette felt herself drawn inside, but she decided she was too tired. She wanted to go home.

Picking up the pace, Bette walked to the greystone. When she was within a block of her house, she looked up and something caught her eye. Was that a light in the downstairs apartment? She was sure it had been dark when she and Barbra had left for the bank, and surely no one had been inside since then. For a moment the light shone more brightly, then in an instant it was gone.

II

Bette's school, Odom School, was a magnet school. A magnet school was, well, like a magnet. It drew kids from different parts of the city.

There were many different kinds of magnet schools in the school system. Some focused on languages, others on literature or science. Odom's magnet program was performing arts. Most kids who went to magnet schools had to travel, sometimes long distances, to get there. Bette was lucky. She had had to pass a test to get into the performing arts program, but Odom was her neighborhood school, too, so it was just three blocks away.

Of course, just because performing arts were at the center of the curriculum, didn't mean that the students could avoid the regular subjects every other kid in the world had to take.

Once, some friends of her parents had come to visit with their gum-chewing daughter. Apparently, they'd mentioned Bette's school. "So let me get this straight," the girl said, gum cracking, "you go to a school where you stand around and sing all day?"

Bette had bristled. "We take the same classes you do. Math, English, science."

But what she didn't admit was that all those subjects were infused with a lot of music, singing, and acting. The school's manifesto listed two main points: *to encourage students' creative and artistic expression, and development of interest in visual arts, music, dance, and drama.* And two: *to integrate the arts into classroom instruction.* Sometimes getting "creative expression" into the curriculm was a stretch.

In the first grade, they learned basic arithmetic by putting on a little play in which a group of children played the sum while other kids added themselves and others were subtracted. Even at age six, Bette thought it was lame.

In the fourth grade, while studying American History, the two fourth grade classes enacted the meeting of the Second Continental Congress, which culminated with the signing of the Declaration of Independence. The teachers were thrilled because there were fifty-six delegates, which meant enough parts for everyone. But as it turned out, there were only a couple of good ones: Jefferson, Franklin, John Hancock. Bette had gotten stuck with the role of Stephen Hopkins of Rhode Island. About all she did was wear a wig and sign the fake Declaration her teacher had prepared.

By the time Bette was in the fifth grade, each student was offered special training. The obvious choice for Bette was singing. Her mother had enrolled her in the performing program because she thought Bette might grow up to be a famous singer. Bette's household was very musical. Even though her parents had jobs that dealt with dry things like numbers and case law, what they both loved was music, all kinds.

Mr. and Mrs. Miller had met at a rock concert, and after they got married, they had kept going to concerts of all kinds. It was jazz that moved Mr. Miller the most. Mrs. Miller loved women singers, everyone from Ella Fitzgerald to k. d. lang to Fergie. One of Bette's fondest memories was listening to her mother sing along with all sorts of incredible ladies while she was cleaning the house, even though, truth be told, her voice wasn't that great. Mrs. Miller had even named her daughters after two of her favorites singers, Barbra Streisand and Bette Midler, which Barbra in particular hated because Streisand, wanting to be unique, had dropped the second *a* in Barbara. Unfortunately, no one expected Barbra Miller to have a unique spelling of her name, so it was consistently misspelled the conventional way. She spent a lot of time correcting it. To add insult to injury, Barbra didn't even like Streisand's music. She preferred reggae.

Bette wasn't crazy about her name either. Nobody was named Bette—or Betty, as some people pronounced it, which really drove her crazy. But she didn't mind Bette Midler's music, even though it was totally retro. She liked singers who could belt out a song. The first one she personally remembered was Annie. Well, the girl who sang the role of Annie in the musical. As a little kid of three or four, Bette had listened to Annie sing "Tomorrow" so many times that even her music-loving parents came to despise that song.

Despise, that is, until Bette sang it for the first time. And it wasn't as if she was singing along with the CD. She just climbed up on the couch, using an old baby bottle as a microphone, and sang "Tomorrow."

Her parents had been sitting next to the fireplace reading quietly. "I thought at first we were just hearing the CD again," her mother used to tell her. "Then I realized there was no music. Just singing. Just you!"

Bette still smiled when she thought about how many times her mother had told her that story.

So Bette's talent, the thing that made her feel special, was singing. Her parents had been so happy when they found out that Odom School had a program for the arts, and thrilled when she had been accepted. School had been great until fifth grade, when her mother died in March. After that, Bette hadn't felt like singing.

All the teachers at school had been totally sympathetic. The principal, Mrs. Wu, had taken her aside and told her she shouldn't even think about singing until she was ready. When she hadn't felt like singing in the sixth grade either, the staff grew concerned and recommended delicately to Mr. Miller that perhaps Bette needed some "help."

Mr. Miller had said, "Sure, sure," and for a short time, Bette had met with a grief counselor. The conclusion they came to was obvious. Singing reminded Bette of her mother, and so she didn't want to sing. The counselor told her to take it slowly.

Well, now Bette was in the seventh grade, and she still didn't feel like singing. She didn't know how much more slowly she could take it.

At the beginning of the year, she was assigned to Mr. Perry for her special training in singing. Her dream, back in the fourth grade, had been to one day play the part of Annie. She figured she had a head start, since she already knew the words to every song. But that dream had died the day her mother did. Now she had to figure out how she was going to get through a performing arts curriculum when the last thing she wanted to do was perform.

Bette's class before lunch was with Mr. Perry. It was a group class with all the singers in the seventh and eighth grades. Since they weren't doing solos yet, and there were plenty of kids in the class, it wasn't terribly noticeable that Bette's singing was really nothing more than mouthing the words. But on the Monday after Bette found her angel medallion, Mr. Perry had made an announcement. "I have some wonderful news."

The kids looked at one another surreptitiously. They would be the judge of that.

"As you know, part of Odom School's mandate is to partner with our many arts organizations in the city."

Uh-oh, Bette thought. It was true that the school tried to use the resources of the Chicago arts community to bolster their curriculum. Sometimes that worked out great: free tickets to shows and concerts. But more often than not, it meant second-rate actors and musicians coming to speak to them about working in show business. Sometimes they'd come alone, sometimes in small groups. The faint odor of failure often wafted around them.

After one particularly bad speech by an out-of-work actor, one of the kids had raised his hand and asked, "If your career is going so good, what you doing here?" Mrs. Wu had been really mad about that.

But as Bette began listening more closely to what Mr. Perry was saying, it seemed as though this time Odom School had scored a coup.

"As some of you know, the Maple Tree Theater is a small but prestigious theater group that has a space on LaSalle Street. They are going to let us use their theater to put on a production of *Big River,* which is a musical based on Mark Twain's book *Huckleberry Finn.*"

Ah, Huckleberry Finn, Bette thought. That fit. *Huckleberry Finn* had been an option on their summer reading list.

"Maple Tree is going to mentor the production," Mr. Perry continued. "It's going to provide help with the staging, music, wardrobe, sets, and one of the actors from the company is going to direct the play. Sometime in the spring, we'll take it to the stage."

Bette looked around. She could see the other students were impressed. At lunch, all the talk was about *Big River.*

If she hadn't had enough losses in her life, Bette's best

friend, Vivian, was being homeschooled this year because her asthma was so bad. It was decided that she ought to take it easy at home, work with a tutor, and practice her piano, the talent that had gotten her into Odom. Bette had friends at school, but no one who was going to take Vivian's place. That was one of the downsides of going to a magnet school. Most kids lived so far away, it was hard to get together anyplace but school. But you can't go to a school for seven years and not have people to eat lunch with.

The three kids Bette ate lunch with were Andy Minkus, Vivian's twin brother, Lucy Washington, and Fred Engberg. Andy played the violin, even more exquisitely than his sister played piano. Lucy was a singer. She had a great big voice that had been honed singing gospel music in her church. Fred could do it all. He was an actor, dancer, singer, probably the most talented kid in the school. And they were all excited about *Big River.*

"It's going to be a real production," Fred said with satisfaction. "Finally, I'm going to get to be onstage."

Fred harbored some resentment against his parents, who wouldn't let him try out for any professional gigs. Some of the kids at their school did audition, but Fred's parents didn't want him going that route yet.

"How do you know you're even going to get a part?" Lucy said with an innocent look. She was just giving Fred the business. If anybody was going to get a part, it was Fred.

He didn't even bother to answer her. "I wonder how many tickets we can get? Maybe I can get an agent to come see me."

"There's gotta be something for me to do," Lucy said, waving around her tuna sandwich. "I saw a movie about Huck Finn. One of the main characters is that black guy, Jim. I don't remember, but he must have had a wife or something."

"Most of the characters in *Huckleberry Finn* are male," Andy told her.

"Well, there better be some part for me," Lucy replied with a scowl.

"So are you going to try out?" Fred asked Andy.

"I don't think there's a role for a short violin player," Andy said drily. "But they're going to need music."

An uncomfortable silence settled over the group. Bette knew the next obvious question was *Bette, are you going to try out?* But nobody wanted to go there.

Bette cleared her throat. Everyone looked at her expectantly. "Does anybody want anything from the counter? I'm going to get some milk."

With as much dignity as she could muster, Bette got up and went to the small counter that served cold sandwiches, chips, and drinks. Odom School was old, so old that when it had been built, most mothers didn't work. Kids went home at noon, and their mothers fed them a hearty lunch before sending them back to school for a grueling afternoon of learning.

Now, of course, no one went home for lunch, but Odom didn't have room for a real cafeteria. Instead, kids either brought something from home or they grabbed a sandwich at the rather sad-looking lunch counter.

Bette didn't really want any milk, but she bought some anyway in case her friends were watching. Then, feeling awkward, she decided to go drink it outside. There was a small playground where the younger children played and benches where the older kids sat in cliques and gossiped. Since it was nippy, most of the regulars were inside, leaving some of the benches empty. Bette plopped herself down and stuck her hands in her pockets for warmth. For the past few years, Barbra had always made sure she had a hat and gloves when the weather turned. *Note to self,* Bette thought. *Try to find a pair of gloves before January.*

Bette watched some of the young kids keeping themselves warm by running around. Sitting alone on another bench, she noticed, was Joe Garcia. He took up one of the few school slots allotted to neighborhood kids, usually because there was some compelling reason they had to attend the school closest to their home. Bette had no idea what that reason might be. Joe was in the seventh grade, too, but Bette had never exchanged even a hello with him. If pressed to come up with a word to describe Joe, the one that came to mind was "lurker." He always seemed to be hanging around, just watching things, looking belligerent. Some people said he was a bully, but he had never bothered Bette.

As Bette stuffed her hands in her pockets more deeply, she felt something nestled in the corner. It was her angel coin. Pulling it out, she examined it once more. Funny, she didn't remember putting it in her jacket. In fact, she distinctly remembered putting it on her dresser, so she wouldn't lose it.

"What are you doing here?" she quietly asked the angel, as she held the coin in her hand.

Bette didn't expect an answer, and there wasn't one.

Were there really angels? Bette wondered. She sort of hoped so, but if there were angels, didn't that mean there was a God? After her mother died, Bette had wished she did believe in God, if only to be mad at him. But she didn't really believe, and in the part of her where belief might have been, there was only a void.

Her life was empty and still—inside and out.

III

Bette walked home after school, and when she got close enough to see the greystone, this time there was no doubt that a light really was shining in the downstairs apartment. Bette didn't know whether to be scared or not. She had a vague memory of her dad saying that the apartment needed to be painted before it could be rented. Maybe there were workmen inside.

The old tenants had moved out in July. They were nice enough, a young couple named Ben and Mary. Ben worked at Mr. Miller's law firm, and Mary was a librarian. Even though Barbra and Bette had tried not to bother them very often, it was good to know that if their father wasn't home, there were two adults just downstairs. One evening, Barbra had almost sliced off the tip of her finger while cutting bread; Ben had driven her to the hospital and stayed with her till she got stitched up. Mary, who was a pretty good baker, was nice about bringing them cookies, which made a welcome change from the store-bought kind.

Barbra had been furious when Ben and Mary bought a house in the suburbs and left right before she was supposed to leave for college.

"Barbra, they're having a baby," Bette pointed out reasonably.

"So? People in the city have babies." Barbra looked around busy Chicago Avenue, where she and Bette were shopping. "There's one," she said, gesturing to an infant in a buggy. "There's two more," as a stroller passed with twins.

"But they probably think they need more room."

"The apartment has three bedrooms," Barbra muttered. "Just like ours. We didn't have to move to the suburbs, and we grew up fine."

Bette knew that Barbra didn't really begrudge Ben and Mary a house in the suburbs, if that's what they wanted. It was all about feeling guilty that she was leaving Bette alone in the greystone.

Even though Bette kept telling Barbra that she'd be fine, and Mr. Miller had new locks put on all the outside doors, truth be told, Bette was not thrilled about being home alone, especially at night. Days weren't too bad. She'd come home after school, watch some really stupid talk shows while she did her homework, and then would make herself dinner. Well, "make" might be too glamorous a word. Often she just poured cereal into a bowl and added milk. Sometimes she'd take something Barbra made out of the freezer and nuke it in the microwave. Then she'd watch more TV, go online, or read until she was tired enough to fall asleep.

It wasn't that she was afraid, exactly. She knew the neighbors on both sides, and their phone numbers were pinned to the bulletin board in the kitchen. Mr. Miller had given Bette a cell phone, and as he'd promised Barbra, he did try to get home before midnight, which was a bit of a sacrifice since the last set at the club started at eleven. He didn't know that Bette put her phone under her pillow if he wasn't home by the time she went to bed, where she practiced punching 911—just in case.

As Bette walked up the front stairs, she peeked in the big picture window of the first-floor apartment. There was no one in the living room, but to her surprise, there was now a couch across from the fireplace, and a floor lamp, which was lit, and there were a couple of cardboard boxes on the floor. She crooked her neck trying to peer into the dining room, but no one was there. Then she heard something coming from the apartment. Singing. But it was so faint, she couldn't make out the tune.

Now what? Bette thought with a scowl as she clomped up the stairs. Should she knock on the door? Bette knew Barbra would kill her if she did that without knowing who was inside. For a few fleeting seconds, she thought about phoning her sister, but she hated to do that. Barbra would just come flying into the city as fast as the El could carry her. There was nothing to do but call her father.

But when Bette opened the door to her apartment, she was surprised to see her father was home, waiting for her.

"Dad, there's somebody downstairs. I guess you know that?" Bette asked, though she hoped that it really wasn't a question.

"Yes, that's why I came home, so you wouldn't be scared."

Bette didn't want to tell him that she had been scared already, at least a little.

"Do you want a cup of tea?" her father asked, heading into the kitchen. Bette followed him. Normally, she would grab a water or stir up some instant hot cocoa, but having her father home this time of day was such a novelty: If he wanted tea, tea it would be.

Bette sat down at the kitchen table while her father filled the electric teakettle with water. It wasn't as if Mr. Miller was never around. He was there in the mornings before she went to school, and he tried to be home on Saturdays, though sometimes he had to get to the club early to solve scheduling problems or meet with the artists coming in to play. If he had errands to run, he always asked Bette whether she wanted to go with him. She usually said no, making up some excuse about homework or going to visit Vivian, just because she couldn't endure the awkward silence in the car. Sometimes, though, she went, just because she couldn't bear to say no all the time.

She once asked Barbra if their dad had always been so uncomfortable with his children. Sometimes it was hard for Bette to recall what life had been like in the time she thought of as "Before." "I mean, he used to take us to the zoo and stuff. I remember that. And we had fun when we went on vacation, like when we visited Grandma and Poppy in Arizona."

Barbra looked a little wistful. "He always worked a lot. But Mom made sure he spent time with all of us. It was her he really loved being with."

Bette wasn't sure she agreed. Barbra seemed invested in this idea of her parents having a great romance, but there had been plenty of fights. That Bette did remember. They always made up, though, and he had never gotten angry at his girls. Even when Barbra had been a bratty high schooler and had started smoking, among other appalling things, and her mother was pulling her strawberry curls out of her head—Barbra had put greens streaks in her own curls—Mr. Miller just tried to reason with Barbra or make her smile, whenever possible. Now her father not only didn't bother trying to make Bette or Barbra smile, he didn't smile much himself.

Mr. Miller brought the mugs of tea to the table, Bette's laced with the half-and-half he knew she liked.

"Thanks, Dad," Bette said, watching the steam rise from the fragrant drink. He seemed lost in his own thoughts, so Bette, to move the discussion along, asked, "So who's the new tenant?"

"Well," began Mr. Miller, running his hand through his short, dark hair. "She's not exactly a tenant. In the sense that a tenant pays rent."

Bette couldn't help herself. "Have you told Barbra that?"

Though it still wasn't a smile, Mr. Miller's mouth did move in some approximation of turning upward. "I haven't spoken to her quite yet. She's not going to be happy about the loss of income, as she keeps calling it. But, the thing is, this woman showed up at the club. I think she's a friend of Marty's, the piano player. Anyway, we got to talking, and she said she was new in town and was having trouble finding a place she could afford." Her dad's brow creased with puzzlement, as if he was trying to remember exactly how everything had gone down. "So I told her about the apartment, and we agreed she could move in on a temporary basis."

"Just like that?" Bette put down her mug in disbelief. After hearing that he was basically giving away the apartment, Bette had assumed the woman was an old friend.

"Well, she's going to be doing some work in the apartment. She's going to paint it . . ."

"She's a painter?" Bette asked.

"Uh, I don't think she's a professional housepainter if that's what you mean. But she's going to be doing some other things, too."

"Like what?" Bette asked suspiciously.

Mr. Miller sipped his tea. "She's going to be looking out for you."

"For me!" Bette practically shrieked.

"Now Bette . . ."

"Let me get this straight. Some woman wanders into the club, someone who is *maybe* a friend of Marty's, and you talk for a while, and you invite her to move downstairs, rent free I might add, and in return she's going to be my nanny." Bette's voice practically quivered with disgust.

"Not a nanny. She's just, well, going to be available for you. And she's going to paint the apartment," he finished haplessly.

"But, Dad . . ."

Mr. Miller tried to regroup. "Bette, I've been really uncomfortable about leaving you here alone at night. It's not safe. It's not like Gabi is going to be babysitting you. But she'll be here if something comes up, an emergency, or if you just need someone to talk to."

"Why would I want to talk to her? I don't even know her."

Mr. Miller warmed his hands on his mug. "She's really easy to talk to. That's the funny thing. We spoke for about an hour, and I felt like I'd known her forever."

Bette didn't know what to think. This wasn't like her father at all. True, he hadn't been the most practical of guys since her mother died. Giving up his law practice and buying the club hadn't made much sense. Still, it wasn't like him to invite a stranger into their lives.

"Dad, what if this doesn't work out? Then you've got this woman . . ."

"Gabi."

"Fine, Gabi. You've got her in the apartment, and you've got to get her out. It looks like she's already moved in. There's a *couch* in the apartment," Bette said, her voice rising, as if the couch were proof positive what a stupid idea this was.

"We've already talked about this," Mr. Miller said. "If you don't like Gabi, then I'll go to Plan B."

"What is Plan B?"

"I haven't gotten quite that far yet."

Bette slammed her mug down and bolted for her room. Her father followed her in before she could shut the door on him.

"Look, Bette," he said, "I know this doesn't sound like it makes much sense, but I'm going with my gut here."

"I think you have a stomachache," Bette said, throwing herself down on the bed.

"Just meet her," Mr. Miller implored. "See what you think. She's a very nice person. Very nice."

Bette lifted her head. She had a thought. "Are you . . . interested in this woman?"

Mr. Miller looked confused for a moment. Then he frowned. "No. No, not the way you mean. It's just that she seemed so sincere."

"I'm sure most con artists do," Bette replied witheringly. Really, had her father never watched a crime show?

Sitting down at the side of her bed, Mr. Miller said softly, "I know this looks like it's come out of the blue, but I need you to give it a chance. I've been so worried about you being alone."

He had? This was news to Bette. Up until a few minutes ago, he had never said a word about being worried.

"Gabi came in, and she wanted to help. It was like an answer to a prayer."

"Wait until Barbra hears about this," Bette muttered.

Her father suggested that they bring a pie down to Gabi as a welcome-to-the-greystone offering. Of course, first they had to come up with a pie, since the only thing in the cupboard that was even close was a box of graham crackers. So with some coaxing from Mr. Miller, Bette accompanied him over to the Jewel Foods, where they picked an apple pie.

"Okay, so we'll go downstairs as soon I change my shirt," Mr. Miller said when they got home.

Change his shirt? Her father liked to dress well, and there was nothing wrong with the shirt he was wearing, as far as she could see. Once again the suspicion seized Bette that her father might like this Gabi person a little more than he was letting on.

She looked down at her own outfit. Hoodie with a peanut butter stain on the sleeve from yesterday's dinner; jeans that probably should have been washed on Saturday; running shoes with a hole in the toe. Yeah, she looked fine.

Still, Bette couldn't say she wasn't nervous when she went downstairs, pie in hand. But she did her best to put on a bored "whatever" attitude. It would show Gabi that while she may have persuaded Mr. Miller to give away his apartment, Bette was impervious to her charms.

That changed the moment that Gabi opened the door and ushered them into the apartment with a smile.

There was something dazzling about Gabi, but what exactly that was Bette couldn't quite say. As she shyly handed her the pie, the immediate impression Bette had of Gabi was an odd one. She seemed so, well, clean. Pristine even. Her straight blond hair, which fell into a long Dutch bob, was almost as white as the blouse she was wearing. Lacy, with wide, pleated bell sleeves, it was the color of new-fallen snow. The blouse topped just a pair of ordinary jeans, although, unlike hers, they had obviously been washed and creased before last Saturday. Considering that it was quite cool in the apartment, it was a bit strange that Gabi wore no shoes, but her toenails, like her fingernails, were painted with a clear polish, which added to the freshness of her look. Her only jewelry was a thin, gleaming gold necklace.

"Hello, Bette," Gabi, said, taking the pie Bette offered. "How lovely of you to bring this."

Bette looked up into Gabi's eyes. For some reason, she expected them to be blue, but they were a deep gray, the color of the earth before the spring flowers bloomed.

"Shall we have some?" Gabi asked. "I can rummage up a few paper plates."

"We haven't had dinner yet," Mr. Miller demurred. "We just wanted to come down and say welcome."

"I can't eat this all myself," Gabi said with a musical laugh. "Perhaps you'll come back later."

"Well, I have to get to the club." He looked a bit pleadingly at his daughter. "But maybe Bette will join you."

Gabi turned those penetrating gray eyes on Bette. "What about it, Bette?"

This could all be so easy. Bette could see that now and, yes, understand how her father had come to offer the apartment. There was a warm pull to Gabi that made you want just to relax and be drawn in. But her earlier resolve kicked in, and Bette decided to put up a fight. She stood up a little straighter, wanting to prove to Gabi, and herself maybe, that she was no easy mark.

She tore herself away from Gabi's glance and looked around the apartment. "How did you get furniture so quickly?" she asked abruptly.

"Bette!" Mr. Miller said, clearly thinking her question was rude.

But Gabi replied, "On my way here, after your father so kindly offered me the apartment, I saw a Goodwill store. I stopped in, and I bought a few things, the couch, among them. Luckily, a delivery truck was just going out, and since the apartment was so close, the Goodwill people agreed to deliver it right away."

Bette felt her face redden. Gabi had offered a perfectly reasonable explanation for her furniture. And that only made her madder. "I can't come down later. Sorry. I have things to do."

"Oh, like what?" Coming from someone else, the question would have seemed confrontational, but when Gabi said it, in her clipped accent, which was impossible to place, it simply exuded interest, perhaps laced with a bit of concern.

Bette decided to play mysterious. "Just . . . things."

"Then let's chat now, even if it's for a moment." Gabi waved her hand toward the couch, and Mr. Miller dutifully sat down. There was nothing for Bette to do but plop herself down beside him.

Gabi pulled up an old wooden chair that Ben and Mary had left behind. Now that she had a moment to actually stare at Gabi, Bette was no longer sure how old she was. She had presumed that Gabi was about her dad's age. Now, looking more closely, she wondered if Gabi wasn't much older. Her hair seemed as much silver-gray as blond, and there was something about the look in her eyes that made Bette think of her grandmother. Then Gabi smiled at her, and her expression was so full of expectation that suddenly she looked younger, closer even to Barbra's age.

Weird, thought Bette.

"So . . . ," Gabi began, and Bette felt herself stiffening again. Here we go. *What grade are you in, what's your favorite subject . . . the same questions every adult asks.*

Instead, Gabi continued, "Don't you find life interesting?"

"Interesting?" Bette repeated, thrown off by the way the query had veered. It took a moment for Bette to organize her thoughts, but when she did, her answer came out forcefully. "No, actually, I don't."

Gabi raised an eyebrow.

"It alternates between monotonous and depressing, so no, I don't find it all that interesting."

Mr. Miller looked as if he were about to leap from his seat and phone her grief counselor.

Bette patted his hand. "Sorry, Dad. She asked."

Smiling at her affectionately, Gabi just said, "Interesting, of course, isn't synonymous with happy."

There was that sea-tide pull again, but once more, Bette fought it. "I know that," Bette replied. "Dad, I'm starving. Aren't you hungry?"

"Oh, sure." He rose, gave Gabi a small frown, and shrugged his shoulders. "We'll go out for dinner."

Bette politely reached out and shook Gabi's hand. "Nice to meet you," she said impersonally, but when Gabi's grasp produced an undeniable warmth in her own hand, it took every bit of acting talent Bette had to keep her expression passive.

"See you soon," Gabi said, heading toward the door.

The old childhood taunt came to mind. *Not if I see you first.*

Bette took some pride in this meeting. She hadn't succumbed, even though that's what her father—and Gabi—had clearly expected. But if interesting wasn't synonymous with happy, being proud of her defiance wasn't the same as being happy either.

Come to think of it, she wasn't sure she could remember exactly what happy was.

IV

Bette had pinned her hopes on Barbra. She was sure that when her sister came over for her weekend visit, she would talk some sense into their father, and Gabi would disappear.

It had taken an act of will not to visit Gabi for the rest of the week, but by hanging out at the library, even doing some grocery shopping one day, Bette had managed to avoid stopping in at Gabi's after school. It annoyed her that she even wanted to. Yet she couldn't deny the longing she felt when she saw the cheery light coming from Gabi's apartment, brightening the fading autumn dusk, or when she was confronted with the mouthwatering smell of cookies or pies—who knew what home-baked delectable—wafting in the air every time she tromped up the stairs.

Somehow, some way, Barbra would put an end to all this, Bette told herself. She'd make Gabi's magnetism dissipate; turn the aroma of spun sugar and heady vanilla, floating through her kitchen window, into the stinky smell of cooking cabbage.

Of course, that's not what happened. Barbra took one look at Gabi and fell in love. After some tea and sympathy and a few butter cookies on her regular Saturday visit, Barbra had bounded upstairs, looking more relaxed than Bette had seen her in, well, years.

"You're so lucky, Bette. She's terrific."

"She's living downstairs, free," Bette reminded Barbra for probably the fourth time since her sister had arrived. "And *how* am I lucky?"

Barbra looked out the living room window, at what Bette wasn't quite sure. "I think she can show you things."

But before Bette could even ask her what great things Gabi was supposed to show her, Barbra was putting on her jacket. "I almost wish I could stay here and get to know her better."

"Well, why don't you?" Bette asked with a scowl.

Barbra didn't even have the decency to look guilty. "I can't. I have a paper to write for economics, and a major French test I'm studying for . . ."

"Fine. Fine. I hope it's not all work and no play." Bette was trying for sarcasm, but since she did truly hope her sister was enjoying college, the comment lost its edge. Barbra suddenly looked shy.

"Barbra," Bette asked with shocked realization, "are you dating somebody?"

Barbra had had lots of boyfriends in high school. Accent on the "friends." But she had never dated anyone, although Bette was aware of several guys who had crushes on her pretty sister, and she had teased her appropriately. Bette didn't know why Barbra hadn't gotten serious with anyone, but if she had to guess, she thought it might have something to do with breaking up. What was the point of getting close to someone when inevitably he'd leave—one way or another. That's how she would have felt anyway.

"I wouldn't say 'dating.' Not at all," Barbra said. "We've gotten together to study a couple of times."

Bette flopped down on the sofa. "What's his name?"

"David."

Oh, Barbra was gone for this guy. Just the way she said

Da-vid, two simple syllables, it was like she was having a Zen moment.

"So are you going to have a real date?"

Barbra turned away and pretended to look for her backpack, which, as both of them knew, was hanging on the front doorknob, because that's where Barbra always put her backpack.

"Oh, well, we're going to the movies tonight. David wants to see that new football movie."

"Sounds romantic."

Barbra straightened up and shed some of her embarrassment. "He's nice, Bette. Maybe sometime you'll meet him. If this goes anywhere."

After Barbra left, Bette curled up in her bed so she could analyze her feelings. She had recently read about the technique in a style magazine in the dentist's office. The article said that if you quietly and objectively looked at your feelings, they didn't seem so scary. At the particular moment she'd picked up the magazine, her thoughts had been about having a cavity filled. Intense examination concerning her feelings about a guy in a white coat coming at her with a drill, she knew, would not calm her down in the least. But Barbra's visit was so unsatisfactory; Bette decided this seemed a good time to try the technique, because her feelings were certainly in a jumble.

Was she sad, mad, or just lonely? As she examined the words, each made a little scratch on her heart. The longer she looked at the words, saw them from different angles, perhaps, they did get a little less frightening. But they didn't become any less painful. She idly wondered how memories, which you couldn't touch or feel, could hurt just as much as a drill at your tooth.

Enough! Bette told herself. All this introspection was getting too boring, too claustrophobic. *Think about something else,* she commanded. *Move on to something practical.* Looking around, Bette had an inspiration. What could be more practical than redecorating her room? Barbra, who loved playing with fabrics and paint swatches, had asked her a couple times if she wanted to do something to her room, but it had always seemed like too much trouble, or maybe she wasn't quite ready for another change.

Even though she had been only six or seven at the time, she could clearly remember her mother coming home with the pink-and-white-striped coverlet and matching pillow shams that still adorned her bed.

"Doesn't it remind you of peppermint, Bette?" her mother had asked with a happy smile. "So fresh and clean."

Bette really wasn't a fan of peppermint candy—it wasn't sweet enough—but she did like the way her bed looked after it was made and had asked her parents if the walls could be painted pink as well. Now, however, if one was to extend the candy metaphor, it seemed as if the peppermint had had one too many licks. The spread and pillowcases were faded, so were the painted walls. Shabby. Sitting up, Bette thought about what colors she would use for her room if she did it over. Blue was her favorite, but green might be nice. Clean green. Fresh, like peppermint, but in a different way. Bette was sure her father would spring for redecoration, but then her thoughts drifted back to how excited her mom had been all those years ago, bustling into Bette's room with the crisp bedclothes. "She picked these out. For me," Bette murmured, smoothing a crease in the coverlet.

Glancing at the clock on her dresser, Bette saw that it was only one o'clock. Usually Barbra's visits lasted later into the afternoon. Mr. Miller was at the airport, picking up a trio who was starting a gig at the club tonight, and though he said he'd take her out for dinner, Bette wondered if he'd make it.

Well, there was no point in just suffocating in her pink room. Maybe Vivi was up for a visit. Unfortunately, with Barbra not around to drive her anymore, she'd have to take two buses. One down Clark Street, then another east on Fullerton to where Vivi and Andy lived in a spacious high-rise apartment overlooking Lake Michigan. Depending on how the buses were running, it would take at least an hour, but Bette had nothing if not time.

After exchanging texts with Vivi, Bette dug into her jeans' pockets to see how much money she could muster up. She felt the satisfying smoothness of dollar bills, thirteen dollars altogether, and in the other pocket, a handful of change. And the angel medallion.

Bette sat down on the edge of her bed and gently rubbed her thumb over the embossed angel. "You again?" Bette said aloud. How did this little token keep winding up in her pocket? Bette looked at it more closely. You could barely see the angel's face, and Bette wished she had the magnifying glass her grandmother sometimes used when reading tiny print. Was the angel smiling?

Well, what the heck, Bette thought. Maybe she should just keep it with her as a good luck charm. She shoved the token back in her jeans and headed out the front door.

"Hello there."

Darn. Bette had hoped by going out the front, Gabi wouldn't catch sight of her from the kitchen window. But here was Gabi leaving her apartment, her knitting in a plastic bag under her arm.

"Hello," Bette muttered.

"Where are you off to?" Gabi said in her musical voice.

Bette sighed. She had been raised to be polite. "I'm going to visit my friend Vivian."

"I'm going to the knit shop." She lifted the bag a little, and Bette could see something made of a grass-green yarn inside.

"Do you knit?" Gabi asked conversationally as they walked along.

"Uh, we learned in third grade, but I wasn't very good at it."

"What are you good at?"

"Singing," Bette replied before she could censor her answer. Why had she said that? Well, it was true of course, at least it used to be. No need to share with Gabi the fact that she hadn't sung in years.

"I like singing, too," Gabi said. "It lifts the heart, don't you think?"

Lifts the heart? Who said things like that? "I suppose," Bette reluctantly answered. She glanced sideways at Gabi. Today she was wearing a sky-blue sweater, light and lacy. "Did you knit that?" Bette asked.

"Why, yes, I did."

Bette had to admit she was impressed. For someone who mostly wore her sister's hand-me-downs or got stuff at the Gap, this was prettier than any piece of clothing she had seen someone wearing outside a magazine. And to think Gabi had made it herself.

"Perhaps you'd like to try knitting again?" Gabi suggested. "I'm quite a good teacher."

Bette could feel herself buttoning up. "No. That's okay. I don't really have time." As soon as she said the words, Bette cringed. Might Gabi guess how much of that particular commodity she had available? Bette glanced over at Gabi: If there was pity or, even worse, a smile on her face, she would be tempted to smack her. Not that she would of course, but definitely tempted.

But Gabi's expression was something else, and Bette couldn't put her finger on it. Thoughtful, yes, but tinged with a sparkle of inquisitiveness. "Time is interesting, isn't it, Bette? It should go at regular pace, minute by minute, hour by hour, day by day. Yet sometimes it races and sometimes it drags as if it's pulling a mountain."

Bette felt her own heart race a bit. She had thought similar things herself, but she was surprised someone else had noticed. Her life before her mother had died, in retrospect, had moved along briskly. Since then, it was as if most days were in slow motion.

"Time is very important, though," Gabi continued. "It's really all we've got. So if you think you're wasting your time, you're squandering something that's quite precious."

Bette was momentarily panicked as all the ways she had wasted her time recently flooded her memory. The easiest way to distract herself was to argue with Gabi.

"How can time be the only thing we've got? We've got a million things. Books, bedspreads . . ."

Gabi cut her off. "Before you go through all the *b*'s, let me just say books can get lost, bedspreads tear or fade . . ."

Bette stared at Gabi. Did she know Bette had just been caressing her own fading bedspread?

". . . any possession can go missing."

"What about family?" Bette argued without thinking. "We've got them."

Gabi said simply, "Do you?"

Duh. If anyone should know family can disappear, it was

Bette. And not just her mother. Barbra for all practical purposes was gone, and even though he lived in the same house, so was her dad.

"But as ephemeral and obstinate as time can seem to be, you do have it. And it can be put to use."

This conversation was getting way over Bette's head. She looked at Gabi's knitting. "Did that take you a long time to knit?"

Smiling, as if she knew that Bette was just changing the subject, she answered, "I'm a fast knitter."

"What is it?"

"A comforter."

Bette jerked her thumb to her left, toward the stone building they were passing. "That's the Church of the Holy Comforter."

"There's a coincidence. If you believe in coincidences."

Bette asked curiously, "You don't?"

Once again there was that Christmas-bells laugh. "No. I believe in plans."

Really, thought Bette. Gabi turning up at her father's club was pretty coincidental. Or was it? Maybe people who needed rent-free apartments had to have a plan.

"Well, I leave you here," Gabi said. "The knit shop is just down the street."

Bette nodded and watched as Gabi strode away. As she pulled her cell phone out of her jacket pocket to check the time, her angel medallion fell out. Scooping it up, she noticed Joe Garcia sitting on the stoop in front of a nondescript apartment building next to the church. He was tossing a small jackknife, watching it stick in the ground, picking it up almost robotically, and throwing it again.

Feeling unsettled, Bette considered walking across the

street to avoid Joe, but he looked up and saw her, as he grabbed the knife once more. "Hey," he said.

"Hi," Bette said, hoping to just walk past him.

"What's up?" Joe asked.

Oh, great, Bette thought. Now, Mr. I-Never-Say-a-Word wants to talk. "Not much."

Apparently, Joe didn't have that many conversations. Clearly, he didn't know that after one person said something, it was then the other person's turn. An awkward silence ensued. Instead of taking this as a welcome reason to extricate herself from the situation, Bette searched for something else to say. She wasn't quite sure why. True, now that she had a moment to actually look at him, not just as a part of the school wallpaper, he was kind of cute. His dark hair curled in the way she wished her own did, and the tight, taupe turtleneck he was wearing showed off broad shoulders. "So," she said, "you live next to the church?" What an idiotic thing to say, she told herself as soon as the words passed her lips. Simply inane.

Joe glanced over at the church as if seeing it for the first time. "Yeah."

"It's a nice church." Okay, now it was official. Could she sound any stupider? Despite the chill of the day, Bette could feel tiny beads of sweat forming inside her blouse.

"Do you go to this church?" Joe asked with a frown.

Ah, a question. "No. That is, sometimes, I just go in there and sit."

"Why? If it's not your church?"

Joe wasn't looking quite so cute anymore. He looked belligerent. Almost angry. She almost said, "You don't own the church," but that sounded babyish, and besides, she didn't want to get into it with him.

"Joe . . ." A voice so thin called the name from a second-floor window that Bette wasn't sure she heard it, but Joe jumped up like a yo-yo pulled by its string. Without a word he turned and walked into the vestibule with its cracked black-and-white tile.

"So that was weird," Bette said later as she recounted the story to Vivian.

Vivi took a sip of the hot chocolate her mother had made for the girls. "He's a weirdo. His first day at Odom, he took Andy's best pen, and I had to steal it back from him. Then I *accidentally* stomped on his toe."

That sounded exactly like Vivian. Well, the old Vivi. That Vivi was one of the most in-your-face kids Bette had ever known. She was small, though not as small as Andy. Considering they were twins, except for their size and their clear, blue eyes, they didn't look a bit alike. Vivian was all gold and pink, a little doll like her mother; Andy had sandy hair and a substantial nose like his dad. But where Andy was quiet, Vivian always spoke her mind and didn't take anything from anyone. She was a fabulous piano player, and even though her asthma was bad enough to keep her wheezing and coughing, it never stopped her from doing much. She just ignored Mrs. Minkus, who was always telling her daughter to lie down and rest.

Then in June, the asthma had gotten really bad. Vivi had had to go to the emergency room several times and the doctor put her on a stronger medication. Her mother was so worried she talked to Vivi about being homeschooled. At first Vivi just laughed at her. Once the medicine had kicked in, Vivi had felt a little better, but it had some unpleasant side effects. The worst, as far as Vivi was concerned, was the weight it had put on her and the way it gave her face a round moon shape.

The effect on her appearance depressed Vivian. She got quieter, and when, during the summer, her parents had once again mentioned homeschooling, Vivi had agreed.

"Who's going to teach you?" a confused Bette had asked when Vivi told her about the plan. "Not your mother?"

Vivi's laugh held little mirth. Mrs. Minkus was nice, but she wasn't the brightest bulb in the closet. Dr. Minkus was smart, but his medical practice would hardly leave him time to teach Vivi. "They're getting a tutor for me."

"Are you sure you want to do this?" Bette had asked. "It's going to be kind of lonely, isn't it?"

Vivi had nodded listlessly. Bette had the distinct feeling that being alone was just what Vivian had in mind.

Once the decision had been made, Bette really noticed the change in Vivian. Before, she had fought the asthma, ignored it, even joked about it. (Sometimes there was a whistle in her breathing, and when there was, she'd try to push it into a tune like "God Bless America.") Now, she just stayed around the house, read, and practiced the piano. When Bette called, it was hit or miss whether Vivi would see her, and Vivi rarely called or texted Bette. As near as Bette could tell, the only person she regularly saw besides family was the tutor, who, Vivi reported, smelled like yogurt and got crumbs caught in his beard. As she sat watching her friend, Bette thought that time must pass very slowly for Vivian, too.

"Let's go out," Bette said, feeling suddenly restless.

Vivi shook her head. "What's wrong with staying here?"

"Vivi, you stay here all the time." Not that it was an unpleasant place to be. A wall-to-wall picture window in the living room looked out on the lake, and the large apartment had a decorator's flair that Bette admired.

"Where would we go?" Vivi asked.

"Well, we could go shopping." Wrong answer, Bette immediately realized. With the medication putting weight on Vivi, the last thing she would want to do is go shopping for clothes. "Or we could just go to the Starbucks around the corner."

"We're drinking hot chocolate now." Vivian held up her mug and took a sip as if to make the point. Then even she had to giggle a little. "Okay, this is really bad hot chocolate."

"Chocolate-flavored water. Hot," Bette agreed, though her voice was soft. She didn't want to hurt Mrs. Minkus's feelings.

Looking more determined than she had in weeks, Vivi got up off the couch. "Let's go get us some real hot chocolate."

When the girls told Mrs. Minkus the plan, she looked deliriously happy for a moment. Then her usual worried look settled on her face. "Bette, is it windy out?" Wind was bad for Vivian's asthma.

"No, not really."

Mrs. Minkus looked out at the panoramic view of the lake, hunting for whitecaps that might disprove Bette's words. "Well, you'll wear a jacket," she told Vivi.

"Yes, Mom, it's October. So I'll wear a jacket."

"All right, have fun then," Mrs. Minkus said, looking happy again.

"God, I feel like I've been let out of prison." Vivi giggled as she punched the down button on the elevator.

A prison of your own making, Bette thought about saying, but it felt so good to be going somewhere with her friend again—even if it was around the corner—she bit her tongue. She looked closely at Vivi while they waited for the elevator. It was undeniable that Vivian was, well, puffy. But it wasn't as if she looked freakish or anything. People who passed Vivian on the street probably still thought she looked pretty. The weight made only a dent in the all-American image of beauty that was a cascade of blond curls and baby-doll blue eyes. She could understand how Vivi didn't see it that way. How many times had Bette dispiritedly stared in the mirror at a chain of pimples breaking out on her forehead or contemplated her split ends as though they told the tale of her future? Looks mattered.

Once they got outside in the crisp air, Vivian glanced around as if she were stepping out of a dream.

"When was the last time you were outside?" Bette asked with a frown.

"Oh, I go out. It's just I'm usually with my mom or dad."

"So let's go out more. Every time I call, you say you're too tired to do anything."

"Well, I'm not tired today," Vivi said with determination. "Let's not go to Starbucks. There's a cute new coffee shop up on Armitage."

Armitage was almost a mile a way, but Bette was up for it if Vivian was. They started out, but after five or six blocks, Vivi, breathing a little heavily said, "I don't know, it's kind of far. Let's just go in here." She pointed to yet another Starbucks a few doors down.

"Good thing there's one of these on almost every corner," Bette joked, but Vivian just grimaced.

When they finally settled into worn but comfy chairs, with grande hot chocolates, sprinkled with cinnamon and decorated with swirls of whipped cream, Vivian needed time to regroup, but that didn't dampen her enthusiasm for hearing all about the mystery woman living in the downstairs apartment.

"I've got to see her," Vivian said.

"So come see her," Bette replied encouragingly. "I'm sure your mother would drive you to my house."

"Yeah, well, I will."

"How about tomorrow? Sunday would be a great day to come over." Sunday, otherwise known as the loneliest day of the week.

"Yeah, maybe." But the initial enthusiasm in her voice seemed to taper off a little. "So what's the deal with *Big River*?" Vivian said, changing the subject. "Andy is really in a twist about it."

"It's going to be a big deal," Bette admitted. "Almost everybody in seventh and eighth grade is going to be involved in some way or another." Immediately, Bette felt bad. Why had she said that? Vivian, the best pianist in the school, wasn't going to be involved. Then Vivian said something that brought her up short, kind of like a punch.

"Well, not everybody, Bette. You won't be in it. You don't sing anymore."

Bette stared at Vivi. Unaware that she had done anything other than speak the truth, Vivi was busy getting rid of excess calories by spooning whipped cream off her drink and onto the saucer.

The truth, Bette decided, was highly overrated.

V

Bette looked around the stuffy school auditorium. The custodian had turned the heat on too early, and kids were taking off extraneous clothing or fanning themselves with notebooks. Bette peeled off her own sweater, wishing momentarily that she had ironed the blouse underneath. Not that she ever ironed. But sometimes she thought it might be nice if she did.

The seventh and eighth grades had assembled during last period to watch a video of the Broadway production of *Big River*. "And Monday we're going to see how *Big River* was performed in a smaller venue with minimal scenery and staging." Mrs. Wu was fluttering with excitement as if she were going to be playing all the parts herself. Well, she always was the enthusiastic type.

Bette folded up her sweater and sat on top of it. It made the hard seat marginally more comfortable. She had to admit she was a little excited, too. Certainly, curious. How did you take *Huckleberry Finn* and turn it into a musical? It was pretty controversial as a book.

Adventures of Huckleberry Finn (Bette couldn't figure out why there wasn't a *"The"*) had been on the suggested summer reading list. Since it was only suggested, most of the kids hadn't read it, of course. But Bette, who had plenty of time on her hands, did. She knew the story. Tom Sawyer's un-couth friend Huck Finn and Jim, a runaway slave, find a raft and journey on the Mississippi River. Huck's running away from his drunk of a father, and Jim's trying to get North to freedom. Unfortunately, they get lost in the fog and head into the heart of the South. She had expected it to be a pretty good adventure story, but as Bette read on, there was so much more.

"Have you read this book?" she demanded of Barbra when she'd finished.

That was two weeks before Barbra started Northwestern, and she'd been frantically flinging clothes around her bed-room as she tried to figure out what to bring to school.

Barbra glanced at the paperback copy of *Huck Finn* Bette was waving in her hand. "They're letting you read this in seventh grade? I don't think I read it until high school."

"So what did you think of it?"

"Good. Great. An American classic." Barbra sounded as if she was repeating the blurb off the back flap. Clearly, her mind wasn't on *Huckleberry Finn*.

That was as far as Bette got with Barbra. She had surpris-ingly better luck with her father. That conversation had come out of desperation. It was one of those times when Mr. Miller, feeling he was neglecting Bette, had taken her out for dinner to a real restaurant instead of just grabbing something at McDonald's.

This night he had chosen a new Thai restaurant in Lin-coln Park that would probably become trendy once people found out how good it was. Right now, it was just pleasantly full, no waiting. Bette was looking forward to the Pad Thai, but she wished she was eating it as takeout in front of the TV. On the rare occasions that she and her father went somewhere together, a destination, there was always the stench of Making an Effort. Mr. Miller seemed to be trying to reacquaint himself with Bette, as if he hadn't seen her every day of their lives for nearly thirteen years. There was only one word to describe these times. "Awkward."

On this particular night, though, they did find something to talk about. Mr. Miller had noticed that Bette was hauling around her copy of *Huck Finn,* and he had asked her about it. At the time, of course, she hadn't known about *Big River.* She had plenty of questions about the book, though.

"It's pretty amazing," Bette replied when her father asked how she'd like it.

"How so?" Mr. Miller asked.

Bette wasn't an idiot. Her dad was a great reader, he could probably write a paper on *Huck Finn* without even picking it up again. He was just trying to draw her out. Well, for once, that was fine.

"So, at first I didn't get it. Huck gets everything wrong. He thinks slavery's okay, he doesn't even hate that creepy father of his, even after Pap almost tries to kill him. And he acts like he's doing the wrong thing when he's usually doing the right thing."

"Like when he decides to steal Jim out of slavery?" Mr. Miller suggested.

"Yeah. He thinks he's going to go to hell for that."

" 'All right, then, I'll go to hell . . . I would take up wickedness again, which was in my line, being brung up to it,' " her father quoted.

"You know everything about this book, don't you?" Bette said accusingly.

"Hey, it's one of the most famous lines in American literature," Mr. Miller protested. "Huck chooses what his conscience is telling him is moral rather than just doing what society says is right, in this case, slavery."

And with that they were off. They picked apart the characters in the book and talked about why Huck turned out the way he did, and how Jim treated Huck better than Pap did, and the way some people's beliefs didn't stand up to the truth of a situation.

Bette nodded at that one as she used her chopsticks to grab some more Pad Thai. "The Widow, the Judge, even Tom Sawyer think they're so moral. But they don't care that people are being sold like farm animals."

"That's part of the irony. You know what irony is, don't you?"

Oh, Bette knew what irony was. Having a terrific voice and going to a performing arts school while never wanting to sing—that was irony.

"One thing really bothered me, though, Dad," Bette said. "Twain wasn't being ironic when he uses the N-word in the book, is he? And he uses it all the time."

Mr. Miller shook his head. "I think he used it because that was what people said at the time. But Twain's making it a slur, too."

Bette thought about that. "Like when Huck's Pap goes nuts because he sees a black person who is educated and well dressed. He keeps calling him that word."

"That's ironic, isn't it? It makes Pap feel better to put down the man, when it's clear Pap is about the lowest life form on earth."

Sitting in the hot auditorium, watching the video of *Big River,* Bette was pleased to see that the word was nowhere to be found in the production. What was amazing, though, was the way the play captured the essence of the story in the music and songs.

The play starts with the Widow Douglas and Miss Watson, Huck's guardians, joined by the other upright citizens of the town, singing that Huck is never going to get to heaven if he doesn't get some learning and read the Bible. But Huck isn't thrilled about being "sivilized." After a romp with Tom Sawyer and some of the other boys, Huck has a run-in with Pap, who, in a drunken rage, tries to kill his son. After Pap passes out, Huck spills pig blood around so people will think he's dead and then runs away. That's when he meets Jim, another runaway, who doesn't want to be sold.

Bette looked around during the song "Muddy Water." It was a big production number whose centerpiece is Jim and Huck getting on their raft to ride the Mississippi to a spot where Jim can get to safety. It was such an upbeat song, a lot of the kids were nodding their heads or tapping their feet along with the music.

Things got much more sober with the next song. A group of slaves sing about crossing to the other side, though whether they mean getting to the other side of the river or into heaven, Bette wasn't quite sure. She did know that Lucy's gospel voice would sound beautiful leading the chorus. Act One ends with Huck and Jim meeting two scoundrels, the Duke and the King, con men pretending to be royals.

Mrs. Wu gave the seventh and eighth graders a few moments to stretch between acts. Bette was sitting next to Andy Minkus.

"There are some great violin solos, did you notice?" Andy asked. "More like fiddle music, but I can play that." When Andy got excited, his nose twitched, making him look a bit like a rabbit.

Bette hadn't noticed. What did please her was that she hadn't seen or heard anything that made her want to try out for the musical. The show was terrific to watch, but except for the Widow Douglas and Miss Watson, and the female slaves, there weren't any parts of note for girls. Bette felt like she had taken a bath in relief. No temptation, no stress, no worries. She would sign up to work on hair and makeup. That would be fun. Working on costumes would be okay, too. Just something nice and quiet backstage so she could feel part of the production.

With that decision made, Bette rearranged her sweater under her butt and settled back in her chair to watch the second act of *Big River*. After making some money on one of the Duke and the King's cons, Huck goes back to the raft and cruelly pretends to be a slave hunter. Jim's fear, then his disappointment in Huck, forces the boy to think about Jim in a different way.

Bette knew what was coming up next. The Duke and the King learn about the death of a wealthy local man and try to steal his inheritance off his daughter Mary Jane. Huck feels sorry for Mary Jane and her sisters and foils the plot.

What she didn't know was that the interplay gave Mary Jane the opportunity to sing two great songs.

Uh-oh, thought Bette as Mary Jane started singing.

The first song was called "You Oughta Be Here with Me," and Bette felt her heart twist like a piece of taffy as Mary Jane stood beside her father's coffin and sang, "If you think it's lonely where you are tonight, then you ought to be here with me." Then as Bette was catching her breath over that one, Huck, Jim, and Mary Jane, each in a different part of the stage, harmonized on a song called "Leavin's Not the Only Way to Go."

Wasn't that the truth. Bette, without thought, dug around in her pocket and curled her fingers around her angel. *People can really leave, or you can be living in the same house with someone, seeing them every day, and yet they're gone, gone, gone.*

Bette tried to pay attention as the play steamed along to its satisfying conclusion. She was moved by Huck's raw yell that he'd go to hell for stealing Jim out of slavery. She tapped her finger in time to the music, as the cast sang "Muddy Water" in a final, rousing reprise. But mostly her mind was on Mary Jane's two songs and the plaguing question of what she was going to do about them. Simple, yet haunting, they weren't just pieces of show music, she knew that for sure. They were speaking, calling even, to her. Bette hated choices, but now, deep down in a place she couldn't hide from, she knew she had some choices to make.

The seventh and eighth grade teachers handed out copies of the *Big River* CD to all the students as they filed out of the auditorium. There was a little sticker on each, saying the music had been provided to Odom by one of the school's local benefactors. Bette shoved the CD in her backpack and headed toward her locker. Lucy Washington, who had the locker next to hers, was already there, putting on her jacket.

"So that was pretty good," Lucy said as Bette began fiddling with her lock.

"Yeah," Bette muttered.

"Crossing to the other side," Lucy crooned in her melodious voice. "I know which part I'm going to try out for."

"You'll get it," Bette said mechanically.

"There's competition." Lucy brooded. "Kia Sweet. Letisha Hawkins."

Bette threw her history book into her bag. "I wouldn't worry too much."

"That Mary Jane is a good role," Lucy said tentatively.

Nodding, Bette closed her locker.

"Okay, see you on Monday." Lucy hurried out to get her bus.

Bette followed slowly behind. Pushing open the heavy school doors, she was pleased to see the day had turned as gray and gloomy as she felt. Heading for home, she crunched the dead leaves strewn across the sidewalk. It made a satisfying sound.

Now what? Now what? Rain began falling in time with her chant, it seemed. *Now what?*

Bette stomped up the stairs of the greystone. Once inside, she dropped her backpack on the floor, flung off her jacket, and headed into her bedroom to change out of her drippy clothes. "It's Friday," she muttered. "I'm not even going to think about this stupid show until Monday."

As she threw on a robe, Bette remembered that she was going out with her father and Barbra tonight. Barbra had something going on tomorrow—probably Da-vid—so she'd arranged for an early dinner this evening. Good, that would take up a couple of hours. Riffling through her closet, Bette tried to find something to wear that would cheer her up. It soon became obvious this was a lost cause. Thinking that maybe Barbra had left something wearable behind, Bette went to check out her sister's dresser drawers. The phone machine in the hall was blinking red, so Bette punched up the messages. The first was from her sister.

"Bette, baby, I'm going to have to cancel tonight. I'm still busy tomorrow, but I'm hoping we can do it on Sunday. Okay? I'll try you on your cell phone."

Message two was from her father. "Bette, Barbra said she had to cancel, so we'll do it on Sunday maybe. I'll come home at the regular time. About midnight."

Oh, damn. Not tonight.

Bette went into the living room and sat down on the couch. Alone again. Well, she was used to it anyway. But tonight, she wanted to be with people, even if it was just Barbra and her father. If she wasn't going to think about trying out for that stupid musical, she needed some distraction.

"If you think you're lonely where you are tonight, then you ought to be here with me."

"I'm not thinking about the play," Bette told herself sternly even as she could feel herself falling into a slough of despair. "I'm going to call Vivi." She sat on the couch for a long time anyway, before getting up to find the walk-around phone, which always took some time, too.

Even though she and Vivian had promised to get together more often, Bette was pretty sure that neither one of them felt like going out in the chill and rain. Well, at least they could talk, though it would be hard to have a conversation without topic number one coming up.

But Vivian wasn't home. Mrs. Minkus said Dr. Minkus and the twins had gone over to their grandmother's house for Friday night dinner. Bette could almost see Mrs. Minkus's sour expression as she explained. She didn't get along with her mother-in-law.

Now Bette began feeling a little desperate. The evening stretched out endlessly in front of her. She was just about to turn on the TV—thank goodness for cable—when she heard a knock at the door. Frowning, she went over and looked through the peephole.

"Hello, Gabi," Bette said, not opening the door too widely.

"Bette, I've heard from your father."

"Is there something wrong?" Bette asked, her throat suddenly tightening.

"No, no." Gabi shook her head. "It is just that he told me

your plans fell through this evening. He wondered if perhaps we might have dinner together."

For a second, Bette wondered why her father hadn't called her. Oh, because she would have ignored his suggestion. "Thanks," she replied, trying to be polite, "but I'm kind of busy." Was her nose growing?

"I'm making Hungarian goulash. It's quite good."

"Goulash? Isn't that like stew?" Stew was one of her favorite dishes, but since her mother died, Bette had been reduced to eating it out of a can.

"Something like stew, but with noodles."

Bette was sorely tempted. A home-cooked meal and a change of scene. Well, sort of, since the downstairs apartment was a mirror of the Millers'. And of course, the food came with Gabi. Still . . .

"I eat early. Perhaps you can come down in an hour or so." Gabi smiled at her.

"All right," Bette said, capitulating. "I'll be down in an hour."

"Lovely."

Bette went into her room and found pants that weren't too wrinkled and a sweatshirt. Then she dug around in her backpack and came up with the CD. She couldn't help it. She wanted to hear those songs one more time.

Her first impulse was to listen to the music on her computer, but then she decided to go into the living room. Mr. Miller might be somewhat neglectful about the apartment, but he was a maniac when it came to having a state-of-the-art music system. Bette popped the CD in the stereo, grabbed the remote so she could find Mary Jane's songs, and nestled into a ball on the couch, as the crystal clear voice filled the air. Her intention was to listen to each song just once. Just once. But with the remote control on her lap, it was impossible for her not to keep hitting it, popping them up, over and over.

Soon she wasn't so much listening as absorbing the music, all the while thoughts of her mom swirled around Bette. She had been aware for a long time that she consciously made the effort not to think about her mother. Now, as she lay on the worn velvet couch, she realized that somewhere, in the back of her mind, her mother was with her every hour of the day and often into the dreams of her night. Whether it was looking at Barbra, who so resembled their mom, or using the imported Italian dishes Mrs. Miller had loved or wearing her favorite cozy red sweater, the one Bette had kept, after all the other clothes had gone to charity, so many little things made Elizabeth Miller an enduring presence. That understanding, right there on the couch, brought Bette heart-bursting happiness and incredible longing.

She fished around in her pants' pocket for her angel medallion. Gently rubbing her thumb over the angel, Bette wondered what she should do about her singing now. Playing the part of Mary Jane would have made her mother so proud, so happy. Bette could picture her smiling in the audience. But though the essence of her mother was all around, it wasn't as though she would really be there to watch her perform. And now, it had been so long since Bette had sung, it seemed like a skill lost and forgotten. She couldn't quite imagine it, any of it. Not walking up the steps of the stage to audition, much less opening her mouth to sing. Rehearsals, a show? Out of the question.

Glancing at the antique clock sitting on the mantel of the fireplace, Bette saw that it was almost time to go downstairs. She was regretting her decision already, but it would be beyond rude to cancel now. If there was one thing her mother had instilled in both her girls, it was common courtesy. The angel in her hand was as inscrutable as ever, but Bette felt comforted just by its presence. She decided she would at least run a comb through her hair before she went downstairs; the weather had made it look a little worse than it usually did. In the bathroom, Bette was aware the rain was now pounding outside the window. Maybe she wasn't thrilled about going to Gabi's for dinner, but the commute was easy and the travel time was right.

Bette had barely knocked before Gabi opened the door. "Right on time. Come in," she said with a smile.

Bette was curious to see what she had done with the apartment, but except for the freshly painted walls, the living room looked pretty much the same as the day Gabi moved in.

"No, I haven't done much in the way of decorating," Gabi remarked, following Bette's gaze. "I told you I would not be staying long."

"Oh, I thought . . ."

"The plan was always to stay for a limited time. Besides, I haven't really lived up to my part of the bargain. I've painted, but I've hardly been looking out for you as I told your father I would. This is the first time you've been down here." Gabi didn't say it accusingly. She was just stating a fact.

Still, Bette bristled. "I told you, I told my father, I don't need a babysitter."

"No, of course, I realize that." Gabi's voice was soothing. "However, you're here now, so let's enjoy our time together."

Bette nodded. She was too confused and tired to take on Gabi. Besides—as usual—heavenly smells were coming from the kitchen, and Bette was hungry.

"We'll eat in the kitchen, all right? I don't have a dining room table."

If the living room was still bare, the kitchen was much cozier. Gabi had painted the round wooden table and chairs that the last tenants had left a cheery yellow. Inexpensive yellow and red dish towels were draped over the oven handle, and fresh flowers, golden mums in cups and glasses, were placed all around—on the table, the window sill, and the counters. Bette wondered briefly if Gabi had gone out to buy the flowers special for their dinner, but that was silly, the weather was awful, and you'd have to walk pretty far to get to a store that sold flowers. She must just like having fresh flowers around for no reason. Something about that endeared Gabi to Bette.

"Uh, can I do anything to help?" Bette asked.

"No, please, sit. I hope you're hungry. I've made quite a lot."

Bette realized that she was absolutely famished. "Yes, I am."

Gabi smiled at her, then proceeded to ladle out a steaming portion of the goulash over a hearty portion of buttered noodles. With a deft shake, Gabi decorated the food with paprika. "That's the final touch," Gabi said as she handed Bette the plate.

"Are you from Hungary?" Bette asked as she waited for Gabi to come to the table with her own food.

"Oh, no," Gabi answered, as she slid into her chair. "I just like making the goulash."

"Where are you from?"

For the first time, Gabi looked a bit startled. "Ah, here, there, and everywhere, I guess you could say."

Bette tasted the goulash. It was as delicious as it looked. "Why did you come to Chicago?"

Gabi shrugged. "I thought I had found work here."

"And there wasn't a job?" It occurred to Bette she rarely saw Gabi outside the apartment.

"Well, it's complicated. Things may still work out."

"So what do you do all day?" Bette asked bluntly.

"Oh, I knit and I cook and bake . . ."

Helping herself to the crusty bread on the table, Bette asked, "Did you make this?"

"Yes."

"There will be a lot of food left over." Bette reddened. She hadn't meant to sound like she was asking for a handout. Anyway, Gabi had brought some baked goods upstairs now and again.

Gabi didn't seem to notice the gaffe, or pretended not to. "I usually bring extra for the women's shelter on Fullerton."

Bette thought of Gabi's knitting. "Do you knit them things, too?"

"Sometimes, but even scarves can take a while. Food is the more efficient way to go."

"That's so nice of you," Bette mumbled.

"Well, we all try to use the talents we have," Gabi replied serenely.

The irony of that comment wasn't lost on Bette. Unfortunately, Gabi had not forgotten Bette's mention of singing when they had strolled together.

"You must get many opportunities to sing at your school," Gabi continued.

"There are opportunities," Bette answered carefully.

Gabi cocked her head, her fork poised. "Do you take them?"

That was direct. "Not for a while."

"Isn't that difficult?"

"Not really," Bette said, helping herself to more of the

goulash. "It's a regular school, too. And I don't have to sing. For instance, if we were putting on a play, I could work backstage."

"Mmm. But you have a beautiful voice, don't you?"

Now Bette was getting uncomfortable. "I don't know about beautiful."

Gabi had an odd, faraway expression on her face. It was almost as if she could hear Bette singing. She glanced back at Bette without a word.

Without knowing quite why, Bette found herself saying quietly, "Some people said it was beautiful."

"Your mother?"

Bette's words caught in her throat. "Yes. She thought so."

And then, to her utter surprise, all the other words, the ones she had locked up for so long, began spilling out. Even more amazing, Bette wasn't embarrassed about the torrent of memories that shaped with the words. It was almost as if she had duplicated herself in time. She was sitting in Gabi's kitchen, but she was also the little girl singing show tunes to the delighted applause of her family; then she was the eager student, accepted at Odom, her mother so happy that day she seemed like sunshine; next came the Bette of just a few years ago, singing along with Mrs. Miller in the car. As she spoke, Bette could feel the happiness that saturated her memories, but they were now so brittle she thought they might break into a hundred tiny pieces.

When Bette finally stopped talking, Gabi, her eyes wet, said, "How you must miss her."

"I miss her."

"I can see why singing must seem so impossible for you. You always sang for your mother."

Bette felt tired. She nodded.

"You don't want to sing for yourself? I'm just asking."

Bette took the question as seriously as Gabi asked it. "I don't think I can."

"You mean you haven't before," Gabi corrected her. "People reach new understandings all the time. Take a second look, maybe change their minds."

Bette sat up straight, startled. "What did you say?" Gabi had just recited lyrics from "Leavin's Not the Only Way to Go." How in the world did she know that song? It was hardly well known, and in any case, Gabi seemed more Beethoven than *Big River*.

Gabi smiled and pointed upward.

Confusion colored Bette's face. Did she mean the song had come from heaven or something?

"This greystone is very well built, but if music is played loudly enough, over and over, well, you can hear things," Gabi explained.

Relief. For a moment, Bette had thought something spooky was going on. She grimaced as she remembered just how many times she had played Mary Jane's songs. Poor Gabi. She knew the songs so well now, she could probably audition herself. "Sorry," she mumbled.

"Ah, well, it was clear the music had touched you in some way."

Bette couldn't deny that. "The songs are about dying and leaving . . . and changing your mind."

"What are they from?" Gabi asked.

"*Big River*. It's a musical we're putting on."

"And perhaps you'll do the makeup for it." Gabi got up. "Are you ready for dessert?"

Bette just stared after Gabi as she went to the refrigerator and pulled out a chocolate cream pie. That was it? No pressure?

"I shall cut us both large slices. We deserve it. Do you drink coffee?"

"I'd rather have milk," Bette said. She hoped that didn't sound too babyish.

"Milk it is."

Bette got up and cleared the table. As they ate their pie, rich chocolate topped with snowy drifts of cream, she kept waiting for Gabi to move the conversation back to singing or auditions, but she did not. Finally, Bette couldn't stand it anymore.

"So what do you think I should do?"

Gabi didn't insult her by asking about what. "Bette, I think you should listen to your heart and decide. There are only two choices. Either you audition or you do not. As the song says, you will take a second look and maybe change your mind. Or not. One way or another, a decision will be made."

"But . . ."

"It's Friday night, why not rest on it a few days? You have only one decision to make right now."

Bette raised her eyebrows.

"Would you like more pie?"

VI

A s it turned out, Bette learned you can make a decision without really deciding anything.

After Mrs. Wu showed the video of the scaled-down version of *Big River,* the seventh and eighth graders broke up into small groups and discussed the lavish Broadway production and the more intimate version of the musical that relied on the audience using their imaginations. Bette sat and listened, but she didn't join in.

Throughout a damp, dismal autumn, the music teachers played the score, and the acting coaches organized scenes from both the book and the play. English and history teachers tried to bring the issues raised in *Big River* and *Huckleberry Finn* into the classroom. Bette participated as minimally as possible.

And when it came time to sign up for tryouts, Bette . . . just . . . didn't . . . sign up.

It wasn't like she forgot. It would be impossible to be a functioning human being and not be aware that auditions were going to be held the week after Thanksgiving. It was pretty much all the kids talked about. At lunchtime, Bette got used to sitting and just listening while Andy, Lucy, and Fred discussed the show.

"I can't believe we have to wait until after Thanksgiving

for the auditions," Fred said for, what seemed to Bette, the hundredth time.

"Hey, Thanksgiving is next week," Andy replied. "So we've got to calm down. We're like horses smelling the barn."

Lucy gave him the fish eye. "What does that mean, Minkus? And what do you know about horses or barns, living up in that high-rise like you do?"

"It's just an expression. After a ride, horses get excited the closer they get to their stalls," Andy explained patiently.

"Huh." Lucy grunted. "I'm no horse, Minkus. And I'm not excited in a happy way. I'm excited in a nervous, sick-to-my-stomach kinda way."

Fred waved his peanut butter sandwich around. "You'll do fine. We'll all do fine." He frowned. "Though I wouldn't mind if Bennett Fitzgerald broke his leg over the holiday."

Bette finally got into the conversation. "That's creepy. What if he said the same about you?"

"How about a case of laryngitis?" Lucy suggested. "Something that would get him out of the way for just a little while."

"I don't know," Andy said mischievously. "Even with a sore throat, he might sing better than Fred."

Bennett, an eighth grader, Fred's only real competition for the role of Huck, did have a better voice than Fred, but he couldn't dance at all and his acting skills weren't much better than his dancing.

"Don't worry about Bennett," Bette told Fred, but to her surprise, he just scowled at her.

"Easy for you to say. You don't care if you get a part. You're not even going to audition."

"I haven't decided that yet," Bette said defensively.

"Ah, yeah, Bette," Andy said in a gentle voice. "I think you have."

Bette thought about that for the rest of the day and into Thanksgiving weekend. She really had believed she still had choices, but of course, all her actions—or lack thereof—had made sure that they had dried up.

Thanksgiving came as a welcome relief. For the last couple of years, she, Barbra, and her father had spent the day with family friends, musicians, who roasted their turkey with Cajun spices and invited any stray trumpeter or bass player who didn't have somewhere to go that day. There was always plenty of sweet potato pie for dessert and jamming after dinner, and no one asked Bette or Barbra questions they didn't want to answer.

Bette had worried that Gabi might be alone for the holiday, so her dad suggested they ask her to come along. "It's always the more the merrier at the Wicks," he told her when he offered the invitation. But Gabi had her own plans. She was going to the homeless shelter to serve Thanksgiving dinner. It sounded like something Gabi would do.

Despite their heartfelt conversation several weeks earlier, Gabi had not pushed or prodded to find out what Bette's plans were for *Big River*. Bette had been spending more time downstairs, but instead of heavy discussions about making choices, Gabi taught Bette how to bake cakes, and she'd shown her the basics of knitting. Sometimes Bette wondered why Gabi wasn't asking more questions about what was happening with the play, but her overriding emotion was relief that she was being left alone to make her own decisions.

Since Gabi wasn't putting any pressure on her, Bette was almost shocked when after a belt-busting Thanksgiving feast, Mr. Miller asked her if she'd like to take a walk, with an oddly determined look on his face. Clearly, her father had something on his mind, and Bette had a sneaking suspicion what that was. The school sent regular bulletins to the parents about all the exciting things that were happening at Odom, and since there had never been anything as exciting as *Big River,* at least since Bette had been in school, breathless updates were now arriving frequently.

They bundled up and headed outside into the lazy dusk. The Wicks lived in one of the fancier suburbs on Lake Michigan, and some of the residents must have spent Thanksgiving Day putting up their holiday decorations, because twinkling lights brightened several of the large homes.

"I'm glad I don't live out here," Bette commented. "It would be kind of boring, but the houses do look pretty, all lit up."

Mr. Miller just nodded; he was gathering his thoughts. Finally, he blurted it out. "Bette, I keep hearing about this musical your school is putting on."

"Yes," Bette said vaguely. "I think I told you about it," she added, knowing full well she hadn't.

"So are you going to try out for it?"

"I . . . I don't think so."

Even in the dusky light, Bette could see him frown. "It sounds like a pretty big deal."

"I guess."

Mr. Miller drew a breath. "Maybe you'd like to transfer to another school, Bette."

Bette almost stumbled. She had expected her father might say a lot of things, but not this. "Why would I want to do that?"

"Well, what's the point of being at a performing arts school if you don't want to participate in the programs?"

"I can still participate," Bette told him. "Like with *Big River,* I'll probably do costumes or something."

Her father shook his head. "That would be okay for some kids, but not you, Bette. Not with your voice."

So there it was. Her father had known for years she hadn't been singing. Parent-teacher conferences had let him in on that, she was sure, but he had never talked to her about it. She didn't know if that was because he didn't think it was that big a deal or if he just didn't care. She liked to think that he let her be because he understood how hard it would be for her to sing.

"But Odom is so close to home," Bette finally said.

Their eyes met under the light of a streetlamp. Bette was the first to look away.

"Yes, it's convenient, I guess. But convenience isn't everything."

"You want me to change schools?" Bette asked, feeling a little panicky.

"Bette, no one at school has said anything to me, not yet, but their patience has to be running out. I don't even know if Odom can let you stay if you don't want to sing. Competition to get in there is fierce . . ." Mr. Miller's voice petered out.

Bette felt a little shock run through her. Did everyone at school think she was just taking up space?

They turned a corner, bringing them back to the Wicks' house. As soon as they were inside the door, Bette caught Barbra give her father a questioning look. He responded with a slight shake of his head. Oh, so she was in on this, too. Bette could feel herself getting angry. Whatever. Let them put their heads together. *Cluck-cluck.* This was one decision she was going to make all by herself. She thrust her cold hands in her pants' pocket, where her angel token lay nestled. She clearly heard the words, *Well, make it. One way or another. But really make it.*

Bette twisted her head around. Did someone actually say that? But the guests were all busy, drinking coffee, chatting, standing around the piano while a woman with dark curly hair caressed the keys. Pulling her hand out of her pocket, she went to find Mrs. Wick and ask if she could help with the cleaning up.

If electricity could crackle the air, so did tension. Bette was sitting in the audience, watching the tryouts, and she would have thought it might have gotten a little boring after the first ten or so kids. Each hopeful sang something from the show and part of the big finale number to see how his or her voice would fit in with a group. Stage left sat Mrs. Wu, several teachers, and Gary Klein from Maple Tree Theater, who would be directing the production. Bette eyed him closely. Surely *he* must be bored watching a bunch of amateurs, kids no less, but he didn't seem to be. He actually looked enthusiastic, smiling and nodding at each of the hopefuls, even the lesser talents. There was something about him that was just . . . nice.

Bette hadn't planned to go to the auditions, but finally decided she should be there to support her friends. Lucy had just finished "Crossing to the Other Side," and Bette thought she nailed it. Fred was still waiting nervously in the wings.

She pulled out her angel token and rubbed it absently. It usually made her feel better to touch it, but now it just felt cold.

"What is that thing anyway?" a voice behind her said.

Bette twisted her head. Joe Garcia.

"It's . . . a good luck charm, I guess."

"What do you need it for? You're not tryin' out for the play."

"How do you know?" Bette bristled.

" 'Cause you're sitting down here, just like me."

Bette turned her attention toward the stage, but Gary

Klein had called a ten-minute break. She had decided to go back to the lunchroom when Joe slipped into the seat next to her, blocking an easy exit.

"See," he continued, "they're not going to let kids like us try out for their big-deal *Big River.*"

She looked at him curiously. "What do you mean, 'kids like us'?"

"The neighborhood kids," he replied impatiently. "The ones with no talent."

Bette didn't know what to say. He thought she was at Odom because she lived nearby? Finally, she muttered, "Anybody can try out."

Joe's laugh was unpleasant. "Right."

Bette scowled. Joe didn't know what he was talking about. Mrs. Wu wanted to get kids involved in school activities no matter why they were at Odom.

"The teachers were telling all their favorites to try out," Joe continued. "Anybody ask you? No? Me either."

"Why should anyone ask you?" Bette asked with irritation. "All you do is skulk around here."

From his puzzled frown, Bette assumed Joe didn't know what "skulk" meant. That didn't stop him from answering back. "And what do you do around here? You couldn't have passed the test to get in. You don't do anything. Never heard you sing, never saw you get up onstage. You hardly talk in class."

"Maybe I don't want to," Bette said fiercely.

"Besides," he went on as if Bette hadn't even spoken, "I've seen you in the neighborhood. We talked in front of the church. You can't deny that, unless you're saying you've got amnesia or something."

"I live in the neighborhood, and I sing," Bette informed

him. "Both." She was practically yelling now. "A student can do both."

Joe leaned back in his chair. Clearly, he was enjoying getting her goat. "Okay, maybe someone can. But you can't. Leastways, you don't. A singer, huh? You're a nobody here, like me. Why don't you just admit it?"

Bette's anger was so hot she could feel her face flush. "What's wrong with you? I could go up there right now and audition if I wanted to."

"So who's stopping you?" Joe asked with a smirk.

"No one. No one is stopping me." As if to prove it, she shot up out of her seat and pushed her way past Joe, practically kicking him in the shin, as she hurled herself into the aisle.

"Mrs. Wu," Bette called up to the principal, who was on the stage, talking to Gary Klein. "Can I still try out for the play?"

The kids and teachers standing around stared at her. She hadn't meant to say it so loud. She wasn't sure she had meant to say it at all. But now that she had, she stood looking up at Mrs. Wu, hardly breathing as she waited for her answer.

"Why . . . Bette." The principal seemed as startled by her request as she was. Then she broke into a smile. "Of course you can. We're just about to start again. Why don't you try out right now."

Bette nodded gratefully. Somehow Mrs. Wu knew that if she didn't get up on the stage and sing right this minute, she would turn around and walk right out of the auditorium and through the heavy metal doors and out of the school—and not just for today. Yet in some part of her, maybe the biggest part, that wasn't what she wanted to do at all.

"Do you know what you want to sing?" Mrs. Wu whispered to Bette as she led her up the stage steps.

Bette nodded. "Maybe 'Leavin's Not the Only Way to Go.'"

Later, Bette barely remembered the singing. Other things stood out more clearly. Mrs. Wu introducing her to Gary Klein, who smiled, then looked at his roster of singers with confusion, trying to figure out who she was. Mr. Lewis, one of the music teachers who was playing the piano for the singers, winking at her happily as he waited for her to begin.

Two memories she might never forget. One did involve singing, when she came to the line, "People reach new understandings all the time, they take a second look, maybe change their minds." Even though she had listened to them so many times, those words sounded wholly new, bubbling out of her like fresh water from a fountain. The second thing she remembered was glancing at Joe, still sitting in the audience, looking as surprised as if a duck had gotten up on the stage and started to dance.

When it was all over, Bette knew she had nailed it. Feeling lighter than she had in a long, long time, she didn't even care if she actually got the part of Mary Jane. Maybe someone else would do it better. What mattered was that she had opened her mouth and sang, and she had been good, and she felt happy. Practically skipping off the stage, she headed out of the auditorium, only stopping at the aisle where Joe was sitting, still not quite over his surprise.

"See," she said pleasantly. "I told you I could sing."

VII

Joe looked around furtively and pulled the angel coin out of his jeans' pocket. He didn't know why he was so nervous. So what if someone saw it? He was in a church. No one here, of all places, would think it was weird that he was carrying around a small coin with an angel on it.

Moving past the font of holy water and heading for the pews, Joe realized it had been a while since he'd seen the inside of the Church of the Holy Comforter. For a time, when they first moved to the neighborhood, he used to drop in regularly. Then he noticed that a visit calmed him down, and sometimes he wanted to be angry. After Bette said she came here, too, he had avoided the place because he didn't want to run into her. She made him nervous in that boy-girl way he wasn't used to. Which was stupid, because even after they had talked in front of his house, she kept right on ignoring him at school. What a friggin' snob.

Without genuflecting as he had been taught, Joe slid into one of the worn wooden pews. The elderly woman in the row across the aisle frowned at him, but Joe just lowered his head, opened his hand, and looked at the coin. Okay, so maybe he shouldn't have taken it. And come to think of it, while churchgoers like that old lady might think nothing of a medal with an angel on it, God probably wouldn't be too thrilled about him carrying stolen property into church. Joe shook off the twinges in his stomach. God? Really? Shouldn't He have better things to get mad about?

Anyway, it wasn't like he had planned the thing, not exactly. It was more like a crime of opportunity. Joe rubbed his thumb across the raised image of the angel. He thought he remembered from some long-ago Sunday school class that angels weren't male or female. But the only angel he could think of with a name was the archangel Michael, a man's name. This angel in his hand was wearing some kind of long robe, and although Joe couldn't see its face very well, the image did seem more masculine. He understood why Bette liked the thing. It felt good in his hand, solid. The rubbing didn't seem to make it warm up, though. The coin or medal, whatever you wanted to call it, was cool to the touch.

The old woman left the church, and Joe had the place to himself. "It wasn't like I was looking to get you," Joe whispered aloud, feeling a little silly. "But . . ."

Yes, but. There were reasons that Joe was thrilled to get his hands on this little bit of metal. For one thing, there was no denying that he had been pissed off by Bette's performance. Impressed, embarrassed, and pissed off. She said she could sing and could she ever. He even felt the tiniest bit of the glory, because he knew she had gotten up there and auditioned to show him up. What he mostly felt, though, was mad. He had thought she was like him, just a neighborhood kid stuck in a school where everyone else had some talent, and it turned out that she was probably the best girl singer in the joint. Which left him alone. Again.

So when they were taking their math test, a couple of days after the audition, and she pulled out the coin, he had taken notice. He remembered that she had been playing with it before she marched up on the stage to sing. Now it was sitting on her desk while she scribbled, erased, and scribbled again. It must be some sort of a good luck charm. Did it help in tests? Joe knew he could use some help. The questions were hard and many of the answers evaded him. When the bell rang, everyone turned in papers, and Bette had hurriedly grabbed her book bag and headed out the door. Joe was slower stuffing things into his own backpack, and it was as he was slinging it over his shoulder that he spotted the coin still sitting on Bette's desk. He reached over and grabbed it, and for the first time noticed the angel embossed on its face. For a second or two, he looked at it and then quickly shoved it into his bag and hurriedly left the classroom, almost charging into a returning Bette, who must have realized what she'd left behind. Joe pretended not to see her.

The small medal meant a good deal to Bette: That was clear. Almost immediately "lost" notices popped up on bulletin boards, in classrooms, and in the cafeteria. She had even managed to get one posted in the boys' bathroom. There was mention of a reward. Joe considered that, but there was no way he could give the thing back without it being obvious he was the one who had taken it. Besides, this coin was something special—at least Bette thought so—and he wanted to have some of that specialness for himself.

Yet for reasons Joe didn't quite understand, he had left the angel medallion in his backpack. Didn't even take it out to look at. Here in the church was the first time he had really held it, examined it. Joe wasn't quite sure why he had chosen the church for this moment, except maybe it was a place where there was some space to breathe. Even though only he and his mom lived in their apartment, it was so small, sometimes it seemed hard to turn around in there, much less have a private moment. Now the place seemed even more cramped with his mother's friend Gene visiting all the time. It was like Gene took up all the oxygen in the apartment, and there wasn't that much of it to start with.

It had been bright when Joe stepped inside the church, the sun playing with the colors in the stained glass windows. Now the light had faded, and so had the afternoon. It was time to go.

Slipping the coin back into his pocket, Joe walked out of the church. He was supposed to pick up a couple of things at the small market on the corner, and he tried to remember what those things were. Milk, although he hated milk; spaghetti maybe. He didn't think he was supposed to get bread. Joe wished his mother would keep up with the shopping, or at least make him a list, but she often worked late, and she was so tired when she got home, it was hard for her do the things he assumed other mothers did. Joe had learned how to make the beds and do the laundry. It had been that way for a lot of years. He didn't mind too much, because after all it was just the two of them, and they had to pull together, take care of each other. Then Gene had started coming around. Joe kicked at a pile of leaves. Maybe he should turn the laundry over to Gene.

Joe walked the block and a half to the tatty market on the corner. There was a huge Jewel farther down, but Joe's mother preferred that he do what shopping he could at the Ortiz Family Market, as the peeling paint on the sign out front proclaimed.

"But you can't get anything there, Mami," Joe had protested more than once.

"The Jewel, we go there, of course, for big things, but, Joey, the Ortizes need to make some money, too. They were here before the Jewel, and we should support them."

That would be fine, Joe grumbled to himself, if the small grocery ever had anything you needed or if the things you needed hadn't passed their expiration date. Finding something decent in the market was like going on a treasure hunt, where the treasure was fruit without bruises.

Mrs. Ortiz, an elderly woman with steel-gray hair pulled back in a bun, sat behind the counter, reading a Spanish-language newspaper and chewing on a stick of licorice. She glanced up and nodded at Joe, and then went back to her reading, trusting him enough to walk around the store without shoplifting. Joe had been in the shop when her eagle eyes didn't leave kids roaming the compact aisles, so he supposed he should be flattered, but there was a piece of him that wanted to stuff something in his pockets just to see if he could get away with it. The problem was there wasn't anything in the place worth stealing.

Instead of taking a small basket, Joe grabbed some pasta, checked the date on the milk, put that in the crook of his arm, found a few bananas that looked decent, and added a box of Oreos to the food he was juggling. He almost bumped into another customer at the counter deciding which newspaper to buy, a blond woman who smiled at him.

"Buenos días," Mrs. Ortiz said as he dropped dinner on the peeling plastic counter.

"Hi," Joe muttered.

Mrs. Ortiz grabbed the items and started adding up the prices on the register, and Joe fished around in his pockets for some money. For a long time, he never had enough, but lately, he had found a way to get some extra cash. He pulled a pack of Juicy Fruit from the little metal rack next to the register. Then he added another one.

"Eight dollars and sixty cents," Mrs. Ortiz said.

Joe threw eight singles and some change on the counter.

Mrs. Ortiz counted out the coins and then held up the angel medal, which Joe had accidentally tossed out with the change. She looked at it curiously.

"Oh, I didn't mean to give you that." He reached out for it, but Mrs. Ortiz was still looking at it.

"Here's a quarter," Joe said, finding one in his pocket and pushing it toward her.

"What do you have there?" the other customer asked in a lilting voice. She appeared behind Joe, startling him a little.

Mrs. Ortiz handed the coin over to the woman, much to Joe's displeasure. "Can I have it back?" he asked sullenly.

The woman glanced at it for a moment, then shifted her gaze to Joe. Her very gray eyes looked frosty for a moment, but then she stared at Joe deeply, making him feel profoundly uncomfortable.

"Very unusual," she said, as she handed it back to Joe. "Where did you get it?"

"Found it," Joe muttered. He didn't want any more questions. But all the woman said was, "I hope it brings you good things."

Joe took the cheap plastic bag from Mrs. Ortiz and practically ran out the door.

That was stupid, Joe said to himself. *You were acting like you were guilty of something.* Well, of course, he was guilty. But crashing out of the store would only raise suspicions, though why a stranger would care about some stupid little medallion, he couldn't understand. Still, he felt as if he had dodged a bullet.

Heading home, passing a couple of houses decorated with lights and reindeer, and one with a big, fat Santa, Joe wondered what the Christmas-present haul was going to be like. His mother would manage to come up with something, and his grandmother always knit him a hat or a scarf that he wouldn't be caught dead in. His father, out in California, was about as hit or miss with presents as he was with child support. His new wife was a little better about putting something in the mail.

Thinking about the present he was working on for his mother calmed him a little bit. He hadn't been able to buy her anything for a long time, but for her birthday or Christmas, he carved her a wooden figurine, usually an animal. By now, she had a small menagerie. The earliest figures were simple, a fish, a butterfly. Now, his carving had progressed, and on his mother's last birthday, he had made her an elephant with big ears and a tiny tail. This year, he was going for something special. Something he was pretty sure she was going to like a lot.

Pushing open the front door to his apartment building, Joe made his way up the worn carpeted stairs to the second floor. Some people might think the second floor was better than the third, but they didn't factor in the *clump-clumping* overhead. Joe rarely caught sight of the upstairs neighbor, but he had seen enough to know he was big; walking around upstairs, he sounded like a giant. "Fee Fi Fo Fum," Joe often muttered to himself at the sound.

Joe put the groceries on the counter. He guessed he would make his fall-back dinner, pasta with grated cheese on top. Checking the fridge, he was pleased to see the brick of cheddar cheese was orange, not green, and there was even some lettuce, which could join the single tomato on the counter for a salad.

The pasta was almost finished cooking when Joe's mother walked in. Lots of people thought she was Joe's sister if they didn't look too closely. Mother and son were about the same height, and Luisa wore her straight black hair loose with a couple of barrettes to keep it off her face, which, along with her huge dark eyes and innocent smile, added to the girlish look. But Joe always noticed the tired lines and dark circles under her eyes.

"How was work, Mami?" Joe asked as he dumped the pasta into the colander, splashing boiling water here and there.

"Fine, *hijo,* fine." She always said this, even though Joe knew the clerical work she did was boring and that her boss was a jerk who yelled at his employees far more often than he praised them.

Mrs. Garcia hung up her red jacket and pointedly looked at Joe as she hung up his jacket as well. As Joe grated the cheese into the spaghetti, his mother grabbed the teakettle and filled it with water. She had been sick last year with a cough that didn't go away and then turned into pneumonia. The expensive medicine the doctor had prescribed had finally worked, but Luisa had also given credit to a special herb tea she had gotten down in the barrio. After she got better, she kept brewing it, almost as if it was her own good luck charm.

Joe winced. The tea smelled funny, and he wished his mother would stop with it already. It made him think of the frightening time when she was sick. He didn't think it was doing her any good anymore, if it ever had, but it was her choice, he guessed. There were far worse things she could pour herself than a cup of tea every night.

"How was school today, Joey?" his mother asked, bringing her tea over to the rickety table and pulling up a chair.

Joe considered the question. His math test had come back with a score so low he was just breaking double digits. The rest of the school was singing and dancing around him, all Huckleberry this, Huckleberry that, until he wanted to puke. And once again he had twisted Andy Minkus's arm with businesslike efficiency until the runt had finally handed over a wad of dollar bills.

"Okay," Joe said, putting a steaming plate of pasta in front of his mother. "The usual."

VIII

"Come on, hand it over." Joe's tone was almost more weary than it was menacing.

Andy Minkus shook his head. Today, apparently, was the day he was going to take a stand.

The boys stood close to each other in the dingy gangway between two apartment buildings that abutted the back of the school. Joe gripped Minkus's upper arm tightly, shoving it behind his back. It was clear Andy had used the colder weather to his advantage by layering what seemed to be several sweaters under his jacket. Joe cussed. It had been much easier to take firm hold of Andy several weeks ago.

Twisting fiercely, Minkus almost got away, but Joe tripped him and Andy fell hard to his knees, the grit of the sidewalk making tiny holes in his pants. So much for taking a stand.

Staring up from the broken pavement, Minkus looked like a cornered animal, with the same wide-eyed expression he had worn the three other times Joe had shaken him down for money. But now, Joe noticed, there was something more. Resignation, yes, but wait . . . was that a dollop of pity in Andy's gaze as well? Just the idea it might be infuriated Joe.

He gave Minkus a kick in the butt while he was down. "The bell's going to ring any minute. Give me the money. Hurry up."

Minkus hurried. Moving shakily to his feet, he put his hand in his pocket and pulled out the dollar bills and handed them over.

Joe knew from past experience there were nine. Never ten, always nine, which was the first amount Joe had gotten off Minkus. Joe realized Minkus somehow took it as a show of strength to never relinquish a penny over nine dollars. Who cared? It was nine dollars more than he had yesterday. Joe stuffed the money in his pocket. Up until that moment, the only thing in there had been the angel medallion he'd been carrying around, and he thought he felt a little current of electricity as paper touched metal.

Joe said, "Thanks," and then cringed as the word came out of his mouth. He had to quit doing that. Thanking the person you're shaking down wasn't really part of street etiquette. Too bad his mother had pounded manners into his head so thoroughly that when someone gave him something, he automatically said thank you. "Now get out of here," Joe added gruffly.

Minkus got. He scooted out of the gangway and ran along the school's chain fence toward the front entrance. Joe took the more direct route, climbing the high fence and then dropping to the grass on the other side. Strictly against school rules.

"Where were you?"

Joe, who had been scuffing the few remaining dead leaves as he made his way through the playground toward the school, jerked his head up at the sound of Bette's voice.

"What do you mean?" he answered, frowning.

"Why were you back there by the fence?" Bette had a look on her face that Joe could only describe as suspicious. He scowled and shoved his hands in his pockets, his right fist knocking up against both money and medallion. He seriously did not want Bette suspicious of him.

"Taking a piss in the bushes."

That shut her up, Joe thought with satisfaction as he pushed past Bette. Well, her mouth was open, forming a great big *O*, but at least no words were coming. Joe made sure he was well ahead of Bette as he strode toward the homeroom they shared.

As he slid into his desk, Joe watched the door. Since, for the most part, the seventh graders stayed in homeroom while their various teachers moved in and out, Joe and Bette were sitting across from each other practically all day. Minkus was in the room, too, but at the rear. Joe had barely been aware of him before the money began changing hands back before Halloween, and even now it was easy to ignore him.

Just as the second bell was ringing, Bette finally walked into the room. Joe noticed her shiny brown hair. It looked like she was letting it grow longer, probably for her role in *Big River.* Her eyes were brown, too, and that combination could be kind of boring, but Bette's eyes were big and full of questions. As she sat down next to him, her eyes were questioning right now.

"You were *not,*" she whispered to him.

Joe could feel his face reddening. What was up with Bette? Any other girl would have been shocked at his crude explanation and let it go. He supposed that's what made Bette more interesting than most, but jeez, she really needed to put a lid on it.

Fortunately, he was spared answering when their homeroom teacher, Mrs. Abrams, walked in. In a sea of singing and dancing, Mrs. Abrams, who also taught them English, was an island of stability. She had a rough voice, as if she had smoked cigarettes for a long, long time, and Joe imagined if she sang, it would sound like a dog growling. As for dancing, if she did any at all, short, square Mrs. Abrams probably looked like a toy robot scooting around the floor. She often wore a bemused look as if she was wondering how she had been placed at a school where "talent," whatever that was, was valued more than knowing how to identify an adverb.

"Good morning, everyone. Let's get started. We've got a lot to accomplish."

Today, Mrs. Abrams's expression was sour. Joe figured it was because it was Wednesday, with less time for class work. Wednesdays and Fridays were short days. Seventh and eighth classes let out early so that most of the kids could practice for *Big River*. It was a drag for Joe, too. Even though he wasn't participating, he wasn't allowed to leave school early. That meant spending the last period of the day in the library. Joe wasn't much of a reader, but at least there were some cool car magazines in the library, so he spent his time leafing through those. It bugged him, though, that he had to sit around while everybody else was showing off.

"We're going to start working on our biographical essays," Mrs. Abrams continued, "so this morning I want you to begin by outlining what you're going to write about." She began passing out sheets of paper. "We've discussed proper outlining, but this will remind you of the correct procedure."

Joe glanced down at the paper. Mrs. Abrams had outlined the biography of a fictional student to show how it was done. The way Mrs. Abrams talked about outlining was almost reverential. A key to all knowledge. Like if you knew how to outline something, you could get everything straight in your mind.

He looked more closely at the biography of the imaginary Malcolm Jones Mrs. Abrams was handing out. Malcolm had a pretty sweet life. He had two parents, a sister, and a dog. He played soccer. In a nod to Odom Magnet School, Malcolm's talents included playing the saxophone, and he also sang. Not at the same time, of course.

"Start thinking about your life and begin outlining it," Mrs. Abrams told the class. "Let's work silently—silently—on your outlines for about twenty minutes."

Joe almost laughed out loud. Think about his life—and outline it!—in twenty minutes. Still, he was ready to get started. Maybe Mrs. Abrams had gotten to him, but there was something that intrigued Joe about outlining. There were so many things about his life that were disorganized. Outlining, if it was done properly, followed along sensibly, one step after another. It was a little like carving. You started with a block of wood that could be anything, but you shaved off a piece here and another chunk there, and suddenly the wood began to resemble something recognizable.

Glancing down once more at the happy life of Malcolm Jones, Joe could see how neatly it was outlined. Roman numerals for the main ideas. A capital letter for each sub-idea under the main ones. If you had points to make about those sub-ideas, you broke them down with regular numbers. It wasn't that hard, and if it got complicated, he would just follow along after Malcolm.

Joe looked down at the blank paper for a while, then picked up his pen. Writing about his life made him nervous and a little resentful, but there was something compelling about it, too. In capital letters he wrote:

THE LIFE OF JOSEPH GARCIA

Joe stared at Roman numeral one. "Early Life." That should be easy enough, right? He checked out Malcolm's early life. Very average. Grimly, Joe began his own outline.

I. Early Life
  A. Parents: Luisa and Ramón Garcia.
    1. Luisa is pregnant with Joe when she and Ramón get married.
    2. Luisa is 19 when Joe is born.
  B. Ramón splits to California when Joe is 4.
  C. Luisa and Joe live in 6 different places by the time Joe is 10.
    1. Most of them suck.
    2. Only pet—ever—a goldfish dies and is flushed down the toilet of apartment 6.

Joe looked at his paper. This was turning out to be easier than he thought, at least the outlining part. But he could feel a spark of anger start to burn inside him as the numerals and letters became memories. The crummy apartments. The times his mother was out of work and couldn't pay the rent on those. He glanced around the room. He bet none of the other kids had to worry about that. The anger burned a little brighter as he thought about Ramón. His father. His father with his new life in California. Sheila, the wife, and their kid, Paul, who was two, and according to Ramón, "the cutest kid in the world." He didn't look so cute in the photos Ramón occasionally sent. He looked skinny and sickly and more like Sheila than Ramón. He, on the other hand, was the spitting image of his dad. For some reason, that thought made Joe even madder. The hell with Ramón.

Trying to calm himself down, Joe glanced at the example Mrs. Abrams had handed out. Malcolm's Roman numeral two was all about his extended family. Joe didn't have many relatives. He scribbled down a line about his grandmother who lived out in the southern suburbs, too far away to see often, and his grandfather who was dead. That's all he wrote, that his grandfather was dead. He could have written much more about his *abuelo,* but he didn't want to, not when he felt like kicking something.

Roman numeral three was "for something important in your life." Soccer, it appeared, was important to Malcolm. He was a goalie, and his team last year had a five–one record.

Joe didn't play sports. But he did have something that was important to him.

    III. Child Support
        A. After his parents get divorced, court orders
            Ramón to pay Luisa and Joe $600 a month.
        B. Ramón usually pays late.
        C. Never $600.
           1. Once $450.
           2. Mostly $200, $300.

Joe appreciated the way the numbers marched across the page. Of course, real numbers never worked in his and his mom's favor. But on paper they were sterile, not dripping with emotion the way they were when Ramón and Luisa were screaming about them over the phone. Joe felt sorry for his mom. She tried so hard to get what was coming to them. Once, when she had scraped together a little money, she had gotten a lawyer, who had filed some papers in some court, but as Luisa had told him with a sigh, "More money went out than came in."

The next subject the fictional Malcolm tackled in his out-line was school. Well, at least he wouldn't have to write any more about his family. School at least was just stupid. Especially this school, especially for him. Should he make it clear that going to a school for the arts was a bunch of bull when you can't sing a note? Or dance. Ha! Dance.

Joe felt someone behind him, and sure enough, there was Mrs. Abrams looking over his shoulder, reading his outline. His immediate thought was to cover his paper with his arm, the way kids did to keep someone from cheating. Not that anyone ever wanted to cheat off him. Ha! Anyway, why cover his paper from the one person who was actually going to read it? Still, he immediately turned his fury on himself for being so honest, for putting so much on paper before he had decided whether he was going to hand in this outline or maybe do another. One that had been prettied up to sound, if not like happy Malcolm, at least a little more normal.

As he waited for Mrs. Abrams to say something, Joe noticed that he was holding his breath. But she didn't say anything. She just patted him on the shoulder and moved on.

The impression of her touch lingered, and he rubbed his shoulder as if to erase it. He didn't like people touching him, not even his mom. Well, he hadn't minded when his grandfather took his hands and showed him how to carve. That was different.

It took a while for Joe to shake off the weird mix of mad and indifference that this stupid outline had brought up in him. Finally, after English and math class and silent reading period were over, he felt normal enough to go to lunch. When Joe had first come to Odom, last spring, he kept to himself. But this year, once the weather had turned cold, he found himself eating with two other neighborhood kids. Ollie was a big bruiser of a guy; he seemed as big to Joe as Joe probably did to Minkus. Ollie was sweet, though, always offering to share his food, which was pretty great because his parents had a catering business and brought home the leftovers.

Lane, on the other hand, was not so sweet. At first Joe assumed she was one of the magnet kids, because she looked kind of arty, with her spiky red hair and perpetual black pants and turtlenecks. One day, he saw her come out of a big gingerbread Victorian house a few blocks from his apartment building.

"You live here?" he asked with surprise.

Lane had narrowed her eyes. "Yeah." Unspoken were the words, "What's it to you?"

"So do you sing or dance or are you just a neighborhood kid?"

"Neighborhood. They had a spot open and since my parents were going to have to send me to private school if I didn't go here, they made a big stink and Mrs. Wu let me in."

"Why were they going to send you to private school?"

Lane looked at Joe a little oddly. "Ah, because this is the only decent public school around, and my parents didn't want me being bussed all over the city at the crack of dawn?"

"They just let you in?" When Joe had first come to Odom late last spring, his mother had been sick and out of work, and he had to take care of her, so the school admitted him. Once his mom got back on her feet, the reason for his being there seemed to have been forgotten. No one told him he had to leave, so he stayed. It was easier than transferring.

"My dad's a lawyer. He knows someone who's on the school board."

Didn't that just figure, Joe had thought at the time. There had been all kinds of hassle before he registered at Odom. He bet all it took for the big-shot lawyer was one phone call.

Lane apparently took that conversation to mean she could

eat lunch with him and Ollie, who needed to be close to home so he could help take care of his autistic sister after school. Ollie hadn't thought it was strange when Lane sat down. He just asked if she wanted a crabmeat finger sandwich, but Joe had glared at her. Lane ignored the look and took the sandwich. Joe got used to her, but he didn't particularly like her.

"So has Mrs. Wu gotten to you yet?" Lane asked, her mouth full of today's goodies, tiny hot dogs wrapped in a croissant. Joe had taken, like, five. Despite the fancy wrappings, they were still hot dogs.

"Yah," Ollie said.

Joe looked between the two of them. "Mrs. Wu? About what?"

"About getting involved in *Big River*," Ollie informed him.

"But we don't do anything," Joe said.

Lane sniffed. "Speak for yourself. I can do plenty. She asked me to work on costumes."

Joe almost snickered. Good luck to Huckleberry Finn and whoever else was in that stupid play if Lane was doing the costumes. Huck would probably be dressed in a black jumpsuit and have glitter in his hair.

"She asked me," Ollie said, "if I would help with the props. I wasn't sure what those were, but she said they were the things the actors used in the play. She said there weren't too many of them."

Lane caught Joe's eye. Clearly, they were thinking the same thing. It was probably smart of Mrs. Wu to put Ollie in charge of something there wasn't much of. As genial as he was, Ollie wasn't known for his power of concentration.

"Well, she better not ask me," Joe said gruffly. "I don't have time."

As if on cue, Mrs. Wu appeared from out of nowhere and

stopped at their table. "Joe," she said. "I'd like to see you last period in the auditorium."

Joe was determined not to roll over. "I've got studying to do, Mrs. Wu."

Mrs. Wu nodded. "I'm sure you do. But take a few moments off and come to the auditorium. There's someone I'd like you to meet."

When Mrs. Wu was out of sight, Lane shrugged and said, "You're stuck."

"Did you have to meet anyone?" Joe asked.

Lane shook her head, and Ollie said, "Nope. She just said she could use my help."

Joe grabbed one of the cream puffs Ollie had put out for dessert. "So who am I meeting?"

Ollie shrugged. "Guess you'll have to wait and find out."

With a social studies test and a Spanish class, Joe's best subject, the rest of the day passed quickly. When last period rolled around, though, it felt weird to Joe to be heading to the auditorium with the singers, dancers, and musicians. He saw Minkus lugging his violin case, but studiously avoided looking at him. He patted the money in his pocket to make himself feel better, but he must have moved it. All he felt in his front pocket now was the angel coin.

While the other kids scurried off to the stage or the orchestra pit, Joe looked around for Mrs. Wu.

"She's backstage," one of the teacher's aides told him, pointing toward the curtain.

Joe hadn't ever been backstage of the Odom auditorium. He was surprised at how large the area was. Dingy, yes, junked up with pieces of scenery from other plays and skits, but a substantial space nonetheless. Yet as big as it was and bustling at that moment, the stage was dominated by the man standing with Mrs. Wu. Joe didn't know how tall the guy was—he was very tall—but it was more his presence than height that made him seem so imposing. And while Mrs. Wu was smiling at Joe, the man with her was not. In some of the rougher neighborhoods where Joe had lived, you'd walk by someone and get an unsettled feeling that made you want to hurry past because you knew the guy was trouble. As Joe glanced at Mrs. Wu's guest, Joe felt disoriented for a minute. This guy was different. He didn't feel like trouble in the usual way, but Joe had the distinct feeling he might be trouble for him.

"Joe, I'd like you to meet Mike Sullivan."

Normally, Joe might have shaken Mike's hand, but he kept his own tightly curled in his pocket, where his fist touched the angel.

If he noticed, Mike didn't show it. "Hello, Joe."

Mike Sullivan's voice was smooth, but strong. He still didn't smile, but there was a look in his brown eyes of such intensity—as if he were looking inside Joe and considering what was there—that Joe almost turned away.

"Mike is from the Maple Street Theater and he's going to plan and construct the scenery. And we'd like you to help with that."

Who's we? was Joe's first thought. Mike didn't seem like he wanted Joe coming anywhere near the scenery. His second thought was to say no, no thanks, too busy, can't do it, don't want to, but the word that came out of his mouth was a simple "Okay."

For the first time, Mike's lips curled upward in, if not a smile, at least a semblance of one. "Good," he said.

For some reason he couldn't explain, even to himself, Joe felt as if he had passed a test. The sense of relief that surged through him made him a little shaky, upset even. Why should he care that Mike was going to take him on?

Striving to get back some control, Joe asked as if the answer didn't matter, "Uh, so what is it you want me to do?"

Now Mike did smile. "Not now. We'll start after Christmas vacation."

"Joe?" The second time, the voice was a little louder. "Joe, can you hear . . ."

His father must have the worst cell phone service in the world, Joe thought, doodling on the pad of paper his mother kept near the kitchen phone.

"Can you hear me now?" Ramón repeated.

"Yeah, I can hear you." The fact that he could hear his father made it no less surprising that his father was calling at all. He would have expected a call on Christmas, maybe, but Christmas was a couple of days away.

"So you're probably wondering why I'm phoning."

"Mmm-hmm."

"I got some good news, *hijo.*"

I'll be the judge of that, Joe thought to himself.

"I'm coming to Chicago."

"You are?" Joe didn't even try to keep the surprise out of his voice. His father used to visit Chicago at the holidays, but not since he married Sheila and Paul was born.

"Yeah," Mr. Garcia said eagerly. "My friend Dizzy, you remember him?"

"Not really."

"Well, he was my best friend . . ."

The phone crapped out again. From what Joe could gather

from the words he caught here and there, Dizzy was getting married, and his dad had found a cheap airfare, so he could be there.

"When are you coming?" Joe said loudly.

"What?"

"When are you? . . ."

"Oh, late on the thirtieth. The wedding is New Year's Eve. New Year's Day, we'll get together, watch some football. How does that sound?"

Joe felt a flutter in his chest. He knew that feeling, and he didn't like it. It was the feeling of hope. "Yeah?"

"Yeah. I'll call your mother. I know she's kinda mad at me . . ."

Kinda. Right.

"But when I tell her we're both excited . . ."

Now the phone completely broke up, and then the line went dead. Joe hung up and sat on the couch. His dad was pretty shrewd. He must have figured that talking to him first would ease the conversation when he talked to Luisa about the visit.

Sure enough, when his mother came home from work later, she looked at him tentatively as she unwrapped the scarf from around her neck and took off her gloves.

"I guess you know who called me today," she said, running cold water into the teakettle.

Joe took a seat at the kitchen table. "Yeah." It was as if nobody wanted to say his father's name first.

Mrs. Garcia busied herself getting out her special tea and sugar from the cupboard. "You want some hot chocolate?"

"No thanks."

"What did you do all day?"

His mother worried that he'd get into trouble during

vacation while she was at work and he was home alone. In truth, it was more likely she'd come home and find him bored to death. He had hoped that maybe this vacation he would hang around with Ollie a little bit, but when he had embarrassedly broached the subject last Friday before school let out, Ollie only said, "Maybe." Christmas season was a busy time in the catering business, and he had to stay around home helping either with the food or looking out for his sister.

"You didn't just watch TV all day, did you?" his mother fretted. "The weather is nice for December. You got out for a walk, didn't you?"

Mrs. Garcia looked so anxious, Joe just nodded and said, "Yeah, I got out." Well, it wasn't a lie. He had gotten as far as the front stoop and sat outside while he did some whittling, finishing up his mother's present, a Persian cat, the fluffy kind. It was the cat she wanted in real life. Every time his mother would see a Persian in a commercial, she'd *ooh* and *ahh,* and then she'd sigh because they were so expensive. Pedigree or something. Anyway, it cost money to feed a cat, even one that came from a shelter.

Sitting down with her steaming mug, Mrs. Garcia reached over and put her hand over Joe's. "So your father says you want to see him."

Joe was pretty sure he hadn't said that. Maybe it was what his father thought he had said when the phone crapped out. Joe shrugged. "I don't care."

Mrs. Garcia frowned. "Well, technically, he does have visiting rights. Not that he should with what he pays!"

His mother was usually so mild mannered. It always unnerved Joe when she raised her voice. For a fleeting instance, he thought about how she would react if she ever found out he was shaking down Minkus. Taking a breath, he told himself that he was stupid. She'd never find out, and besides, whenever he had extra money, he was doing his mother a favor. Not having to bug her for cash. Picking up a little extra food. Having enough for her Christmas present. When he focused his attention back on his mom, he could see she was working herself up. "And where are you going to watch this football? He's staying with his cousin Al, and I never liked him . . ."

"Mami, I don't have to go," Joe interrupted.

Mrs. Garcia refocused on Joe. "What?"

"I don't care if I see him."

Taking a calming sip of tea, his mother said, "No, you should see him. You should see him. You don't get that much opportunity."

"Huh?" Joe looked at her with surprise. He thought she'd be happy if he said he wouldn't go.

"He's your father," she said flatly. And that seemed to end the discussion.

"Okay," Joe replied. "It's not for a while anyway." New Year's seemed a very long time away. There was still Christmas to get through.

Usually, Joe and his mother spent Christmas with his grandmother and some other elderly relatives in the south suburbs. Sometimes they took the El downtown and then caught the commuter train; once in a while someone picked them up. But this year, Joe's grandmother was going to Mexico to see her sister. She had saved up for the trip for years. "It might be the last time," she had told Luisa. "I'm not getting any younger."

Joe figured they would spend the day with the relatives, but his mother had surprised him when she said, "I don't want to go all the way out there on the train if *mi madre* is going to be in Mexico."

"So what will we do?"

"I'll make dinner at home. And we'll ask Gene."

"Gene? On Christmas?"

The cheerfulness on Luisa's face was replaced with an embarrassed flush. "Why not? His family isn't here. He'd be alone if we didn't have him over."

"Doesn't he have friends?" Joe muttered.

"Of course, he has friends. I am his friend." She took a gulp of her tea. "He would be your friend, too, if you let him."

Joe held his tongue, but his mother knew exactly what he was thinking. "Don't look like that. You could use some good male role models."

That was it. Joe got up and slammed his chair against the table. "I don't get you. First you don't want me to see Papi. Then you do. Next you're bringing some stranger over and saying he should be my role model. I don't need anybody to show me how to act. I know how to act."

"Do you?" his mother said quietly. "That's good if you do, because I wouldn't want a son to grow up yelling at his mother or doing the wrong things."

Joe stomped out of the room. Ha! His mother had a son that was doing both. Merry Christmas.

By Christmas Eve, Joe was resigned to his fate. He'd be spending Christmas with Gene and New Year's Day with his father, and he wasn't very happy about either holiday. The worst thing, he figured, was coming up with something to talk about. And it depressed him that he'd probably have more to say to stupid Gene than he did his own dad. At least Gene had been around lately.

The one thing, the only thing, Joe felt good about was his Christmas present for his mom. It was finished and it looked great. The way he had carved it, you could see almost every hair on the fancy Persian's coat. It was his best work ever, and he knew in part it was because he was able to buy such a good piece of wood. Thank you, Minkus.

There was even plenty of Minkus money left for some really fancy wrappings. A silver-and-gold box with paper and a bow to match had caught his eye at the card store. For a while he had toyed with using the money for another gift, maybe perfume, but he decided he preferred to have his cat presented in the manner it deserved. When he put the glittery box under the small tree his mother had bought the day before Christmas, when trees were cheaper, she looked at it with surprise.

"*Hijo,* it's beautiful. Where did you get such expensive paper?"

"Oh, it was on sale," he lied.

"And you wrapped the box yourself? You are so handy." She walked over to him and gave him a hug. "I can hardly wait to open it, even though I don't want to tear the pretty paper," Mrs. Garcia said with a laugh.

"I think you'll like it," Joe said confidently. He could hardly wait either. Now he just had to get through Christmas Eve. Joe and his mother had always been irregular church-goers. But when they moved next door to Holy Comforter, Luisa had been excited. "This will make it easy to go to church."

Joe liked to make his mother happy, so sometimes he went with her, but Luisa hadn't made much of a fuss when he didn't. Midnight Mass, though, they had never missed, and this year, it presented a problem. Since this stuff with Minkus started, he hadn't gone to confession, and if you didn't go to confession, you couldn't take Holy Communion. And if he didn't take Communion during Midnight Mass, his mother would start asking questions, and she wouldn't stop.

He supposed he could go to confession. Joe would spill the beans about the Minkus money, the priest would forgive him, tell him how many Hail Marys and Our Fathers to say for penance, and he'd have to say he wasn't going to do it again. That was the rub. He was pretty sure that he was going to ask Minkus for money again. Well, maybe "ask" wasn't the right word. Okay, straight out, as soon as he got back to school, he was going hit up Minkus, because the piggy bank was empty. He didn't want to lie right to the priest's face. So screw Communion. He might be a bit of a bully, but he wasn't going to be a hypocrite. He felt righteous for about ten seconds until he realized his stand wasn't solving the problem about Midnight Mass.

Joe spent all Christmas Eve day worrying about what to do. Finally, he decided.

"Mami," he said about nine o'clock, "I don't feel well."

His mother turned from the stove where she was making flan, a delicious custard, for tomorrow's dessert. "What's wrong?"

Putting on what he hoped was a pathetic expression, he said, "My head hurts."

Mrs. Garcia wiped her hands on her apron, and came over and touched his forehead. "You're not warm."

"It just hurts really bad. And I already took something for it about an hour ago, and it still hurts. And now I'm getting the chills." He tried to shiver and hoped it didn't look too fake.

"Go lie down," his mother instructed. "I'll make you a hot water bag. I hope you won't be sick for tomorrow," she fretted.

There was the opening he needed, but he waited the hour or so until his mother came into his darkened room. "How are you feeling?" she whispered.

"Maybe a little better. If I stayed in bed . . ." Was she getting his drift? "But I want to go to Midnight Mass." His words were soft, his tone plaintive.

"I know you do." Luisa came and sat down on his bed and stroked his hair, which made Joe feel terrible. "And it is nearby . . ."

Joe held his breath.

"But we want you to be well for Christmas, so I think maybe you should stay in tonight. Go to bed right now and get a good night's sleep."

Relief washed over Joe, but it was mixed with sadness. He had always liked going to Midnight Mass with his mom.

After he heard the door slam, Joe went to the living room, where he could see the church from the window. Even though the service wouldn't start for a while, people were pouring into Holy Comforter because seats were always tight for Midnight Mass. It was odd to see the church lit so brightly in the middle of the night, making the stained glass windows look like they were on fire.

Joe padded over to the couch and clicked the TV remote. There was at least one thing he'd been looking forward to this evening. On the few nights he was up this late, he couldn't watch television because he'd wake his mother. Now he settled in on the couch under a brown tweedy afghan his grandmother had knit, ready to watch some late-night TV. After pounding away on the remote for a few seconds and finding nothing but talkers, reruns of old shows, and really old shows, and—ha!—a local broadcast of Midnight Mass, he turned off the TV and went back to bed. It was hard to get comfortable. His bed was small because his alcove was small, and it seemed as if every day he was getting bigger. Pretty soon his feet were going to be hanging over the edge of the bed.

Tossing fitfully, Joe tried not think. There were so many things he didn't want to think about. Christmas with Gene, New Year's with his father. He didn't want to think about school, and he didn't want to think about the look on Minkus's face when he handed over his money. Then another face came to mind, and Joe knew for certain he'd never fall asleep if he started trying to figure out Mike. Pulling his cover tighter around him as if for protection, Joe willed Mike's reflective brown eyes out of his mind.

What could he think about? He desperately tried to come up with a neutral topic. Finally, it came to him—the Chicago Cubs. Last year, the team had been lousy, but Joe had seen a lot of the games on TV. He started going through the lineup, trying to figure what kind of trades the Cubs could make to move them up in their division. He beefed up the pitching staff, got the team a new catcher, and finally fell asleep considering how the Cubbies could revitalize second base.

X

"Oh, Joe, it's wonderful!" Mrs. Garcia said yet again, her fingers smoothly touching each part of Joe's carved Persian cat, the ears, the tail, even the delicate whiskers. She looked at him with wonder in her eyes. "Like your grandfather always said, you have a gift in your hands."

Joe beamed with pride. His mother's reaction to the cat was everything he had hoped for: chatting about where she would put it—"in the living room where everyone can see it, or in my bedroom, where it will be special just for me"— putting it down, while she went to refresh her tea; and then picking up the cat again and talking about how amazing it was that Joe could "make wood look fluffy."

Joe liked his presents, too. Their TV was too old to be rigged right for the new video games, but his mother got him a couple of handheld ones that were pretty good. She also got him a black sweatshirt.

"I wanted to get you more clothes, but it's so hard to figure out what you think is cool . . ."

Smiling at the idea of his mother trying to measure the coolness of clothes, Joe told her, "This is great. Black. Sweatshirt. Never goes out of style." The scarf knit by his grandmother, as usual, was a bit more problematic. Colorwise, he guessed she was going for festive, but the red, green, and gold scarf was a little out-there. It might come in handy if it was cold. But only if it was really, really cold.

There were a few other gifts scattered around. One of his mother's cousins had sent a book about making birdhouses, which might be an okay thing to do sometime, and his aunt Graciella in Arizona had sent gloves to both him and Luisa. Every year, Graciella sent gloves, her way of gloating that she had finally escaped the cold.

So, kind of slim pickings, but okay. Usually, there was some sort of present from his father, who always got his size wrong and never knew what kind of game or book he was interested in, but this year there was nothing.

His mother, watching him peruse his loot, said, "Your father is probably bringing his present with him."

Joe hadn't thought of that. "You think so?"

"Mailing things is a hassle, so I'm sure he decided it would be easier to bring it along."

That made Joe feel better. Although, come to think of it, it was going to be hard to look enthusiastic when he opened one of his father's gifts while actually sitting next to him.

Christmas Day always had a smooth slowness to it that Joe enjoyed, at least until it was time to leave for his grandmother's house. This year, the sweet-molasses feeling ended even earlier, as Luisa bustled around getting dinner ready. While his mother fussed with the turkey breast—she said a whole turkey would be too much, but too expensive was more like it—and the tamales and the salad and the green bean casserole, Joe lay down on his bed and played with his games.

Finally, his mother came in, exasperated. "Can I get a little help, *hijo?*"

"Help?" Joe barely looked up.

Luisa stood in front of him. "Yes, help. I need you to set the table and clean the bathroom."

That got Joe's attention. "Clean the bathroom?"

"Yes. Gene will probably have to use the bathroom at some point, and I'd like it to look nice."

Joe didn't want to fight with his mother on Christmas Day, but clean the bathroom. Really?

His mother ignored the look on his face and just headed back into the kitchen. "Why don't you start with the table."

By the time Gene rang the doorbell, the table was set with their best dishes, which meant the three that weren't chipped, and the bathroom looked clean, if not the "nice" that his mother had requested. What did nice even mean when you were talking about bathrooms?

"Will you get that, Joe?" Luisa called from the kitchen.

Without replying, Joe buzzed Gene in downstairs and then waited until there was a knock at the door. Opening the door wide, Joe was unprepared for what he saw: Gene carrying one good-size package, badly wrapped, and another box with handles; weird little noises seemed to be coming from within. Handing the wrapped present to Joe, Gene put the other box down in the corner of the hallway and pointed to it, putting his finger to his lips, asking Joe not to give away the secret.

That would be easy, since Joe had no idea what the secret might be.

"Hello," said Luisa, coming in from the kitchen, wiping her hands on her apron. She looked like she wanted to give Gene a kiss but just patted him on the arm.

Staring hard at Gene, Joe could see nothing at all kissable about him. He was probably the most average-looking guy in the world. White bread seemed exotic compared to Gene Fulton with his medium-brown hair, medium-brown eyes, average height, a stocky body bordering on flabby, and wire-rimmed glasses that slipped down on his nose with alarming regularity. He wasn't even interesting enough to be nerdy.

Gene smiled at Luisa, and then at Joe. "I'm so glad to be here."

He was probably glad to be anywhere, Joe thought, wondering how often Gene had gotten out before Luisa had taken pity on him. It had to be pity, because Joe refused to believe that his mother could have anything approaching feelings for this guy.

Not that he wasn't affable. That word had been one of their vocabulary builders in English. It meant pleasant. Gene was affable, but females didn't get swoony over guys who were just affable. Did they?

Joe remembered very clearly the day his mother had started talking about Gene. It was the first day of school. Luisa was always eager to hear about his teachers and how his classes seemed, and it was no different that day. But when they started talking about the kids in his class, she asked, "So do you see maybe making some new friends?"

"No," Joe wanted to say flatly. What was the point of making friends, when they'd probably move again by summer. So in answer, all he did was shrug.

"I've made a new friend at the office," his mother said shyly. "Gene," she added.

Joe didn't pay much attention; his mother naturally made friends. He also assumed that "Gene" was a woman named "Jean." It wasn't until Luisa was readying herself for their first date that he figured it out.

"Gene and I are going to the movies," she'd said that day,

as she put on her lipstick, then fastened her shiniest gold bracelet.

"You sure look nice."

"Well, I don't have a date very often," Luisa had said, laughing.

A date. Jean? Oh, Gene. Joe hadn't said anything, because he didn't want to look stupid, but the idea of his mother going out on a date was shocking. To say that she didn't date very often was an understatement. Try never. But things had apparently gone well, because since then Gene had turned up regularly and Joe tried to avoid him whenever possible.

Today, Gene looked utterly pleased with himself as he put down the awkwardly wrapped package near the tree. "Hey, Merry Christmas, everybody."

"Would you like something to drink, Gene?" Luisa asked.

"How about some coffee? It's freezing out there. Then we can open our presents."

Luisa went to the kitchen to get the coffee, while Gene settled himself on the couch. "Presents already?" she said over her shoulder.

That's what Joe was thinking. He liked presents as much as anybody, but Gene was certainly acting pushy.

"It's just that I'm so excited about them," Gene said as he took his coffee mug from Luisa.

Now Luisa looked worried. "Gene, I have a few small presents for you . . ."

Gene beamed at Luisa. "I'm sure whatever you got me is great, but it's the presents I'm giving you guys that I'm excited about. It's better to give than to receive, remember."

"Gene, I hope you didn't overdo it," Luisa said a bit sternly.

Gene just grinned.

"All right," Luisa answered, throwing up her hand. "Joe, I'll get you some hot chocolate, and we'll open presents."

While his mother was getting the hot chocolate, Joe sat across from Gene, studiously studying his hands and saying nothing.

"How you been, Joe?" Gene said.

"Fine."

"Everything good?"

"It's all good."

Gene's smile faded a little, but he gamely said, "I hope you'll like your gift."

So do I, Joe thought. He wasn't in the mood to fake enthusiasm. But when he finally ripped open the package, he didn't have to. "A TV!" True, it wasn't a large TV, but it was totally up-to-date and a million times better than the TV they had.

Luisa's expression alternated between delight and exasperation. "Gene, this is too much . . ."

"The store was having a sale, and I had a coupon that made it another twenty percent off. They practically paid me to buy it."

Louisa smiled and shook her head, and Joe took that to mean they could keep the television set. Well, Joe thought, maybe old Gene was good for something after all.

But whatever grateful feelings had bubbled up inside Joe when he unwrapped the television, spectacularly popped with the appearance of the next gift.

"Okay, guys, I'm glad you liked the TV, but the next present is really special. Luisa, it's something I've heard you say you really wanted."

"Oh, Gene . . ." By now, Luisa was giggling.

As Gene walked into the hallway to get the box, everything clicked. Something his mother wanted, the odd little sounds . . .

Luisa took the handles of the box and opened it curiously.

With an intake of breath, she lifted out an orange-and-white-striped cat with huge green eyes, looking around with a mixture of curiosity and fear. Luisa was dumbfounded. Finally, she choked out, "You got me a cat?"

"You love cats!"

"I know." This cat cuddled against her shoulder. "But, Gene, I can't afford a cat. The food, the medical bills . . ."

"The shelter gave it a checkup and shots." Pulling a gift card out of his pocket, he added, "And here's something that'll get you maybe a year's worth of food if you get the big sacks of dry food. I've got litter and a pan in the car." Gene was beaming as if he had thought of everything.

As his mom and Gene smiled at each other, Joe felt his face redden. He wanted to jump out of his chair and tell this interloper his mother already had a cat, and not a stupid alley cat from a shelter, but a carved Persian that was better looking than the hunk of bones he had brought. At the very least, he wished his mother would say something like, "This is my second cat of the day. Joe carved a Persian for me, which by the way is actually the kind of cat I always wanted." But all Luisa did was stare at the squirming cat with a dopey smile on her face, while it tried to claw her blouse.

The rest of the afternoon, the cat was the center of attention. No one even noticed Joe's pouting. His mother tried out various names before settling on Gato, which means "cat" in Spanish. Finally. Gene hooked up the new TV, and Joe was able to ignore Gato and his antics and watch television. At around four, his father called. The conversation was short, but his dad confirmed that he was coming in just like he said he would. He'd go to the wedding on New Year's Eve, and then pick up Joe the next morning, and they'd spend the day watching football games at his cousin Al's house. His mother didn't look thrilled when Joe told her the plan, but she didn't say a word against it either.

The evening seemed to go on forever, and the apartment seemed so stuffed, with people and food and wrappings— and a cat—Joe felt like he could hardly breathe. He wanted desperately to get out of the living room, though he doubted going to his so-called bedroom would help with this feeling of suffocation. Finally, he decided to reuse his lie of yesterday and pleaded a headache.

"He had one yesterday, too," Luisa told Gene with concern.

"Probably just all the holiday excitement. Do you want to go take a walk?" Gene asked him. "Get some fresh air?"

"No," Joe snapped.

"Why don't you go in my bedroom and lie down," Luisa said. "Maybe Gene and I will go for that walk, and the apartment will be quiet for you."

Joe nodded with relief. As he settled himself in her bed, not too comfortably because he knew he'd have to move later, he noticed his Persian on the dresser. It looked lonely.

Joe had been looking forward to the next couple of days after Christmas. Luisa had taken some of her meager vacation, and they had planned to do a little postholiday shopping, maybe go to a movie or two. But all of it was ruined by his mother's infatuation with her new pet. She couldn't stop talking about Gato and cuddling him whenever possible, though he didn't seem to like it much, usually slipping out of her arms. Even when they were out shopping, she spent as much time looking at cat treats and toys as she did trying to find marked-down clothes for him. It was getting harder and harder for Joe not to lose his temper, and it was almost a relief when she went back to work.

December's warm streak was continuing, and Joe was darned if he was going to spend the rest of his vacation in their tiny apartment playing nursemaid to the cat. He'd feed him, like his mother had instructed, but that was it. Let Gato spend the day doing whatever it was that cats did when left to their own devices. As far Joe could tell, that was eating and sleeping.

Throwing on his jacket and leaving his gloves and hat in the closet, Joe gave the door a good slam behind him. He hoped the cat jumped.

Of course, once he was outside, Joe was stuck with the problem of what to do. There was nowhere to go and no one to see. And no one to see him. Sometimes he felt like Harry Potter wearing an invisibility cloak. Of course, if he headed down to bustling Armitage Avenue where there were plenty of stores, he might just try to lift something, and then an invisibility cloak would come in handy.

First, maybe, he'd stop at the Ortiz Market and grab a Coke. Joe rummaged around in his pocket to see if he had any money left over from Christmas, but all he found was that stupid angel coin. He was sick of it showing up when he was looking for money. Next time he was in church, whenever that might be, he was going to drop it in the collection plate.

Roaming aimlessly around the neighborhood, Joe had plenty of time to think, and as usual, thinking turned into worry. What would it be like to see his father again? It had to be three years since he laid eyes on him, and truth be told, Joe didn't feel like Ramón Garcia was his father at all. He was a voice on the telephone, the source of his mother's tears. Dad to a brother Joe had never seen.

Worry became anxiety, which morphed into disgust. Why even bother going out with his father on New Year's Day? So he could sit around and watch a couple of football games he didn't care about with a guy who didn't care about him?

But then, creeping out from a corner of his mind, came the memory of Ramón taking him to the beach when he was a little boy, holding his hands as they jumped what passed for waves in Lake Michigan. Sometimes his father would read him a story before he went to bed, and even though his father wasn't the greatest at reading out loud, Joe liked being in the darkened room with him, just listening to his voice. Being in that room was what it was like to feel safe.

"Fine, okay, I want to see him," Joe admitted out loud, causing a dog walker passing by to glance at him. The admission gave him a stomachache, but yeah, there it was. He wanted to hang out with his father, if only for an afternoon. Did he still look like Ramón? His mother used to laugh and call them Big Twin and Little Twin. The wondering made him want to kick something.

And then, as if by magic, Minkus appeared, getting out of a late-model Lexus. Minkus! Joe almost shouted his name. There was mad, and then there was this feeling, anger so cold, it was hot, and right now he wanted to share it with Minkus.

Striding toward him, Joe was startled to see someone else getting out the car, a girl. He vaguely remembered Minkus's sister was in school last year. Was that her?

By now, Joe was too close to Minkus to avoid him. His fury shriveled into mere awkwardness. The girl glanced at him curiously, but not as if she knew anything about what was going on between Joe and her brother.

For a moment they just all looked at one another. Finally, Joe had to break the silence, but "Ah, hey," was all he could manage.

Minkus just stared at him. Then he turned to his sister and said, "Let's go, Vivi, Bette's waiting."

Joe looked around. A moving van was parked down the street. "Is Bette moving?"

Before Minkus or Vivi answered, Bette came charging down the stairs of the greystone and hurried over to their small, unhappy group.

"I saw your mother drop you off," Bette said. She turned to Joe. "What are you doing here?"

Joe shrugged. "Just ran into them."

"Your name is Joe, right?" Vivi asked. Without waiting for an answer, she told Bette, "He wants to know if you're moving. Seemed a little concerned."

Joe glared at Vivi. "It was just a question."

"No, I'm not. My downstairs neighbor Gabi moved out, and now the new tenant is moving in." Then she added, "It's Mrs. Abrams's daughter."

"Our Mrs. Abrams?" Andy asked.

"Yeah. A coincidence."

"Maybe she can steal test answers for you," Joe joked. Nobody laughed.

Bette, Minkus, and Vivi began moving away, and Joe, to his surprise, didn't want to see them go. Well, Bette anyway. He looked at Vivi, the least likely to have something against him. For the first time, he noticed her puffy face. Weird. "So, what happened to you?" he asked conversationally.

Vivi's rounded face reddened. "Pardon me?"

"You look all blown up." As the words came out of his mouth, Joe realized they didn't sound so good. He really hadn't meant anything mean by the comment, he was just curious. From the expressions on Vivi's and Bette's faces, however, he could see he had said the wrong thing. Minkus, going on the offensive like he never did when Joe was shaking him down, leaped toward Joe, who put an arm against his chest to stop him. "Hey, hey, watch it."

"Leave my sister alone," Minkus sputtered.

Already embarrassed in front of the girls, Joe instinctively understood that hitting Minkus would only make things worse. Not knowing what else to do, he jammed his hands in his pockets and strode away.

With no place else to go, he went home. When his mother called to ask if he wanted to go out for dinner with her and Gene, he barked no.

"Okay, okay. Then I'll come home."

"Don't come home. Go out to eat."

"Joe, I don't want you to be by yourself."

"I'm always by myself," Joe wanted to yell at her. But all he said was, "I'm fine. Gene got me a new television to watch and a cat to keep me company so he could feel free to take you out."

Sarcasm was wasted on Luisa, always had been. She never seemed to get it. "Well, if you're sure. There's some money in my dresser drawer. You can take ten dollars for dinner."

"Sure, sure. Go."

Later, rummaging through his mother's dresser drawer, Joe easily found Luisa's small stash of emergency money. Well, if she thought giving him money for dinner so she could go out with Gene was an emergency, fine. Slamming the drawer shut, he cast a jaundiced eye at the Persian sitting atop the dresser. "Dust catcher," he muttered.

As Joe grabbed his coat from the closet, Gato rubbed up against his leg.

"What do you want? You've got food." He opened the front door, and Gato tried to dash out. "No, you don't," Joe said, nabbing him and bringing him back in. Gato might enjoy having room and board, but he also was interested in exploring. Every time the front or back door opened, the cat was right there.

Figuring he'd go to McDonald's for dinner, Joe headed up the street, but without really making the decision, he turned and found himself walking back to Bette's. He realized how stupid it was to be worried about what she thought of him for making an unthinking remark to Vivi. If she ever found out what he was doing to Minkus, she'd hate him for sure. When he finally got to Bette's house, he stood outside and looked up. Was that Bette at the second-floor window? After staring for a few seconds, willing Bette to see him, he found himself walking up the steps and looking at the doorbells, when a man and a woman came out the front door.

"Hello," the man said.

"Hello."

"Did you want to see Bette? I'm her dad."

"Uh, no."

"Oh, 'cause you were looking up at the window, and now maybe considering ringing the doorbell."

"Well . . ."

"What's your name?" Mr. Miller asked.

"Joe," he said, almost inaudibly.

Bette must have caught sight of them talking from the living room, because she raised the window sash and stuck her head out.

"Joe's here," Mr. Miller said. "Do you want him to come up?"

Bette shrugged. Now what was he supposed to do, Joe wondered.

"Ms. Abrams and I are going to pick up a pizza. We'll be right back. Do you want to join us for dinner?" Bette's father asked.

Another dinner invitation he didn't want. "No," Joe said forcefully, then added a quieter "thanks."

Bette slammed the window down, but she buzzed the front door. With Mr. Miller and Ms. Abrams staring at him, there seemed nothing to do but go upstairs. The welcome he received wasn't warm.

"What are you doing here?" Bette demanded as she opened the door.

"I don't know," Joe answered honestly, not sure if he should come inside, but when Bette pushed the door open a little wider, he stepped over the threshold. "I was just walking past your house, and your father said I could come upstairs."

Bette frowned. "That doesn't make sense. My father wouldn't ask a strange kid to come into the house."

"Okay, maybe I was looking up at the window. And then I was going to ring the bell."

There wasn't much to say to Bette's *hmmph*. The silence lengthened and thickened. Finally, Joe said, "Was that your new neighbor?"

"Yes."

"She doesn't look anything like Mrs. Abrams."

"No, and she's a singer."

That broke the ice a little; they both smiled at the idea of Gravel Gertie Abrams having a daughter who sang.

"How do you know that?" Joe asked. "She didn't come here singing, did she?"

"No. My father has a jazz club, and she auditioned for him. Then he found out she was looking for an apartment, and we were looking for a tenant. Gabi, the woman who lived downstairs, moved. Suddenly." Only someone listening very carefully would have heard the slight wobble in Bette's voice.

"You liked her, I guess," Joe said.

Bette nodded. "She was great, but she got a job, she said, and she had to go."

Joe folded his arms across his chest. "Yeah, well, people go all the time."

"You're telling me," Bette replied quietly.

There was another silence, but this time it was shared with understanding.

"Anyway," Joe said, clearing his throat. "Uh, could you tell Minkus's sister I didn't mean anything when I said that about her face."

"She takes medicine for asthma that makes her look like that," Bette informed him. "And she doesn't want to come back to school because she thinks people will make fun of her," she added pointedly.

"They will," Joe said.

"Yeah, I guess so." There was no point in denying something they both knew.

"So, I'll go now."

"You could stay for dinner," Bette said hesitantly.

Now Joe was tempted. He could even keep the money and tell his mother he'd spent it at McDonald's. But the thought of having to make conversation with Bette, her father, and Mrs. Abrams's daughter scared him off. He shook his head.

"See you in school," Bette said, but Joe was out the door before she could say anything else.

Joe couldn't say he had ever looked forward to going back to school after a vacation, but now Odom shone like a beacon. All he had to do was get through New Year's Day.

Even though he had stayed up until midnight on New Year's Eve with Gene and his mother, watching the ball drop in New York on their new TV, Joe found himself up early on New Year's Day, too nervous to sleep. He went into the kitchen and pulled the juice out of the refrigerator and drank it out of the carton, something his mother hated. Luisa was still sleeping; Joe wasn't sure what time Gene had left, but the apartment was so neat, his mother obviously hadn't gone to bed until she cleaned up and put out a little dry food for Gato.

Joe sat down on the living room couch, not knowing what to do with himself. It was way too early to expect a call from his father. Ramón had even told him he'd probably want to sleep in after partying at the wedding. "I'll call you when I wake up" was as definitive as he had gotten on their last phone call.

By the time his mother got up around ten, Joe had been reduced to doing homework he'd put off for most of the vacation. Luisa seemed almost as nervous as he was.

"How about I make pancakes for breakfast?"

Joe barely looked up from his math. "Whatever."

"Pancakes are your favorite."

"I'm not too hungry."

"You'll feel better if you eat something."

Joe doubted that. Just the thought of pancakes mixing it up with the knots in his stomach made him feel infinitely worse. "Mami, maybe just toast and tea."

"A scrambled egg?"

"Okay, fine, a scrambled egg." He tried not to sound snappish.

By eleven, breakfast was long over. By noon, Joe was reduced to watching a stupid parade on television. Luisa kept looking out the window as if she expected Ramón to drive up rather than call like he said he was going to.

"There are a few flakes already," she said, closing the blinds. "The warm spell is over. It's supposed to snow heavily tonight."

Joe had noticed the sky was as dull and gray as the day was turning out to be.

"I'm going to call your father," Luisa said.

"No!"

"Why not? We don't know what's happening. It's almost twelve thirty."

"He said he was going to call me. Anyway, he told me he was going sleep in."

At twelve forty-five, the phone rang, but it was only Gene. Luisa asked him to come over, "But not till later."

Joe hoped fervently that "later" he would be long gone. But at about one, the phone rang again, and there was something about the tinny sound that reeked of disappointment. Luisa went for the phone, but Joe pushed her hand away and picked it up himself.

"Joe? It's your father."

"Where are you?" Joe asked curtly.

"I'm still at Al's."

"When are you getting here?"

"Well, there's a problem, Joe."

Joe didn't say a word, but his eyes met Luisa's.

"See, they're predicting a big snowstorm tonight. Of course, we're not used to that kind of weather in L.A." Ramón chuckled nervously. "Sunshine Central. Anyway, I was going home late on the red-eye, like I told you, but I'm afraid if I stay, I won't get out. You know how they cancel flights these days.

It's raining somewhere, even if it's not where you are, and they cancel flights, huh? So I called the airline, and I booked myself on an earlier flight. And of course, I gotta be at the airport way early for that whole security hassle. So, anyway, that doesn't leave us much time for football games."

Joe wanted to hang up right then, but his father said, "Hey, Joe, I know you're disappointed. I'm disappointed, too. And I'm going to stop by to give you your Christmas present on the way to the airport. I brought it all the way from L.A., I don't want to drag it home. Joe? Joe, you still there?"

"Yeah, I'm here."

"So I'll see you in about an hour."

Now Joe did hang up.

He repeated the conversation to his mother, and as he expected, Luisa fumed. "This is just like him. Promises. Promises that come to nothing."

Joe felt like doing one of two things, neither of which was an option: smashing his fist through a window or throwing himself down on his bed and crying. Luisa kept asking him if he wanted something to eat or if he'd like to go to a movie later, but Joe just went back to his homework. At two, the doorbell rang. Finally, it seemed, his father was able get somewhere on time.

His mother answered the door, standing in front of Joe as if she was protecting him.

"Ramón . . . ," she began.

"Hey, Joe," his father said, stepping around her and stiffly giving Joe a hug. He handed him a box with torn, tired wrappings that looked as if it had flown halfway across the world, not just the country. "Look, I'm sorry about all this, but I gotta get home. Safer to try and get out early." He looked appealingly at Luisa and Joe.

Joe studied his father. He had his answer about one thing
for sure. Anyone could see how much they still resembled
each other. The curly dark hair and brown, almost black eyes.
The sturdy build. "Yeah, it's okay," Joe said, throwing the gift
down on a nearby chair.

"And Luisa, I've got something for you, too."

"Oh?"

Ramón pulled out his wallet and handed her a wad of
bills. "I know I'm a little behind . . ."

"Was there a poker game last night?" Luisa asked.

His father offered his mother a boyish grin. "You know
me too well. I got lucky, and I said to myself, I'm gonna give
this to Luisa, for my boy."

Luisa looked like she wanted to throw the money in his
face, but shoved it into her pocket instead.

"So, I'm sorry I can't stay longer, but Al's waiting for me
downstairs. He didn't think you were too anxious to see him,
Luisa."

"No," she murmured.

"Joe, maybe you can come out to California. I'll send you
a ticket. Maybe this summer."

His father looked like he expected an answer. "Whatever," Joe said.

"Okay, then," Ramón answered a little nervously. "Well,
give me a hug."

It was the last thing Joe wanted to do, and he just stood
there, but his father hugged him anyway.

"Bye, Joe. I'll see you soon." Then he was gone.

Joe and his mother sat down on the couch. "How much
did he give you?" Joe asked.

Luisa took out the money and counted it. "Two hundred
and fifty. Now he's only three hundred and fifty short for this

month." She gestured to the present Joe was still holding. "What did he give you?"

Joe tore open the present. Inside the box was a sweater. Charcoal gray. The color wasn't too bad, he thought. He took it out and looked it over. A decent enough sweater, okay for school. Then Joe held it against himself, checking it for fit. He could see the answer in his mother's eyes. It was at least a size too small.

XI

Joe never would have believed it in a million years, but he was happy—thrilled!—to be back at school. No more trying to keep busy, no more getting claustrophobic in that apartment, no cat. As he pushed his way through a bunch of kids to get to the front door, he spotted Minkus, and Joe smiled. Yes, Christmas had left him short of money, but Joe felt so pleased just to be around people, he benevolently decided to give Minkus a break and leave him alone for a day or so. Of course, Joe knew that worked to his advantage as well. Minkus always became more nervous when he didn't know when the blade was going to fall.

For a moment, once inside the building, with its particular smell, a mix of disinfectant and kids, Joe felt like he might be on the verge of something new. It was a new year after all, and that's when people made resolutions to dump their bad habits and wipe the slate clean. Slate wiping felt good for about two minutes, until all the things that he'd have to do flew at him: improve his grades, try to get a couple of real friends, stop shaking down the smallest kid in the class. Hanging his jacket in his locker, Joe wondered if anyone ever waited for February to make their resolutions.

Slamming the thin metal door shut with a certain loud satisfaction, he turned around to see Mrs. Wu frowning at him.

"Quieter next time, please, Joe."

"Sure," Joe muttered.

Since she kept standing there, Joe figured Mrs. Wu's appearance wasn't just coincidence.

"In homeroom today, Mrs. Abrams will make the announcement that Tuesday has been added as an extra day of rehearsals for *Big River*."

So? Joe thought to himself.

"And Tuesday is the day you can join Mike from the Maple Tree Theater and help with the scenery. I hope that works for you."

Joe frantically tried to come up with a reason why it didn't work for him, but nothing came to mind. With Mrs. Wu waiting for his answer, all Joe could do was nod mutely.

"Fine. Meet Mike backstage tomorrow," the principal said, smiling brightly before taking off, her high heels clicking on the linoleum floor.

Joe opened the door of his locker, just so he could slam it again. Harder.

At lunch, Joe grabbed some milk and went to sit with Ollie and Lane, hoping that Ollie had enough leftovers from New Year's parties to provide him with something to eat, since his dried-up cheese sandwich from home was barely edible.

Ollie came through. As Joe sat down, Ollie was taking all sorts of tiny sandwiches out of a plastic bag. He had even come prepared with paper plates, handing one to Joe and another to Lane. "Cream cheese and pimento and shrimp salad," he informed them.

"Thanks," Joe said gratefully, taking about six sandwiches and plopping them on a silver plate embossed with the words HAPPY NEW YEAR! "How was your vacation?"

"Busy," Ollie said. "We had lots of parties."

"We went skiing in Colorado," Lane said.

I wasn't talking to you, Joe thought, but he just continued eating his sandwiches.

"What about you?" Ollie asked.

"Oh, my dad came in from California. I spent some time with him." Well, it wasn't a lie. Five minutes was "some time."

"I guess I'm glad to be back," Ollie said. "School is going to seem like a vacation after making canapés practically every day."

"*Big River* is heading into high gear," Lane commented. "I hear they've added an extra rehearsal day."

Joe sighed. All through morning classes, he had tried to avoid thinking about tomorrow. He wasn't sure why working on the scenery for the play made him so uneasy. Under different circumstances, he might have liked getting to do some sawing and painting, but the memory of Mike's piercing eyes disturbed him. Wasn't there any way to get out of this stupid play?

That night, he felt out his mother on the subject. As they were washing up after dinner, Joe said, "Did I tell you about this play they're putting on at school?"

Luisa nodded. "A musical. What's the name?"

"*Big River,*" Joe responded shortly. "It's about Huckleberry Finn."

"That's a funny name," Luisa said as she finished scrubbing the last pot.

"Yeah." Joe didn't feel like explaining about the kid and the book. Obviously, his mother had never heard of it.

"You said the principal asked you to work on the scenery."

Joe put the pot he was drying on the shelf. Here was his

opening. "Yeah, but I'd have to stay after school—a couple of times a week, maybe—to do the work."

Luisa gave him that mother-knows-all look. "So?"

Unlike this morning with Mrs. Wu, Joe had his answer at the ready. "It will take a lot of time away from my homework."

"*Hijo,* I'm sorry to say, you don't spend that much time on your homework."

"Well, you don't want me to have less time to spend, do you?"

Luisa gently took the towel out of his hands and led him over to the kitchen table.

"Now," she said, pushing him into the rickety chair, "tell me why you don't want to work on this play."

Joe shrugged. "It's a waste of time."

"Mrs. Wu doesn't think so. I don't think so either. You do beautiful work with your hands. This will give you a chance to show the whole school your woodworking."

Instead of taking this as the compliment he knew his mother meant to offer, Joe could feel a sour taste rising up from his stomach. He had been watching in the days since Christmas to see if his mother had even picked up his carved Persian cat from her dresser, where she had put it. Since it was starting to get dusty, the answer was no.

But Gato got picked up. Picked up, petted, cooed over, chuckled at. Okay, so sure, a real cat was more appealing than a wooden one, Joe could give his mother that, but he had put plenty of work into the Persian, and he might as well have bought her a stuffed kitten for a couple bucks at the Walgreens for all the attention his gift got. Well, if his mother thought he was going to spend more time working on some project that was literally going to fade into the background, she was crazy.

"It's a big waste of time," Joe muttered.

Luisa coughed. Uh-oh. His mother had started coughing before Christmas. A cough had been the start of all their troubles last time, when she wound up with pneumonia and no job.

"Are you okay?" he asked.

Luisa nodded, clearing her throat. "Joe, it's a break you're at this school, so close to home. Otherwise, you'd be traveling all over the city, and I'd be worrying about you even more than I do now."

"So?" Joe asked sullenly.

"They let you in because it was hardship, and you helped take care of me when I was sick. Now, I think they forgot why you're there. Maybe they still think I'm sick, I don't know. But I don't want you to make a fuss about this. Or call attention to yourself. Just do what they tell you to do."

Luisa's soft brown eyes were pleading. What could Joe say?

"Fine. Whatever." But he didn't have to say it nicely.

His answer seemed good enough for Luisa. "Do you have homework?"

Joe considered. If he said yes, he'd be stuck here at this wobbly table all night trying to figure out some stupid equations. If he said no, he could watch TV. "It was only the first day back," he answered.

Luisa didn't seem to notice this wasn't exactly an answer to her question.

"All right then. Let's watch that new show where they give all the money away. You don't even have to be smart," she marveled. "You just have to pick the right door."

Joe gave a fleeting thought to his page of math problems. With any luck, he could do them in homeroom. Maybe Lane would let him copy her paper. She was pretty good in math. Of course, if he had any real luck, he'd be on that TV show, opening doors and getting buckets of money. He made a mental note to check in with Minkus. His funds were really getting quite low.

Joe stood backstage, hiding in the wings and counting the seconds before he'd have to force himself to show himself to Mike.

Mike. Joe had a clear view of him from this vantage point. He was checking something off on a clipboard, but even in doing that innocuous act, there was a kind of potent energy that radiated from him. To Joe's surprise, Mike wasn't as tall as he remembered him, but he was tall enough and looked as though he worked out, his body taut in his black turtleneck and jeans. His hair was thick, brown, almost to his shoulders. Hippie long. It must have been pulled back the day they first met. Joe also noticed Mike's well-shaped hands, the tapered fingers, and he wondered if Mike carved wood as well as made scenery.

Even though Joe was pretty sure he was hidden, Mike looked up and glanced in his direction. Joe waited until he had settled back to his clipboard before walking from the wings. Mike barely acknowledged him when Joe said, "Hi."

"Hey, Joe."

There was a silence that apparently Joe was expected to fill. The straightforward approach, that's what he would take. "I'm here to work on the scenery."

Now Mike looked up. "Yes, I know."

There was the X-ray look, the one Joe had dreaded. Yet now that Mike was gazing at him, Joe realized he had in some strange way been longing for it as well. A fleeting sensation of relief passed through him. Someone understood.

Then, as quickly as it came, the glance was gone. Mike

turned his head, distracted by a the sound of a chair being knocked over by a clumsy kid, and when he returned his gaze to Joe, there was nothing extraordinary about it in the least.

"Let's sit down, Joe." Mike walked a few steps and righted the chair. He pulled it next to a stack of bundled wooden sheets covered with plastic, and motioned for Joe to have a seat on that while he slid into the chair, his legs stretched in front of him. "So," he began. "Why did you want to work on the set design for *Big River*?"

Startled, Joe didn't even pretend to be polite. "It wasn't my idea."

"Oh?" Mike said coolly, one eyebrow raised.

"I have to," Joe said bluntly. Then he tersely explained about how he came to be at Odom. For some reason, he wasn't in the least worried that Mike would rat him out. "My mother wants me to go along with anything Mrs. Wu tells me to do," he concluded.

"You have to go along to get along, huh?"

Joe shrugged.

"So you have no interest in helping me design and build the sets?"

Another shrug seemed in order. But as Joe looked around the empty stage area, he couldn't deny that turning this, well, nothing into something might be interesting. Not wanting to let down too much of his guard, he finally muttered, "I didn't say that."

"Oh." Mike cocked his head. "Tell me, Joe, do you have any imagination?"

Joe bristled. "Everybody's got imagination."

"I don't know if that's true. Well, maybe everyone has a little," Mike conceded. "But to design sets, imagination is everything. Then, building them is another skill entirely."

Trying to get comfortable on his plastic perch, Joe said, "I've worked with wood before."

"You build?"

"I carve," Joe answered defiantly. "My grandfather taught me."

"Are you any good?"

For once, he could answer something honestly. "Yeah, I am good."

Mike just nodded, and Joe was surprised how readily he took him at his word. "Well, carving is different from building, but they're both done best when you love wood."

Joe thought about how elated he had been when he had found just the right piece of wood for the Persian. The hobby shop he had found in the phone book was two bus rides away, and most of the wood there was pricey, not like the pieces he'd nabbed from the lumberyard near his house. But Joe had known what he wanted, and when he asked the elderly clerk if they had a small piece of white oak, the man had just smiled. "You whittlin'?"

Feeling uncharacteristically shy, Joe had nodded. "I'm making a present."

"Well, you're in luck, boy. We just got some wood in for carving. Oak, maple, ash."

Thankfully, the clerk had left him alone as he looked through the pieces of wood. Choosing a piece of wood seemed a very private matter, at least to Joe. He wanted to touch it, eye it, even give it a sniff, to see if it was the one. Once he found a decent piece, he'd hold it in his hand for a while, almost straining to hear if the wood spoke to him. Oh, not really spoke to him. He wasn't crazy. But there was a vibe that came from a fine piece of wood that was kind of like a voice saying, "Yeah, I'm the one."

Joe refocused. He didn't feel the need to say out loud how he felt about woodworking. To him, it was almost sacred, and even without words, this seemed to be something he and Mike now understood about each other. That settled, Mike became businesslike.

"Designing the sets for this production of *Big River* is going to be a combination of imagination and building. Probably more of the former, since the budget is minuscule. Understand?"

His nod, Joe realized, meant more than just agreeing with Mike about design techniques. He was saying he was in. Well, he didn't have much choice, did he? But somewhere in between his chest and his stomach, there was that flutter again. Hope.

"Now, some things are going to have to be built," Mike continued.

"Like the raft," Joe suggested.

"You're sitting on it." Mike nodded toward the wood under the plastic. "And there will be some other scenery. Let's both be thinking about what's necessary. Are there any good artists around?"

Joe didn't have a clue, but Mike was waiting for an answer. "Uh, most of the kids are singers and musicians, but you could ask Miss Hanlon, the art teacher."

"Good idea."

Joe felt a small rush of pleasure. He had made the obvious suggestion, but it had been a long time since anyone had told him his ideas were good.

"Now, I'm going to need you around every afternoon that I'm here, but I can't be here all the time. I'll give you a schedule."

"Okay."

"Okay then." Mike put out his hand, and this time Joe

didn't hesitate to shake it. For sure, now there was no going back.

After writing down the days Joe was needed to work on scenery, Mike left. Joe was going to head home, when it occurred to him he ought to go sit in the audience and watch the rehearsal. Maybe it would give him some ideas about the scenery requirements he could pass on to Mike.

He plunked himself down in the fifth row of the darkened auditorium. Only a few of the other seats were filled, mostly with kids in the play who weren't in the scene being rehearsed.

Onstage, a group was singing the first song of the show. Widow Douglas and Miss Watson, with whom Huck lived, Judge Thatcher, and Tom Sawyer were telling Huck he wasn't going to get to heaven unless he learned his lessons, followed the right path, did what he was supposed to. Joe had the uncomfortable feeling that they might be singing to him. Well, at least he could tell Mike that since the scene was taking place in the widow's kitchen, it could probably use a table.

By the time Joe got home, it was dark. His mother wasn't home yet, so he fed the ravenous Gato and checked the refrigerator to see if there were enough eggs for omelets. He was looking forward to supper tonight, sitting down and telling Luisa about his day. For once, it seemed, he could tell her something about school that would make her happy. Maybe, for once, he was happy, too.

XII

Joe tried to keep his defenses up. He didn't want to seem as if he actually enjoyed being a part of *Big River,* but he had to admit, if only to himself, that he looked forward to his meetings with Mike. At the second one, Mike had brought Cokes for them, while they sat and went through the play scene by scene, figuring out what they needed to build for each one.

"When Bette sings 'You Oughta Be Here with Me,' there's a coffin in the room," Mike noted. "It will take a lot of our precious wood, but I guess we need it."

"Why?" Joe argued. "The audience knows her father's dead. They can just imagine it."

"It's an important part of the scene. We might not want to push it," Mike responded.

"I think Bette's a good enough singer to make people believe there's a coffin onstage."

Mike considered this. "Maybe you're right. One less thing to build would certainly help us conserve."

Joe couldn't have been more pleased that Mike took his argument seriously. After that, they spent a fair amount of time talking and planning, and if nothing else, Joe thought he was starting to earn Mike's respect. Still, he was anxious to start building things. So on the day they were supposed to start on Huck's raft, Joe woke up excited. From practically the moment he opened his eyes, though, things went wrong.

His mother was usually hustling to get out the door for work when he tumbled out of bed, but today she seemed to be moving in slow motion.

"Are you okay, Mami?" Joe asked after he had thrown on his clothes.

"Yes, yes," she said. "I'll be fine as soon as I drink my tea."

Luisa had gone to the health food store and bought an extra-strong dosage of her loose-leaf tea. This batch smelled particularly vile, but Luisa still drank it religiously.

"You have time for tea?" Joe glanced at the clock over the refrigerator.

"My boss is on vacation, so me and the other girls are taking turns slipping in a little late," Luisa said with a small smile. "It's nice not to rush for a change."

That made Joe's heart hurt. Just having an extra hour or so to herself meant so much to his mom. It didn't seem fair. But his heart hardened at her next words.

"Joe, I'm probably going to be late tonight. Gene and I are going to dinner and then a movie."

Joe grunted.

"Is that okay?" Luisa asked, rather anxiously.

Joe tried to mask his unhappiness in concern. "You're not feeling well. Shouldn't you come home and rest after work?"

"Maybe, but I've been looking forward to this all week." Luisa considered. "If I'm too tired after dinner, I'll come home and skip the movie."

"Whatever," Joe said, grabbing his books and heading for the door. It wasn't his decision to make. Usually, he kissed his mother good-bye if she was home when he left. He knew she liked that. Today, he just said, "Bye."

It was one of those miserable days, cold and rainy, with a wind so sharp it felt like a slap. Never one to carry an umbrella, Joe pulled a baseball hat out of his jacket pocket and tried to keep his head down. Which was why he almost bumped into Bette as she walked ahead of him.

Considering they lived fairly close to each other, it was odd how rarely they ran into each other on the way to school. Maybe Bette went early, or maybe it was because he was usually late, but running into each other, literally or figuratively, was unexpected.

"Oh, hello," Bette said from under her black-and-white polka-dot umbrella.

"Hi." Joe tried to say it loudly and confidently. He didn't like the way Bette made him feel shy.

For a moment neither said anything. Then they rushed to speak at the time as Bette asked, "So, are you building any scenery?" and Joe muttered, "Rehearsals going okay?"

After an embarrassed second or two while both of them waited for the other to answer first, Bette finally said, "Well, what do you think? I saw you watching the funeral scene the other day. Does the song sound okay?"

"Yeah."

Bette seemed to expect more. Joe, however, wasn't in the mood to offer praise. Instead, he asked, "When you sing that song, do you think about your mother? She's dead, isn't she?" As soon as he heard the words coming out of his mouth, he wished he could take them back.

"How do you know my mother is dead?" Bette demanded, her face one big frown.

Joe wasn't sure. Had he heard it somewhere? Or maybe it was because Bette lived with her father, and usually when there was a divorce, kids lived with their moms. Joe tried backtracking. "She's not dead?"

The rain, which had been steady but soft, now became a harder pelting. "Yes, as a matter of fact, she is." Bette picked up the pace. Joe wasn't sure if it was to get out of the rain or to get away from him.

Now Joe tried changing the subject. "Well, I was watching that scene to see if we, me and Mike, need to build a coffin. Or if we could get by with the audience just imagining one."

"So what did you decide?"

"We're not gonna built one."

"You don't think my song's not worthy of a piece of scenery?"

Joe was getting weary. He should have just told her the song sounded great when she asked and left it at that. After all, it did. "No, no. We're just short of wood, and we thought you could make the song work without it."

"Oh." That seemed to mollify Bette a little.

Before Joe could say anything else, the skies opened, and Bette sprinted toward school, leaving Joe behind to get soaked until he started running toward the school, too.

The conversation with Bette bugged Joe all morning. There was something about Bette that made him want to know her better, even though they continued to infuriate each other. And like most of their conversations, this one seemed to move their relationship one step forward and two steps back.

The rest of the day didn't go much better. Mrs. Abrams gave them a period to work on their biographies. What seemed so smart at the time, telling the truth in his outline, now was going to have to be turned into one depressing essay. Why hadn't he come up with some fairy tale about having a dog and playing Little League baseball? Joe could have kicked himself for being such a sucker, for giving away so much information. The only saving grace was that Mrs. Abrams said she was going to be grading primarily on sentence structure and grammar rather than content. Maybe she'd be so busy making sure his commas were in the right place, she wouldn't notice the biography itself was kind of a downer.

At lunchtime, Joe was in for a rude shock. Two, actually. Having stopped at the boys' room, he was a little late getting to the sandwich counter. When he fished around his pocket to pay for a peanut butter and jelly sandwich, however, all he could come up with was a quarter and the angel coin. Angrily, he shoved them back where they came from and waved away the sandwich. The lunchroom lady looked at him sympathetically, and then asked, "Do you want to borrow some money from your friends?"

Joe scowled and shook his head. He wasn't going to embarrass himself by asking Lane or Ollie for money. Oh, he could probably have gotten by with a joke about how he forgot to get his allowance, but that option stung too much, especially since there was no allowance, and there was never going to be any allowance. And, sure, there were plenty of days when he ate Ollie's catering leftovers, but that's when he had brought a crummy sandwich from home, or had the cash to buy an equally crummy sandwich. To Joe, the fact that he didn't have to mooch off Ollie made a difference when shoving the canapés into his mouth. Pulling out the quarter, Joe slapped it on the counter and asked for some milk.

For reasons he didn't quite understand, Joe hadn't hit up

Minkus for money since school had started. *That kid's been coasting along on borrowed time,* Joe thought bitterly. Well, time was up. He needed to get to Minkus and his money this afternoon.

Holding his pathetic carton of milk, Joe went looking for his lunch companions. They weren't at their usual table. Instead, he found them sitting and laughing with Bette, Lucy, Minkus, and Fred. He was about to turn away when Ollie spotted him.

"Hey, Joe, we're over here."

Joe felt trapped. Now what? It would look so weird if he bolted, but sitting down with two kids he barely knew, as well as Bette and Minkus, both of whom made his stomach ache for different reasons, seemed nearly impossible.

But there was smiling, oblivious Ollie, bellowing his name, and Joe found himself walking over to the table. Lucy and Fred didn't seem to have any problems with him joining the group. Bette, on the other hand, was determinedly gazing out the window and Minkus's head was so far down, studying his salad, Joe could barely see his face even after he sat down across from him.

The topic for table discussion was, of course, the play. Fred, who had snagged the role of Huck, was doing some fake complaining about how far he still had to go learning the song lyrics.

Another one who wanted praise, Joe thought to himself. And sure enough, Ollie agreeably told Fred what a great job he was doing. Joe grudgingly gave silent props to Lane when she said, "Put away the pole and stop fishing for compliments, Fred."

Lucy, who along with a couple of other African-American kids sang the haunting "Crossing to the Other Side," pushed it up a notch when she said that Dexter Woods, who played the slave, Jim, had a much harder part than Fred.

"Why's that?" Fred asked with a frown.

"Because he not only has to play his part, he has to make sure you're not hogging the limelight."

Everyone laughed, but not meanly. Even Fred smiled.

"What about you, Joe?" Lane asked. "How's the scenery going?"

Joe took a swig of his milk. He was grateful no one seemed to have noticed his lack of lunch. "Okay. We're going to start building the raft this afternoon."

"What's with that guy Mike?" Bette asked curiously.

"What do you mean?" Joe bristled.

"I don't know," Bette responded, pondering. "He seems so . . . so intimidating, I guess."

Joe was relieved in a way that Bette had noticed how Mike radiated power. Sometimes he wondered if he was imagining it. Mike could be like an ordinary guy, complaining about how much they had to do to get ready for the play. Then, other times, Mike would gaze at Joe so intensely he felt like he was having a CAT scan. "He's okay," Joe said. "Most of the time."

"He reminds me of someone," Bette said. "But I can't figure out who."

"Do you like working with him?" Lucy asked.

"Yeah," Joe said, thinking of how much their afternoon sessions had come to mean to him. "Yeah, I do."

So when Joe hurried backstage after his last class, he was disappointed when Mike was nowhere to be seen. He waited for a while, poking around the paints and other supplies that had been donated for the set design and wondering what to do, when the woman from Maple Tree supervising the costumes hurried past him.

Dressed in a bright red blouse, close to the color of her bright red hair, she was carrying a pile of costumes in her arms.

"Uh, excuse me?" Joe said, stopping her. "Do you know where Mike is?"

The woman, Joe thought her name was Nadine, looked harried. "Oh, are you Joe?"

"Yeah."

"Sorry. I was supposed to tell you, he had something else to do today. He'll see you next week."

"Thanks a lot." He said it sarcastically, so that Nadine would know he didn't appreciate waiting around for someone who wasn't going to show up, but she had walked away so quickly after delivering her belated message, he doubted if she'd even heard him.

Joe was fuming. Why should he be surprised though? He was used to waiting around for people who didn't show up. He felt like picking up one of the plastic crates piled on the floor and throwing it against the wall. Instead, he snatched his backpack off the floor and headed out. When he got to the back of the darkened auditorium, he spied Minkus standing alone near the double doors that led to the vestibule.

Minkus! Immediately, his mind searched for a lonely spot, preferably outside the school, where he and Minkus could have one of their chats. Never had he felt more like shaking down Minkus.

Minkus didn't seem to notice him, which was good. He was such a little rabbit, he might flee if he realized Joe was close. But then something odd happened: Minkus turned and looked right at Joe, and he didn't run. He didn't even move. Joe was close enough, however, that he could see him take a breath.

Before Joe could say anything, Minkus beckoned him over with his finger. Minkus calling to him? *What the? . . .*

"Joe, I want to talk to you," Minkus said with determination.

Joe offered what he hoped was an evil smile. "Great, I want to talk to you, too."

"Let's go out in the hallway," Minkus said.

Joe shrugged. Fine, that might make it easier to get him outdoors.

Standing in the vestibule, Minkus pulled himself up to his full height. He was still a head shorter than Joe. "I've got something for you."

Some sort of trick, Joe thought to himself. "Let's go outside. I've got something for you."

Minkus ignored that. Instead, his hand shaking a bit, he pulled a ten dollar bill out of his pocket. "Here."

A confused Joe asked, "What are you doing?"

"I'm tired of the charade. Maybe you are, too. You obviously need money, so I'm just going to give you money."

Joe looked at the ten dollars Minkus was holding out. Ten, not nine. Minkus was upping the ante, but on his own terms.

"Aren't you going to take it?" Minkus asked, cocking his head. "It's okay. If you need it, take it."

What Joe wanted to do was punch Minkus right in the mouth, even though a fifth grader had just walked by, looking at them curiously. Humiliation washed over him. Minkus thought he was some stupid charity case. Somebody he could hand money to, like a bum on the street. A quiet voice inside his head remarked that people did give money to those in need, but Joe had never thought of his interactions with Minkus in those terms. He had seen himself as a man of action, taking what he wanted. Now he just felt like a jerk. A furious jerk, but a jerk nonetheless.

"Keep it," Joe said through gritted teeth, pushing Minkus's hand away.

Minkus looked at him steadily. "I don't care if you take it. It's not that big a deal."

To you, Joe thought. *Ten dollars means nothing to someone like you.* Now he wanted to beat up Minkus just for the hell of it, and then stuff his ten bucks up his nose. Instead, he turned away and pushed through the double doors and headed outside where he could finally breathe.

Practically running home, Joe could feel tears coming to his eyes. Well, screw that. And screw them all. Mike, for not showing up; his father, for never showing up; Minkus, for thinking he could buy him off; Bette, for . . . for just being Bette.

Pounding up the back stairs, he pulled out his key and opened the door to the empty apartment. And it was going to be empty all evening, Joe remembered. His mother would be out on a date. As he entered the house, he was frightened by a rambunctious Gato, who ran toward him from a corner. As usual, the cat tried to dart around Joe's legs, looking for a way outside. This was when Joe always shoved his shoe at Gato, urging him back in the house.

But this time, Joe didn't care what Gato did. If the cat wanted to run away, fine. Joe wouldn't mind running away himself. Not quite believing what he was doing, Joe opened the back door wide and watched as the orange cat, at first timidly, then picking up speed, fled down the wooden stairs.

For about a half hour, Joe felt great. Letting Gato go seemed a balm for all the wrongs he felt burning him. He was hungry. Starving. There was a frozen pizza in the freezer, the size he and his mom usually shared, but he put it in the micro-wave, and then proceeded to wolf down the whole thing him-self. He watched a stupid talk show while he was eating; the host was trying to convince some skinny teenage girl that starving herself wasn't a great idea. Ha! Someone who prob-ably had a refrigerator full of food and didn't eat it. Well, screw her, too.

Soon enough, though, he began to wonder what he would tell his mother about the cat. He flipped the remote control mindlessly as he decided that it shouldn't be that hard to con-vince Luisa that Gato had slipped out before Joe could do anything about it. Lord knows, the cat tried to escape at every opportunity. So why should his mother be surprised when one day he succeeded?

Yet fingers of guilt began massaging Joe. He could, he supposed, go down and look outside for Gato. The cat pro-bably didn't have time to get too far. A part of him thought that he should do that. A bigger part, the part that liked the real and justifiable way his anger felt and didn't want it di-minished, suggested he should take a nap. Yes, Joe thought, sleep, the kind that blocked out everything. That's what he needed. Suddenly, he was very, very tired.

By the time he awoke, his blanket jumbled and tumbled around his body, it was dark. Joe tried to focus on his table-side clock. Almost eight o'clock. He rolled over, not really wanting to get out of bed. Closing his eyes for a moment, he was back in the crazy dream he'd been having. He was on a bus, and Mike was driving, where to Joe didn't know. Gato was on the bus, too, hiding under the seats, sometimes run-ning madly down the aisle. The whole thing was unnerving. Maybe he did want to get up.

The pizza he'd eaten after school was sitting like a greasy

pepperoni-studded lump in the middle of his stomach. He was not hungry. He was thirsty, however, and as he stood at the kitchen sink, running the water to get it cold, he noticed for the first time, a note from his mother on the counter. It said she'd call later, and she'd taped a ten dollar bill to the hastily torn piece of paper.

Joe took his water and left the money where it was. He was flat broke, but for today, anyway, he wasn't in the mood for Luisa's money any more than he was for Minkus's.

To Joe's surprise, the apartment seemed a little lonely without Gato. Luisa was the cat's favorite, of course, but when Joe was watching television, Gato would sit beside him and occasionally stick his head under Joe's hand for a rub.

Forget about the cat, Joe said to himself. He settled down on the couch to play one of the games his mother gave him for Christmas. It was mindless fun, and time did have a tendency to slip by while he was playing. Yet, he couldn't help but realize that his mother had probably gone on to the movie or she would have been home already. Well, if she got sicker from being out when she should be resting, that was her problem, Joe told himself defiantly, all the while realizing that a Luisa home from work was a problem for him as well.

He played a while longer and started to get bored by the game. He switched on the television and watched a movie. It was *Planet of the Apes,* and even though it was pretty good, he began to drift to sleep again. The ringing of the phone awakened him. A little disoriented, Joe got up and hunted around for the phone; it was never where it was supposed to be. Finally, he found it in the kitchen. He expected it to be Luisa, telling him what time she would be home. So he was unnerved to hear Gene's voice.

"What's wrong?" Joe asked immediately.

Gene sighed. "Joe, I'm at the hospital. I had to bring your mother here. She couldn't stop coughing."

Joe walked over to the couch and sat down. "How is she?"

"She's okay, but they're going to keep her overnight. They don't want her talking on the phone, but she wanted me to tell you she's feeling much better."

"That's good," Joe said quietly.

"She's worried about you, though. She doesn't want you staying alone, so once she's settled in her room, I'm going to come over and spend the night."

"No!" Joe burst out. "I'm all right."

Gene said in a voice more firm than Joe had ever heard him use, "I'm sorry, but this isn't up for discussion. It's what your mother wants."

"It's not what I want," Joe yelled. It felt good to take a stand.

"Joe, I'm sorry, I don't have time to argue with you. I'm at Lakeshore Hospital, so I'm not that far away. I shouldn't be too long. If you want to go to sleep, go ahead. I've got your mother's key." And with that, Gene hung up.

Shaking a little, Joe took the phone with him into his bedroom. He lay down on his bed without undressing, pushing the messy covers aside. Whatever energy he had put into his angry responses to Gene had disappeared like vapor in the air, and now all he felt was spent, sad, and weary.

Luisa was in the hospital again. Yeah, it was supposed to be for only a day, but that's what the hospital had said the last time, and then his mom had only gotten sicker. At least now her new job provided pretty good health insurance, that's what she said anyway. But if she were sick longer than a couple of days, what then? Maybe she would lose her job like last time. Joe felt a little sick, too, with fright, he thought, but he didn't know what to do about it. Turning his head a little, he looked out his window at the darkened church. For a moment, he thought about going over there and saying a prayer, then realized the church was locked up at night. Besides, would God really listen to a prayer from the likes of him?

As he tried to smooth the covers around him, he had a thought. Slipping his hand into his otherwise empty jeans' pocket, he pulled out his angel coin. There was something solid, even weighty about it, as if it had grown more important. He rubbed his thumb over the embossed angel. God seemed far away at the moment, but the angel was right in his hand.

Could you pray to angels? Joe wasn't certain, but surely there was nothing wrong with talking to an angel. Beginning was easier than he could have imagined. He asked for help, wincing a little as he did so. He hated asking for help.

He talked for a long time.

"What's the difference," Joe said aloud, when he ran out of things to say. "I'm just talking to a piece of metal here." Oddly, though, it didn't feel that way. And as he slipped the coin back in his pocket, he realized he felt better. Not good, maybe, but better.

He was just dozing off when he heard the door open. Confused for a moment, he thought it was Luisa, then everything came rushing back, and he realized it was Gene.

Joe's first impulse was to roll over and pretend he was asleep. How could he do that, though, when Gene had just seen his mother? He wanted to know what was happening.

"Oh, Joe," Gene said, a little startled when Joe walked into the living room. "I thought you might be asleep."

Gene, never the sharpest of dressers, looked like he was the one who had been sleeping in his clothes. Everything about Gene sagged with exhaustion, and that made Joe wonder if everything was as okay as Gene had said earlier on the phone. Or maybe things had gotten worse since then.

"Mami?" Joe asked.

"She's doing all right. She's still scheduled to come home tomorrow afternoon."

"That's good," Joe said, relieved. Then, to Joe's shock, Gene came over and gave Joe a big bear hug. For a few seconds, Joe tried to squirm away, but Gene held on. Not quite against his will, Joe felt himself relax into Gene's arms.

"All right," Gene said, letting Joe go, "all right. It's late, and I know your mother would want you asleep."

"I've kinda been sleeping."

Gene gave him the once-over. "Why don't you try it in your pajamas this time."

Joe smiled a little and nodded. Gene walked him back to the bedroom. "I'm going to wash up and then sleep in your mother's room, okay?"

"Yeah." Joe sat down on the bed. "But, Gene . . ."

Gene looked at Joe. "What?"

"Can you tell me what happened first?"

Gene sat next to him on the bed. "We had a nice dinner, then we were headed to the movies. It was so cold. That's what seemed to set Luisa off, going from the warm restaurant into the cold. She started coughing and had trouble stopping, so I drove her right to the hospital. Against her protests, I might add. You know how stubborn she can be."

Joe knew. He had to give Gene credit for getting her to the hospital at all.

"It seemed like we sat in the emergency room forever," Gene continued, "but it probably wasn't that long. Fortunately, there was a really good doctor on duty, a Dr. Raphael. She knew what medicine to give her, and best of all, she calmed your mother right down. I'm just glad I was there with her."

Joe had to admit to himself, he was glad Gene was there, too.

"All right," Gene said, getting up. "I'm going to turn in. Do you want to come to the hospital with me tomorrow? I'm probably going to leave early."

Joe was about to say "of course." Then he remembered he had to take care of something important in the morning.

He had to find Gato. He just had to.

XIII

Joe heard Gene get up in the morning and had to stop himself from jumping out of bed to go with him to the hospital. The last thing he wanted to do was spend the morning trying to find a cat who could be anywhere, an endeavor that could well prove futile. He had to try, though. He didn't want even to think about telling Luisa that Gato was gone.

When Joe heard the kettle whistle, he pulled a sweatshirt over his pajamas and went out into the kitchen. Gene had his coat on, ready to go, but he was standing at the counter drinking a cup of hastily made coffee.

"Joe, I wasn't sure if I should wake you. You got to sleep so late."

"Yeah, I didn't sleep too well." It was the truth.

"Why don't you go back to bed? There's no point in going to the hospital. Your mother will be home this afternoon."

Joe felt guilty, but wasn't that what he'd been hoping Gene would say? "Ah, maybe I will do that."

Gene clapped Joe on the shoulder. "You rest. Last night was hard on everybody."

Then Joe noticed something on the counter, partially hidden by the milk Gene had used to whiten his coffee. Gene followed Joe's gaze. Picking up the Persian cat Joe had carved, he said, "Your mom asked especially for me to bring this cat. She said it's her good luck charm."

Joe couldn't have felt worse if Gene had grabbed knife from the kitchen drawer and stabbed him in the heart.

"By the way," Gene said, "where's Gato? I haven't seen him all morning."

"Uh, sometimes, he sleeps late. In my closet."

To Joe's relief, Gene seemed to accept that answer. He took a final swig of his coffee and put the Persian in his pocket, then pulled out this cell phone. "I'm going to leave this for you, in case I have to get in touch. Oh and, Joe, would you mind straightening up a little? Maybe change the sheets on your mother's bed? I want to get going."

Any other day, this would have been the kind of request that would have made Joe bristle, but now he was thrilled to have something he could actually do to make his mother's homecoming better. As soon as Gene left, Joe madly cleaned the house, so he could begin his search as soon as possible. That was maybe one good thing about living in such a small space. It didn't take much time to make the apartment look presentable.

Throwing on yesterday's clothes, Joe dressed and went outside to look for Gato. At least it was a nice day. Chilly, but the rain had ended and there was no wind to make the day feel colder than it was. Walking down the back stairs, though, a wave of hopelessness washed over Joe. Where to begin?

The easiest place to start, he decided, was to look around the rear of the apartment and the alley. Softly calling Gato's name, Joe checked out the basement area and then methodically searched around the neighboring apartment buildings. He stuck mostly to the gangways and the backs of the buildings, figuring Gato wouldn't be just strolling down the street. It struck him that if Gato had ventured out in front, he could easily have been hit by a car. Shuddering a little, Joe tried not to think about Gato lying in the middle of the street, injured or worse.

After having gone three blocks, with the only sign of animal life a couple of squirrels and a snarling dog locked in its yard, Joe tried to decide whether he should keep on or go back in the opposite direction toward the church and then work his way over to Bette's house. He was beginning to panic, and for a few minutes tried unsuccessfully to quell the scared, nervous feeling. Sticking his cold hands in his pockets, he found his angel coin. Joe remembered how he had spilled his guts talking to the coin last night, and immediately felt both better and a little silly. Rubbing the tip of his thumb over the embossed surface, he wondered if the coin really had any more power than stuff other people hung on to, like a four-leaf clover or a rabbit's foot. Well, Bette had seemed to have faith in the coin, he told himself. That made him feel better until he remembered how he had come by the coin, and then he immediately felt worse.

He headed toward the back of the Church of the Holy Comforter, figuring to ignore the NO TRESPASSING sign and search its rather sizable yard. Covered with leaves that had fallen after autumn's final raking, it made a decent hiding place for a cat, Joe thought.

He passed through the shrubbery closest to the building. "Gato?" he whispered, not wanting to disturb anyone inside the church. "Gato?"

There was a rustling under the leaves, and Joe's heart leaped, but once again, it was only a squirrel. A thorough search of the yard turned up nothing else, but there were lots of bushes in front of the church, Joe remembered. Maybe Gato was hiding somewhere there.

As he was beating around the bushes, quietly calling Gato's name, Joe became aware of people leaving the church. He didn't have a watch, but he figured the daily eight o'clock Mass was over. Not wanting to appear to be lurking, Joe moved toward the stone steps. When the church had emptied out, he'd start again.

Church attendance could be pretty spotty, except for Sundays, so Joe figured the parishioners would disperse pretty quickly. They were mostly elderly women and a few girls dressed in the uniform of the nearby Catholic school. Just as Joe was wondering if any men had shown up for the early Saturday morning Mass, a guy wearing worn jeans and a leather jacket came striding out of the church. It was the last man Joe would have ever expected.

His initial reaction, he wasn't sure why, was to take off. Mike, as formidable as ever, was coming down the steps so quickly, however, he'd probably bump into Joe as he was hurrying by. There was nothing for it but to stand his ground and say, "Hello, Mike."

Mike didn't seem nearly as surprised by Joe's presence as Joe was by his. "Hi, Joe." Still, he asked, "What are you doing here?"

"I live next door," Joe replied a little belligerently. "What about you? You don't live around here, do you?"

If Mike was offended by Joe's tone, he didn't show it. "I like to go to Mass at different churches around the city. I had to drop something off at Odom this morning, so I thought I'd stop in at Holy Comforter."

"Oh."

"Have you been looking for something?" Mike asked.

Joe felt a shock run though him. "How did you know?" he couldn't help but blurt out.

"I was saying good-bye to the priest before I left, and I glanced out the window. You were beating the bushes, and it seemed as if you had lost something."

Well, at least that explained it. "My mother's cat," Joe replied flatly.

"Ran out of the apartment, did it?"

Whatever relief Joe felt at the logical explanation Mike was giving him for skulking around faded at the way Mike asked the question. It was nothing about the words themselves. After all, logically, the cat had run out the apartment, otherwise Joe wouldn't be looking for it. No, what hit Joe hard was the gravity of Mike's tone, as if all of Joe's recent wrongdoings were contained in the question. Joe had the distinct feeling that when Mike asked the question, he knew the answer, the whole of it. Looking up at Mike, with those brown steady eyes taking everything in, Joe was even more certain he was right, even if he didn't have a clue how that was possible.

"I let him out," Joe blurted out.

"Accidentally?"

He couldn't help himself. "On purpose."

Confession was supposed to be good for the soul, but hearing himself say those two words made Joe feel scared and sad. How could he have told Mike, of all people, the truth? Someone whose opinion he valued must now think he was the lowest of the low. He turned away from Mike, afraid of what he would see in his eyes. Then Joe felt a hand on the shoulder. That gave him the courage to look at Mike and what he saw in his eyes was only compassion.

"How long have you been out looking for him?"

"I don't know. A half hour maybe, maybe more."

"It's cold. I was going to get some coffee. Why don't you join me?"

"I don't really have time. My mother will be home soon, and I've got to find the cat before she gets here," Joe said, trying to keep the panic from his voice.

"Have you had anything to eat this morning?" Mike asked.

Eating had been the last thing on his mind. "No."

"Trust me, you'll be able to go a lot longer if you eat something. I'll buy you a bagel and something to drink. It won't take long."

Joe gave in. He tried to tell himself he was just hungry, but truth be told, he wanted, even needed, to be with Mike.

As soon as they were settled with their drinks and food at Starbucks, Joe tried to take back control of the situation. "So where were you yesterday?" he asked.

"I had to visit someone in the hospital," Mike said, sipping his coffee.

There was a coincidence. "My mother's in the hospital."

"What's wrong?" Mike asked, his expression now softened with concern.

Instead of feeling upset, thinking about Luisa being ill, Joe felt himself inexplicably relax. "She has a problem with her lungs. She started coughing last night and her . . . her boyfriend took her to the hospital." It sounded strange to say it out loud, but that's who Gene was, his mother's boyfriend.

"Who's taking care of you?" Mike wanted to know.

"Gene, the, uh, boyfriend, he stayed over last night. And supposedly my mom's coming home today."

"Supposedly?"

"Well, she's been sick in the hospital before and had to stay longer than anyone thought."

Mike nodded. "Let's hope the doctors are right this time. Now, what about the cat? Why did you let him out?"

Joe really, really didn't want to get into all that. Mike knew the worst of it, though, that he had done it on purpose. And he was waiting for an answer. "I was mad," Joe said, and took a bite of his bagel. He hoped he could leave it at that.

No such luck. "Mad at your mother?"

"No," Joe said, startled.

Mike cocked his head and looked at him.

"Maybe a little. That was before I knew she was in the hospital, though." Mike seemed to be waiting for more. "I was mad at a lot of things. I was mad at you," Joe said, defiance slipping back into his tone.

"Because I stood you up," Mike said matter-of-factly. "Who else?"

"Just some of the kids at school." Joe vowed to go no further than that. He wouldn't mention Ramón.

It didn't seem to matter. Once again, the expression on Mike's face made it seem as if he understood everything, even without the words.

"Getting angry doesn't help things, Joe. Neither does getting even."

Joe tried to come up with a suitably sarcastic reply. When none came, he found himself asking, "What does?"

Mike warmed his hands on the coffee. "Thinking things through. Deciding how you can make a situation better, not worse."

Joe shook his head. He wasn't buying that. When did he ever get to make any important decisions?

Smiling, Mike said, "Ah, I can see you don't believe me. But think of it this way. You have a talent for carving wood, yes?"

He didn't see where carving came into it, but Joe shrugged and nodded.

"You begin with a hunk of wood. It has weight, but not form. But you have a vision of what you want that wood to become. Next you choose where to cut or carve or shave the wood, and you see it taking shape before your eyes. Life is like that as well, Joe. Just as you choose where to cut or carve or shave the wood, each decision, made each day, shapes what your life is going to look like. Lying, stealing, that's like hacking away at your life. Small, mean moments—tiny, ugly nicks. Just like a piece of wood you've botched, sometimes just through carelessness, you can be stuck with a life that can't be salvaged. Sad."

Joe didn't like what he was hearing. Angrily, Joe dismissed the image of that misshapen piece of wood that Mike had so firmly placed there from his mind. "Yeah, well, maybe you and a bunch of other people had some kind of a charmed life." Minkus and his money flashed through his mind. "Things haven't been so easy for me and my mom."

"And when you've lashed out, did it make you feel better or worse?" Mike asked simply.

"Sometimes I've felt better," Joe answered. But if he was honest, he had to admit that while he might have felt better for a while, eventually what he felt was ashamed. He didn't like remembering some of the things he had done.

"Well, it's something for you to think about," Mike said with a shrug. "Right now, you have a more immediate problem."

"Gato," Joe said, his stomach knotting. "The cat," he added, in case Mike didn't know Spanish.

Mike looked at his watch. "I guess you'd better get back to looking. It would be helpful if you had a few more pairs of eyes looking with you."

Joe must have looked puzzled, because Mike clarified. "Friends. Can you get some friends to help you?"

No use in holding back now. "I don't have any friends."

"I'm not sure that's true."

"Maybe you're not sure," Joe replied with a halfhearted laugh.

Mike turned in the direction of the door. "What about them?"

Heading into the coffee shop were Bette, Ollie, Minkus, and Minkus's sister.

"They're not my friends."

"You know them. You could ask for their help. I find generally people like to help."

Joe shook his head. "I don't think so."

"Well, it's up to you," Mike said, rising from his chair.

"Where are you going?" Joe secretly hoped that maybe Mike would help him look for Gato.

"I have people I need to see. And you have to look for your cat."

Joe thought that Mike might be mad at him for arguing with him, but the smile Mike gave Joe dazzled him. "Good luck."

Faster than Joe would have thought, Mike was gone. He was left looking over at the round table where Bette and the rest of them were sitting. As at lunch yesterday, Ollie noticed him first. "Hey, Joe."

Joe had a good view of the quartet. Ollie seemed anxious for him to come over. Bette gave him a tentative smile, while Minkus looked resigned. The sister didn't seem to remember him. Or if she did, she was pretending not to.

As if moving under somebody else's steam, Joe got up and

walked over to their table. Maybe he could just mention Gato. If they were walking through the neighborhood, they might see him.

"We were just going to order," Bette said.

"Want something to drink?" Ollie asked.

"I can't." Taking a breath, he explained about Gato, not how he'd gone missing, of course, just that he had. Then, without really meaning to, he added, "My mom's coming home from the hospital this afternoon. She'll freak if the cat's gone." He could hear his voice shake.

"That's awful," Bette said.

"Do you need help looking for the cat?" the sister asked.

"Vivi, you can't be running around looking through bushes for a cat," Minkus told his sister. "It could set off your asthma."

"Fine," Vivi said. "I'll look in the alleys, and I won't run, I'll walk."

"Oh, you guys don't have to," Joe said, feeling uncomfortable. Yet he could feel his hopes rise.

Ollie stood up. "Of course we will. It would be stupid to try and find Gato yourself when we're all here."

It was as simple as that. They decided on a strategy, dividing up the neighborhood and left Starbucks.

Bette said she would look around her house; Ollie around where he lived.

"I said I'd take the alleys," Vivi said. "Why don't I do a thorough search around where you live, Joe."

"I'll go with Vivi," Minkus muttered.

Joe accidentally caught Minkus's eye. He wasn't sure which of them looked away first, but clearly they were both embarrassed. He wished he could just tell Minkus, thanks but no thanks for his help. That, though, would make the situation even more awkward. What explanation could he give for that?

"Let's meet back at your apartment in a half hour or so," Bette suggested.

They all agreed to the plan and went off in separate directions. Joe walked in tandem with Vivi and Minkus. None of them said a word.

Finally, when the silence had become agonizing, Vivi spoke up. "How did the cat get out?"

Joe may have felt compelled to tell Mike the truth, but he had no such compunctions about doing the same with Vivian. "He slipped out the door. He's always trying that."

"Just had to get away," Minkus muttered.

Vivi glanced at her brother oddly. Joe looked down on the sidewalk as he marched along. Okay, this wasn't such a great idea after all.

"Could you slow it down a little?" Minkus asked.

What? Joe thought. Minkus's legs are so short he can't keep up? Then he noticed Vivian huffing and puffing.

"Uh, sure. I was just trying to get home faster."

"Andy, I'm fine," Vivi told her brother.

"We're almost there," Joe said. He pointed toward his building. "It's the one next to the church."

"Why don't you two walk ahead?" Vivi suggested. "I'll be right behind you, and I'll look around for Gato as I go."

"I'm sticking with you," Minkus said.

"No, just go with Joe. He can show you where to start looking around his house. Maybe the cat's already back."

"But . . ."

"Andy, you're going to be like fifty feet ahead of me. All you've got to do is turn around and see if I've keeled over."

Joe didn't want to get in the middle of this. He picked up

his pace, hoping that Minkus would hang back with Vivian. Not so much for her sake; he just didn't want to spend any time alone with Minkus. Minkus, however, plowed along beside him. Finally, Joe couldn't stand it anymore. "Why are you doing this?"

"What?"

Forced to say it, Joe spit it out. "Helping me find the cat."

Minkus allowed himself a small smile of satisfaction. "You're welcome. I'm not doing it for you, though."

"So who you doing it for?"

"Your mother," he said. "And maybe the cat, though he might be better off away from you. And because I have to."

"Have to?" Joe asked with confusion.

"Do you know what a bar mitzvah is?" Minkus asked.

Now Joe was really confused. "It's like a Jewish birthday party?"

Minkus grimaced. "Not exactly. When a Jewish boy turns thirteen, he's considered an adult. There's a special ceremony at the synagogue. Sometimes there's a party. But before any of that, you have to go to Hebrew school for a couple of years."

Joe turned and looked at Minkus. He restrained himself from saying, "What do bar mitzvahs and Hebrew school have to do with a lost cat?"

"Anyway, you don't just learn Hebrew at Hebrew school. You also have to do stuff to get ready for your bar mitzvah, like write a speech."

"Sounds like a lot of work," Joe muttered.

"My speech is about how if you do good deeds, the world will be a better place. Well, I couldn't write a speech like that and not do some good deeds," Minkus continued. "So I decided to do some for you."

"Me!" Joe practically yelped. "Why not do 'em for people you like?"

"It's easy to do nice things for your friends and family. I didn't want it to be easy," Minkus said grimly. "That's where you came in."

Joe let this sink in a minute. "And this good-deed stuff is why you tried to give me the ten dollars yesterday?"

"Yeah. Well, that, and because I wanted to get you off my back."

Joe couldn't quite get his head around Minkus's words. It was crazy, wasn't it, what Minkus was trying to do, especially considering the way Joe had treated him? Joe remembered the priest once talking in the homily about turning the other cheek, and saying the words meant more than simply not fighting back. The idea was to be a bigger person. That had sounded stupid at the time and didn't make much more sense now, but if Minkus wanted to give it a shot, who was he to argue? Joe was so lost in thought, he almost walked by his apartment building. "Oh, this is where I live."

"So, how do you want to do this?" Minkus asked.

"I'll go down in the basement. The door was closed before, but sometimes if someone's doing the laundry, it gets left open. Gato could have gone inside."

"You looked around the church?"

"Yeah, but there's so many places to hide, you could look again."

Minkus nodded, then turned and waved at his sister, a ways back. She pointed toward an alley to her right, indicating that's where she intended to go.

"When Vivi gets back here, make her sit down," Minkus told Joe. "Maybe get her some water. She's not supposed to tire herself out."

Joe had to admit he admired the way Minkus protected his sister. He stood up for her more than he ever had for himself. "Sure," he said gruffly. Leaving Minkus to beat the bushes, Joe went around the back and headed down to the basement, but the door was still locked. Frustrated, he kicked at the door, and tried to think about what to do next. An odd ringing noise distracted him, then Joe realized it was the cell phone Gene had given him.

It took him a few seconds to figure out how to take the call; he wanted to hear his mother on the other end, but it was only Gene. He sounded happy, though.

"Joe, your mom feels much better. The doctor's here now, explaining her new medicine regime. She has to sign a few papers, so we should be home in about an hour."

"An hour," Joe repeated dumbly. For a second, he considered telling Gene the truth. Maybe he could break the bad news about Gato to his mother. But hope—or maybe desperation—stayed his tongue. "Okay, see you soon," Joe said.

As he pounded a few buttons, trying to figure out the right one to shut off the phone, Joe immediately began second-guessing his decision. An hour? That was no time at all. Why hadn't he given Gene a heads-up? Now everything was going to be on him to explain. He could feel the dread spread through him like a fever. Sinking down on the back steps, Joe put his head in his heads.

He sat like that for a few minutes. He knew he should get up and use whatever time was left to keep looking, but it was hard to make himself move. Finally, he rubbed his eyes and stood up.

Right then, Vivi stepped from the alley into the gangway. In her arms, she held a big orange cat.

XIV

"Joe!" Bette called, running up behind him as he headed over to Odom. "Wait up. I want to hear what happened with Gato."

Joe hadn't seen Bette since Saturday. Vivi had texted the other kids, so they knew Gato was found, but now, apparently, Bette wanted more details. "Weren't you relieved?" she asked, as she caught up.

"Totally," he told her.

Vivi and Gato had appeared in the dirty alley almost like a mirage. Joe had wanted to grab Gato from Vivi's arms, just to make sure he was real, but the cat seemed so contented, almost asleep, he hesitated to disturb him.

"Let's get him upstairs," Vivi had said. "Before he gets any big ideas about staying outside."

Joe didn't want to let Vivi, the rich kid, see his apartment, but what choice did he have? At least it was clean. So he led her up the back steps, which she took slowly, holding tightly on to Gato, who, perhaps sensing his fate, was starting to wiggle.

"Where did you find him?"

Vivi laughed. "He was sitting on top of a garbage can, licking his paws. It was like he was waiting for me to show up."

Opening the back door, Joe let Vivi go first, so she could dump Gato on the kitchen floor. The cat made straight for the couch and stretched out.

"He'll probably sleep all day," Vivi noted.

"Yeah. Well, thanks." Joe wondered if that came out sincere enough. He meant it to be, but it also sounded like he wanted to get her out of the apartment, which he did.

"You're welcome." She turned her huge blue eyes on him. "I guess I'll see you at Odom."

"Since when do you go to Odom?" Joe asked with surprise.

"My parents want me to go back to school. So I'll be coming back in a couple of weeks."

"Oh. Well, see you then." He had murmured another thanks as Vivi left the way she came, by the back door.

Joe refocused on Bette, who was looking at him expectantly. "What did Vivi tell you?"

"Just that she found the cat on a garbage can and brought it upstairs."

Joe would've liked to have known if that was all Vivi said, but he didn't know how to pry out more information. Girls' conversations were all mysteries anyway.

"So how's your mom?" Bette asked as they headed inside the school.

"Better. Much better. The doctors put her on this new medicine that they say is really going to help."

"That's good." Bette smiled at him. "And she never knew Gato was gone?"

Joe shook his head. "He had some dirty spots, but he licked them off before she got home." He thought about how his mother had wrapped both of them in her arms when she'd come through the door: first him, then Gato, who she picked up off the couch, much to his squirming dismay. She looked so happy. Joe still didn't want to think about what it would have been like to tell her the cat was missing.

"Vivi was really glad she found Gato," Bette told him, "although she probably shouldn't have been carrying him. She had to use her inhaler when she got back to us."

He hadn't considered Vivi's asthma. The cat didn't bother his mom because her lung problems didn't include allergies. Joe frowned. "She okay now?"

They got to their lockers. "Yeah."

"She said she was coming back to Odom," Joe said, throwing his jacket inside his locker.

"She told you that?" Bette's surprise was evident.

"Why shouldn't she?"

"She's not all that happy about coming back, especially in the middle of the year. She's kind of been pretending it's not going to happen."

"Then why's she doing it?" Joe asked.

"Her parents think she's getting a little squirrelly staying home, and I guess they could be right. She hardly sees anyone and doesn't want to go out. She's got a real thing about how she looks."

Joe remembered his own comment to Vivi and was embarrassed.

Bette continued, "We practically had to drag her out on Saturday."

"Well, I'm glad she was there," Joe said simply. And he was.

He was also ready to put the whole ordeal out of his mind. Yet, at the oddest moments, Vivi would pop up in his mind. Maybe he was reminded of Vivi because his mother was feeling so much better.

"Thank heavens for Dr. Raphael." If Luisa said it once, she said it ten times since she came home. Joe repeated the words to himself. The doctor had come up with a medicine that really seemed to work. Because she wasn't coughing, she was sleeping better, and that gave her more energy, too. There was maybe one downside. Since she wasn't so tired, Luisa was spending more time with Gene. To his surprise, though, Joe didn't mind as much as he might have thought. The way Gene had stepped up during his mother's health crisis had made an impression on Joe. What had really surprised him was how Gene seemed to care almost as much about him as he did about Luisa.

Joe found himself wishing he could do something to make Vivi feel as good as his mom seemed to. He wondered when, exactly, Vivi was coming back to Odom, but he didn't want to seem too interested, so he didn't ask Bette. He certainly didn't say anything to Minkus about it. Actually, in the days that had passed since Gato's escape, the only thing he had said to Minkus was a gruff "Thanks. For trying to find the cat."

Minkus had just smiled.

Minkus seemed to be everywhere these days. In class. At the lunch table where Joe kept sitting, though still saying as little as possible. In the auditorium. Whenever Joe was working on the scenery, Minkus was in the orchestra pit, playing his violin. During the corners of his day, when he was supposed to be doing something else, Minkus's words would come into his mind, about good deeds and making the world a better place. How he wanted to help, of all people, *him*. Who said stuff like that? Or did it for that matter?

Joe couldn't decide if Minkus was some sort of everyday hero or an idiot.

That's what Joe was thinking about on Friday as he was

nailing slats of the raft together while waiting for Mike to show up. He hadn't been around earlier in the week, so this was the first time Joe would be seeing him since the great cat caper.

Fred, as Huck Finn, was upstage singing a song called "Waitin' for the Light to Shine." It was about all the things Huck had done because they were the way he was "taught to run." Now, after living in the darkness, he was waiting for the light to shine. There were two different versions that Huck sang. First the sweet, slow version that Fred was singing now. Then, near the end, a hurried, angrier version, after Huck realizes so much of what he thought he knew was wrong.

As he hammered harder, Joe wondered what he knew for sure. He had thought he knew Minkus, had him pegged. Now, it seemed, Minkus was turning out unpeggable.

"Better pay more attention or you're going to hit your thumb instead of the nail," a voice over his shoulder said. How could Mike tell his mind was elsewhere? Mike must have read the question on his face because he said, "You're nailing 'em in crooked."

"Oh." Joe looked down at his work. Not too good.

"Take five, Joe, and talk to me. I want to hear all about your mother. And the cat."

Joe put his tools neatly away, as his grandfather had taught him, and then pulled up a metal chair next to the one Mike had dragged from the wings. Mike was looking around the stage. "This is all coming together," he said. Turning back to Joe, he continued, "You've done a very good job."

Flushing, Joe muttered, "Thanks."

"We'll finish up the raft, and then work with the lighting director on Tom Sawyer's cave. That will be more effect than actual structure. After that, we'll be down to the details."

Joe felt his stomach knot a little. He had enjoyed working on the play more than he would have liked to admit out loud. He didn't want it to be over.

"Well, the devil's in the details, as they say," Mike told him, noting his expression, "so we're not quite there yet. Now, to more important things. Tell me about your mom."

The whole story spilled out of Joe. He felt the same sense of relief talking to Mike as he had the moment Vivi and Gato appeared.

"So your friends were a help," Mike said with a smile.

Joe answered sheepishly, "I don't know if they're my friends, exactly, but yeah, they helped."

"Maybe they're potential friends," Mike replied.

Joe's thoughts went again to Minkus. He felt funny bringing him up, but if anyone had the answer about Minkus, Joe thought it was Mike.

Slowly, hesitatingly, Joe told Mike about Minkus. "See, I haven't been, well, nice to Minkus, you might say." He prayed Mike wouldn't ask for details, and he didn't. But that meant Joe had to choose what to confide. Skipping over the shake-downs, just repeating that the two of them had "problems," Joe moved quickly to Minkus's generosity of spirit. "I don't know why he's being so nice to me," Joe finished up.

"He told you," Mike pointed out. "He's treating you the way he'd like to be treated. It's not really that complicated."

"Yeah, but even with that bar thing . . . ," Joe stumbled.

"Bar mitzvah," Mike supplied.

"Yeah, what you said. Well, even with that, he could have picked someone else to pay attention to." Joe could hear a little resentment creeping into his voice. Why didn't Minkus leave him alone? Things were finally starting to go good. The last thing he wanted was Minkus hanging around being nice, making him feel guilty.

"Seems to me, there're only two things to do," Mike said. "You can ignore him, or you can reciprocate."

"What does that mean?" Joe asked suspiciously.

"Do something nice for him."

That's where they left it. Not much was said as they finished up the raft, though Mike did clap him on the shoulder when they were done. "Good work, Joe. Good work."

Joe felt the pressure of Mike's hand, long after he was gone.

Respiercate. Reciprikate. Joe couldn't quite remember how the word was pronounced, but he did remember what it meant. He thought about how Minkus could have shut down the search for Gato before it began. All he would have had to do is mention a few twisted arms and outlays of nine dollars, and Bette, Vivi, even sweet Ollie, horrified he was sure, would have turned their backs on him. Gato might never have gotten home if that had happened. Yeah, he oughtta *resipercate. Whatever.*

But what in the world could he do for Minkus? Joe wondered. Throughout the weekend, Joe could think of little else, even when Gene and his mom took him to a pretty good war movie. If Joe was going to do something, he should probably do it soon.

That night, as he got ready for bed, Joe emptied his pockets of change, like he did whenever he had any change to empty. He usually left the money on his desk until he could transfer it to the pockets of the jeans he'd be wearing the next day.

He often thought most of the coins felt too light, like play money. Then his fingers brushed the angel coin. It may have been the size of a quarter, but it had more weight and substance than the real money. He got into bed and took the coin with him. Looking out the window next to his bed, Joe watched the almost-full moon play hide-and-seek as clouds leisurely passed it.

As he held the coin tight, Joe felt like there was an idea inside him that was playing hide-and-seek as well. Sometimes he could almost grasp it, sometimes he wasn't sure he even wanted to. He looked at the moon for a long while. Then he must have dozed, because he felt like he was falling, and that awakened him with a start. As he got his bearings, Joe realized the coin had fallen from his hand.

Then he knew what he should do.

It was funny they were back in the vestibule. Almost in the exact spot where Minkus had tried to give Joe the ten bucks. Joe hadn't planned it that way, but that's where he caught sight of Minkus, both of them a little late getting out for recess. Joe was right behind him, but Minkus hadn't seen him yet. Joe thought, maybe he could just let this thing go, and Minkus would never ever be the wiser. It was tempting. So he called out Minkus's name before he could chicken out.

Minkus whirled around. The sound of Joe calling him seemed to stir up some old feelings, because there was a touch of fear on his face that he tried to hide. It made Joe feel bad.

"Minkus," Joe repeated his name. He really had no idea how to begin.

"Yeah?" Minkus asked, now more curious than frightened.

Joe grasped the angel coin in his pocket, hoping for a little courage. "I want to give you something," he plunged in.

"Give me something?" Minkus repeated.

Joe could barely stand to pull the coin out of his pocket. Now that he was actually doing this, he realized he wanted to keep the angel, probably more than he wanted to give it away. But it was too late now. He shoved it at Minkus.

"What's this?" Minkus asked as Joe dropped it into his hand.

This part Joe had practiced a little. So he wouldn't sound like a complete moron. "Okay, it's this medal thing with an angel on it."

Minkus turned it over in his hand. "Yeah, I can see that."

"And, well, it's brought me good luck."

"You're giving it to me?" Minkus looked up at him with clear blue eyes that Joe now noticed were the same as Vivi's.

"Yeah. It's for you. And your sister, too, her being sick and all. Maybe it will bring you guys good luck, too."

Joe knew what the coin seemed to have brought him was much more than luck. It had given him something to hold on to when everything seemed to be slipping out of his grasp. It had made him feel like there was something or someone out there that was willing to listen, maybe even help. But he didn't feel like he could say any of that to Minkus. Let good luck cover it, he thought to himself, and maybe Minkus, or Vivi, if he shared it with her, would find out for themselves.

By now, Minkus's surprise had turned into something closer to shock. "Let me get this straight. You, Joe Garcia, are doing something nice for me?"

"Well, why not?" Joe asked indignantly. "You said you were going to do nice things for me."

"Yeah," Minkus agreed slowly. "I did."

"So why should that be one way? I can do good things if I want to."

A smile crossed Minkus's face. "You're right," he agreed. "Nobody's stopping you."

Joe nodded with satisfaction. "Nobody's stopping me."

XV

Vivi curled up on her pink satin bedspread, staring up at the lacy pink canopy overhead. She loved her bedroom. It was pretty. Everything in the bedroom that wasn't pink was white, accented with gold, including the shelves that held her collections of antique dolls and perfume bottles. Yes, some people might—okay, did—think the room was princessy. Bette teasingly remarked it reminded her of Sleeping Beauty's gift shop at Disneyland. Vivi didn't care. From the time her mother had decorated the bedroom in fairy-tale colors, she had felt like a princess. What girl somewhere deep inside didn't want to give her inner princess a suitable stage? And whether Bette admitted it or not, that included her, too.

Now, of course, Vivi felt like the princess who had turned into a frog. Or had that been a prince? Anyway, a frog, for sure. Rolling over, Vivi picked up the gilt-touched hand mirror from the end table next to her bed. She didn't know why she kept it there. After all these months, there was no surprise left in looking at her reflection and seeing the puffy cheeks and the rounded face that was a common side effect of the medicine she was taking for her asthma. Even her curly blond hair was less thick than it used to be, and her eyes, so big and blue, seemed smaller.

She threw the mirror down on the bed. It was a good

thing she loved her bedroom because she had no real desire to ever leave it. And the last place she wanted to go was back to school. As long as she was away, the other kids could still think of her as Before. She didn't need to be someplace where they could look at her and so clearly think, After.

"Vivi?" Minkus stuck his head in the doorway.

"Andy. Knock. I've told you a million times."

Minkus nodded sheepishly. "Yeah, right, sorry." He stood tentatively, waiting.

If Vivi was perfectly honest with herself, and she prided herself on her honesty, she was getting tired of Andy. It wasn't his fault. She tried to avoid everybody, almost all the time. Only when she craved company so badly that her head hurt from being nowhere but inside it, would she make a date with Bette. Andy, well, Andy tried hard to be a good brother, a good "womb mate" as the twins used to call each other. Ever since she had gotten really sick, he had made her laugh when he could and was more sympathetic than probably she deserved. But he also probed, checking out her feelings, and pushed, trying to get her to do more than she was capable of.

"What is it?" she asked impatiently.

He didn't answer. Instead, he came in and sat down on her bed. He looked nervous. That was nothing new. She had always been the braver, more confident one of the two. Vivi was inevitably the one who was ready to take a risk. Whether it was sneaking out to play in the elevator of their high-rise when they were little or daring her brother to "borrow" some money from their mother's wallet so they could buy themselves a couple of cupcakes at the fancy bakery down the street, Vivi was the leader and Andy the usually reluctant follower. Sometimes he tried to rein her in, when her schemes seemed too ill-advised, and once in a while, he even succeeded. There had been no doubt, however, that Vivi was always the center of whatever attention was around.

The only time the tables were turned was when they were playing music. Vivi was good, that she was sure of. Sitting down at the piano not only garnerd Vivi plenty of accolades, music also blanketed her with a calmness she very rarely felt otherwise. But Andy did more than play well when he picked up his violin. The music that came out of his instrument was suffused with real emotion. Vivi had once told her brother his music sounded like colors, and if someone couldn't see, all they'd have to do was listen to Andy play and they would be able to "hear" red or yellow or blue. The sweet look Andy had given her melted her.

Andy was looking sweet now, as he approached her bed. Vivi sat up a little and looked at him curiously. "So what's up?"

"I have something for you."

"A present?" The holidays were long over, and Andy wasn't carrying a box.

"Well, kind of." He opened his fist, which was curled in a ball. Vivi could see something that looked like a quarter in his palm.

"You're giving me twenty-five cents?"

Andy smiled his hesitant smile. "No, of course not." He came closer and pushed his hand out so she could see more clearly what was in it.

"Some kind of medal?" she asked, looking at it, and then reached out her hand to take it.

Andy nodded.

The medal—it seemed to have an angel on it—felt good in her hand. Solid, important. Though what could be important about this rather dull piece of metal, Vivi couldn't say.

All she knew was holding it reassured her. It gave her the same feeling you might have after worrying about a test, and then realizing you know the answers.

"Where did you get it?" Vivi asked curiously.

Andy had known that one was coming and had prepared for it. "Someone working on *Big River* gave it to me." It wasn't a lie. Andy really hated to lie. "Said it was good luck."

Vivi frowned. "Why did he give it to you?"

Andy shrugged. "He had been kind of, uh, rude to me." Well, bullying someone and taking his money was nothing if not rude. "And, I, well, guess he wanted to apologize."

"That's sort of a weird way to apologize."

Andy should have guessed Vivi wasn't going to give it up so easily. "He thought it was a nice thing to do."

Vivi examined the angel on the coin a little more closely. It was a long, lean angel in a flowing robe, but it was too small to see the face.

Andy sat down on the bed next to his sister, and Vivi swung her legs over the bed so she could sit up beside him.

"So you'll keep it, right?" He didn't know why exactly, but it seemed important that Vivi not toss it in a drawer like a cheap piece of jewelry.

"Sure," she said with a shrug. "I'm going to need it."

She was going to need it on Monday, when she went back to school. She was dreading it, just dreading it. When she had started being homeschooled, well, tutored actually, it had been a relief. Oh, she had fought it when her mother first suggested it, but last summer had been so hard. She had worn herself out trying to get on top of her asthma. Then, not going back to school had sounded not so much like giving in as, well, taking a breather. Totally ironic, of course, since breathing was what she wasn't doing very well at that moment.

So she told herself that this was a well-deserved break. And told herself again, in an effort to convince. Deep inside, though, Vivi knew that she wasn't leaving school because she didn't feel well or was weary, even though she was both of those things. She didn't want to go back to school because of something she no longer was—herself.

She felt fat and ugly and sick, and that made her feel afraid. Vivian Minkus, who had never been frightened of anything in her life, except maybe rats, and even in the city you didn't see rats that often. Fear, once it came upon her, was not what she expected. It didn't churn in her stomach or make her shaky. It just made her want to lie in her bed, quietly, and do as little as absolutely possible.

Vivi turned to her brother. "Andy, I don't know how I'm going to do this. Going back to school, I mean."

Minkus looked at her with those blue eyes, so like her own. "It won't be terrible. The kids at Odom aren't that bad. I mean, most of them are artistes," he said with a bit of a fake French accent to make her laugh, or at least smile. "They've got more important things on their minds than you."

"Everybody makes time to talk about other people."

"Vivi, you don't look that bad." And no matter what his sister thought, it was true. Yeah, she was heavier, her face especially, and maybe she didn't have that Vivi glow that was so much a part of her. But it wasn't like people would cover their eyes with their hands and shriek when she passed by. He wished Vivi could feel about her medicine the way he did, grateful that it allowed her to breathe. Vivi's twisted face when she was trying to claw for air? That scared him to the tips of his toes.

"I don't look that good," Vivi countered bluntly. "I can't think of one decent thing that can come out of going back to school."

"You won't have to look at the crumbs in Mr. Solanari's beard anymore?" Finally, a real smile, Minkus thought.

"Okay, I won't miss Mr. Solanari. Not only was he a crumb face, he was a lousy tutor. I don't know what Mom and Dad saw in him. I'm probably going to be, like, two years behind in class."

"Yeah, Miss All A's. I'm sure you will have reverted to a fifth grader in the last six months."

"While everything else on me has been expanding, my brain has been atrophying," Vivi said, shaking her head.

Minkus wasn't quite sure what to say about that. With so little stimulation, seeing so few people, doing so few things, maybe Vivi's brain had shrunk a little bit. Fortunately, her mother, with unerring timing, stuck her head in the room, so Minkus didn't have to say anything about his sister's brain.

"It's almost time for dinner. Your dad's home, and he's got some news for you."

Vivi and Minkus looked at each other in stunned silence. Their father was almost never home in time for dinner. For years, Mrs. Minkus had urged her doctor husband to make sure his office hours ended early enough to get him home before they ate. Dr. Minkus tried, but there always seemed to be some emergency or patients who showed up late, making the day last longer than it should. Once he did get home, he rarely had news, or if he did, he didn't share it with his kids. Usually, he ate his dinner quietly with just Mrs. Minkus for company, nursing a glass of wine. Their mom was the one who did the talking, while their father nodded and chewed. Good news? That was a first.

"So hurry up, wash your hands, and come to the table," Mrs. Minkus said, closing the door softly.

"My hands are clean," Vivi said, getting up and slipping the angel coin in her drawer.

"Mine aren't," Minkus noted, looking at his hands, but he made no move toward Vivi's bathroom to wash them.

"What do you think Dad's news is?" Vivi asked.

"Who knows?" Minkus answered morosely. "But I doubt if his definition of good is the same as ours."

So Minkus was pleasantly surprised when they were finally settled at the dining room table, salads and bread at their places, that their father cleared his throat and made his announcement. "You know how I attend the ophthalmologists' conference every year?"

Vivi and Minkus nodded dutifully. Their father was an eye doctor, and apparently the eye doctors thought it prudent to meet every year and discuss what was up with eyeballs and ways to keep them healthy, because their father always made it a point to attend their conventions.

"Well, this year we're meeting in Florida, and the conference is being held the same week as your spring vacation. So your mother and I thought it would be fun for all of us to go."

Vivi and Minkus looked at each other, suitably surprised. Vacations were hardly anything new in their family. But both of their parents liked things orderly, boring even, so vacations were pretty well prescribed. For part of Christmas vacation, they went to visit their mother's parents in Santa Fe. The first two weeks in August, they alternated every other year between renting a cabin in Wisconsin, which their dad loved because he could fish and their mother hated because she was bored, or spending the time in some glamorous city like London or Paris. Dr. Minkus wasn't exactly bored in those places, but he usually looked like he'd rather be fishing.

They had never gone anywhere for spring vacation before. It was a time to "stay home and enjoy Chicago," according to their mother. Not that they ever did too much out-of-the-usual enjoying. Except for the occasional trip to a museum, it was just hanging out with their friends. That was fine, too.

Vivi glanced at Andy. He seemed happy enough with the news. That was Andy's problem, he was too trusting. He rarely looked for ulterior motives.

"Why this year?" Vivi asked her parents.

Dr. Minkus looked perplexed. "I just told you. Your vacation overlaps the conference."

"It has before," Vivi pointed out. "Two years ago, you went to the meeting in Toronto and we stayed home and enjoyed Chicago." You had to be quick to catch the look exchanged between her parents, but Vivi was very quick. "Something else is up." For the life of her, though, she couldn't figure out what it was. Then, as her mother twisted her napkin in her lap, Vivi got it. "This is another plan to get me out of the house, only on a grander scale."

A weary Mrs. Minkus didn't even try to deny it. "It's just that you've been cooped up for so long."

Aha, thought Vivi. So this *was* something her parents had cooked up to help their poor, pathetic, asthmatic daughter.

"I'm about to start school, Mother," Vivi said, and all the fear about that coated her voice with ire. "I'll be getting out every single day to go to a school where I'm going to be a laughingstock."

"That's not true, I told you, Vivi," Minkus murmured.

"Oh, you don't even know when people are making fun of you," Vivi said, turning her anger on her brother. She felt bad as soon as she said it, but it was true. It hadn't escaped the attention of some kids that Andy had a way of wiggling his nose when he was scared that, unfortunately, made him look like a bunny. She'd heard plenty of rude comments behind his back. Once, in the fifth grade, Vivi told eighth grader Josie Peterson that if she ever called Andy "Bunny Boy" again, she'd tell everyone Josie stuffed her bra with Kleenex, and if there wasn't any Kleenex around, she used toilet paper. Since the information was totally true, acquired from Josie's sister, the comments had stopped.

Andy didn't respond to Vivi's accusation, didn't even look at her. He just took a long sip of his water, hiding as much of his face in his water glass as he could.

Instantly, Vivi felt terrible, which made her want to lash out all the more. "So, like you insisted, I'm back at Odom. What, Mother, you couldn't stand to have me around all day? Did it depress you?" This was a low blow, too, because Vivi knew that her mother could get down pretty easily.

"Stop it, Vivi," Dr. Minkus said in a stern voice. "No more. Your mother and I thought it would be good for everyone to get away for some fun and sunshine after a tough year. And that's what we're going to do."

A tough year, Vivi thought to herself. A tough year for who? For her, that's who. Florida didn't sound like fun to her, and as for sunshine . . . sunshine? It suddenly hit her that sunshine equaled pools and pools equaled bathing suits. "I'm not going to sit out by the pool in a bathing suit with everyone looking at me," Vivi said through gritted teeth.

"Oh, Vivian," her mother said with a sigh. "No one is going to be looking at you."

The angry air inside of Vivi seeped out of her like air out of a balloon. Now she just felt sad. There was a time when she liked people looking at her.

"I'm not going to the beach," she began, "and I'm not sitting by the pool, and I'm not . . ."

"Vivian," Dr. Minkus said, carefully buttering his bread.

"Don't go to the beach if that's what you want, but the arrangements are made and we're all going to Florida."

Vivi stood up with as much dignity as she could muster, threw her napkin on her chair, and walked toward the only place she really wanted to be. As she opened the door to her bedroom, she could hear her mother faintly say to her father, "Gee. That went well."

XVI

"Vivian. Bette will be here any minute." Mrs. Minkus raised her voice. "Are you listening to me?"

Vivi turned away from the picture window that looked out onto the lake. It really was a spectacular view. Some people dissed Lake Michigan because it wasn't an ocean, saying it didn't have the majesty that a larger body of water might. But those people had never really studied the lake, had never noticed the way the water could churn one day and look like silk the next. There was grace alone in the color—so many shades of blue—from the turquoise color of Indian jewelry on a sunny day to a blue so steely, it was almost gray. One of the nicest things her father ever said to her was that her eyes changed color, just the way the lake did.

"Yes, I heard you. I think I'll meet her downstairs." It had been a while since she'd even spoken to Bette. The closer it came to going back to school, the fewer calls Vivi had made. Talking about school had made her return seem all too real. Bette had seemed surprised, but happy, really happy, when Vivi had arranged this shopping date.

"Now, you're sure you don't want me to come with you?" Mrs. Minkus asked.

"No, just your credit card will be fine." Vivi said it as a joke, but she could tell her mother was hurt. Today was one of those days when making her mother feel bad didn't seem like much fun. "Sorry, Mom."

Mrs. Minkus plastered a smile on her face. "That's okay, I know it'll be more fun if it's only you and Bette. But you'll buy some new school clothes, won't you? You've put it off until the last minute."

"It's Saturday. I could have waited until tomorrow for the very last minute."

Digging into her wallet for her credit card, Mrs. Minkus said, "Very funny. And don't forget to look for boots. We're getting into slushy season."

Vivi looked outside again. "It seems nice today." Better weather was the very reason Vivi was starting school now instead of at the start of the new semester back in January. No matter how much her mother thought she needed to get out of the house, she didn't want her to do it when it was freezing outside.

Mrs. Minkus handed Vivi her card and said, "Well, without much snow, there's nothing to melt, but that could change." Mrs. Minkus's lips thinned. "It always does in Chicago."

That was true. Even April wasn't too late for snow in Chicago. Her mother had grown up in California, and everyone in the family knew how tired Mrs. Minkus got of winter. For a brief moment, Vivi realized that perhaps going to Florida wasn't all about getting her out of the house. Maybe her mom was just craving some sun, too.

"Now, you've brought medicine to take at lunchtime? And you have your inhalers with you?" Mrs. Minkus continued.

Vivi had two inhalers. One for when her breathing got bad and one for when her breathing got really bad. "Yes, Mom. I have everything."

"Good. Fine." Mrs. Minkus's face cleared.

The downstairs doorbell rang, and Vivi hurried over to the intercom. "I'll be right down, Bette," she said before Bette could even say hi.

"Tuck my credit card in a side pocket of your bag, so you'll know where to find it," Mrs. Minkus instructed as Vivi put on her down jacket and grabbed her purse. "Do you have your gloves? And your hat?"

Vivi put a cute little knit beret on her head.

"What about your scarf?"

She had to dig a little into the closet for the matching scarf, but she came up with it. Without a good-bye, she ran out the door.

Bette was sitting on one of the leather chairs in the lobby, reading *The Prince and the Pauper*.

"What's up with that?" Vivi asked, pointing to the book.

"Oh, after we finished *Huckleberry Finn*, I started reading other books by Twain." She put *The Prince and the Pauper* in her backpack. "*Huck Finn* was better."

Vivi wrapped the scarf she'd been carrying around her neck. "So what's happening with *Big River*?" Vivi asked. Not that she didn't hear about it from Andy, but he had such a positive take on everything. It was one of his great faults. She'd rather get the skinny from Bette.

Bette smiled. "It's going really well. I've got my songs down, and the show opens a couple of weeks after we get back from spring break. Hey," Bette said as they headed outside. "You'll be there."

"Duh."

"Well, I didn't really think about you being back in school in terms of the show," Bette replied as they walked a short half block to the bus stop. "Maybe there's still time for you to get involved."

Vivi looked up the street to see if she could spy the 151 bus that would take them to Michigan Avenue. "No thanks."

"Well, I'm not sure what you could do," Bette admitted. "Flora Kennedy is playing the piano. It's a ton of work."

"I know. I've been accompanying Andy when he practices. How's Flora doing?" Vivi tried not to look too interested, but Flora, a red-headed eighth grader, had been her main competition as a pianist at Odom.

The bus pulled up, and Bette clambered on. Vivi thought she heard her say, "Flora's great." Or maybe she just said "good." Either way, it didn't make Vivi very happy. She rather hoped that Bette might say Flora was "adequate" or "okay." "Lousy" would have been too much to hope for.

"Maybe you could help with the costumes," Bette said as she settled into a seat by the window. "Lane—you know, that friend of Ollie's—she's working on them."

Vivi slid in next to her. "I'll take a pass." She was beginning to get irritated at Bette's persistence.

"Really? Everyone's so into it."

"Too much trouble. So are you going to buy anything today?" Vivi asked, changing the subject.

Bette looked at her shrewdly. She knew exactly what Vivi was doing, but she played along. "I still have my Christmas money. So, yeah, I'm shopping. And I should buy something for Laura. Her birthday is next week."

"Have you considered the fact that if your dad marries Laura, Mrs. Abrams's going to be your grandmother? Well, stepgrandmother, actually, but still."

"I don't think they're getting married," Bette said carefully. "At least my father said they were 'taking it slow.'"

"Would you mind if they did?"

Bette had clearly thought about the possibility and had an

answer ready. "Not really. She's nice. Except for the fact that she loves music, Laura doesn't remind me of my mom. Or any mom, really. She's more like an older sister. An older, older sister."

"What does Barbra think?" Vivi asked.

Bette shook her head. "She's so wrapped up in Northwestern, I don't think she cares much. My father and Laura? It's a big whatever for her. But my dad," Bette added softly, "well, he seems happy."

"And that makes you happy?"

"Yeah," Bette replied thoughtfully. "It does."

Vivi fiddled with her scarf. "So between getting back to singing and stuff at home, you're happy, happy, happy."

Bette glanced at Vivi. "I guess so. What about you?"

"Hey, this is our stop." Vivi pulled her gloves from her pocket and hurried to the front of the bus, Bette scrambling to keep up. They got off across the street from Water Tower Place, the big glass-and-chrome shopping center that dominated north Michigan Avenue.

A stiff breeze was blowing now, and Vivi wrapped the scarf more securely around her neck.

"Do you want to head over to Macy's or stop at H&M?" Bette asked, pointing to the store behind her, where you could get cute stuff pretty cheap.

"There are more stores in Water Tower," Vivi said. "Let's go over there."

Along with a horde of people, the girls crossed the street. One side of the vertical indoor mall was the department store, Macy's, and the other half of the building led to the American Girl store, a five-story doll fest, which had been a favorite stop of both Bette and Vivi when they were younger. Still, the allure wasn't entirely gone. The girls looked at each other and knew what the other was thinking. "Maybe we can stop in before we go home," Bette said.

"Sure, why not," Vivi said, trying not to smile.

"But first let's go shopping."

Vivi tried to let some of Bette's enthusiasm rub off on her. It didn't work. If only the shopping really was limited to dolls. Instead, as they made their way through several stores, there was the taking-off of clothes, exposing too much of Vivi in the mirror for her comfort, the trying-on of tops that weren't flattering, the struggling to get into jeans that would have fit easily last year. An hour and a half later, she had bought nothing and felt exhausted and sad.

As she dressed one more time, she looked at her reflection. Who was this girl? Was the other one ever coming back?

Bette had started the shopping expedition enthusiastically, but progressively Vivi's mood began rubbing off on her. Whenever they had gone shopping in the past, they had always shared a dressing room. But today, at each stop, Vivi had carried her clothes to a small cubicle and pulled the curtain tightly behind her.

"Let's quit shopping and go get something to eat," Bette finally suggested, sticking her head inside Vivi's dressing room. "Do you feel like pizza?"

"Pizza?" Vivi looked at her friend, astonished. "I can't eat anything like that, I've already gained ten pounds. Last year, my jeans were a size four," she wailed.

Bette came in, pushed aside the clothes that lay on the small wooden seat, and sat down. "Maybe you've gained weight because you haven't been doing much but sitting in the house."

"I can't do much. I can't exert myself," Vivi countered, quoting her mother.

"Vivi, you don't do anything," Bette said bluntly.

"Oh, nice. Nice to have such a sympathetic friend."

"I'm sorry," Bette said, "but you've gotta see . . ."

Vivi looked at her watch. "I've got to get home."

"You're not going to buy anything?"

Vivi picked two items off the floor where she had dropped them. One was a red sweater that was loose and sloppy. The other was a pair of jeans that didn't flatter her in any way, but at least they fit. "I'm going to buy these."

Bette shrugged. "Fine." She steamed to herself, but as they waited in a long line to check out, she softened. "Are you sure you don't want to get just a little something to eat. I'm so hungry." She put on a sad puppy-dog face.

Finally, Vivi smiled. She could never resist the puppy dog. "I guess." In truth, despite the disappointing shopping, Vivi wasn't really looking forward to going home.

"How about McDonald's?" Bette asked. "You can get something healthy there, like a salad."

"I guess."

They got their food and finally found seats in the crowded food court. As Vivi put her salad and diet soda down on the not-very-clean table, she felt the little guilty flutter that had become a part of her lunchtime. That was because Vivi had a secret. She had stopped taking her medication at lunch. It was the medication that gave her the chipmunk face, and as the time to go back to school drew closer, Vivi had become desperate to do something about the way she looked. She figured if she cut her dosage in half that had to make a difference. Doing something about her dinner dosage usually wasn't an option; her mother made sure she downed that one, to the point that Vivi was insulted. Didn't her mother think she was old enough to monitor her own medication? The irony wasn't lost on Vivi. She was monitoring it, all right, but in a way that would have horrified Mrs. Minkus.

"What are you thinking about?" Bette asked, biting into her burger.

"Huh?"

"You looked so weird there for a minute."

"Oh, I just remembered I forgot to buy boots. My mother wanted me to get a pair."

"Do you want to look for some when we're done eating?"

"No," Vivi said. "I've had it." This shopping trip was the most she had attempted in a while.

Without interest, Vivi nibbled at her salad. Suddenly, she was startled by Bette reaching over to grab her hand. "Vivi, we haven't talked much lately . . ."

"I know, I'm sorry about that," Vivi interrupted wearily.

"Oh, I understand," Bette said, shaking her head. "It's just that, well, I never really got to talk to you about some stuff."

"Like what?"

"I wanted to tell you about Gabi."

"That woman who lived downstairs from you for a while?" Vivi asked. "What about her?"

"Yeah. I don't know how to explain it, but talking to her was great. She really helped turn things around for me."

Vivi frowned. Where was this going?

Bette stumbled. "It's just that sometimes you meet people, and I don't know, they help you see things . . ."

"Are you telling me I should see a shrink?" Vivi asked bluntly.

"No," a startled Bette replied.

"Because my parents have been telling me I should talk to

someone for a long time. In fact, they tried to set up an appointment for me."

"And you didn't go?"

Vivi's smile was small and contained. "No."

If there had been any moment when Vivi had felt power during a time when she was weak and helpless, it was when her parents had made an appointment with a psychologist.

"I'm not going," Vivi had declared to her surprised parents. Apparently, they hadn't thought she would put up a fight.

"But why not?" her father had asked.

Vivi had just shaken her head. She didn't want to talk to anyone about her illness. She didn't want to be sick, and sitting down and talking about it would just make it more real than it already was. Maybe that didn't make a lot of sense. Vivi was sure her parents could poke all kinds of holes in her argument. So instead of getting into a fight, she had just pursed her lips and shook her head. That course had led to a startling insight: There were things her parents couldn't force her to do. She was too big to pick up and carry to the shrink's office. If they had one come to the house, they couldn't make her talk. Vivi held that knowledge like a precious talisman. Sometimes it made her feel strong.

"But why, Vivi?" Bette asked. "What would be so bad about talking to someone?"

"I just don't want to."

Leaning back in her chair, Bette looked at her friend intently. "I guess you're going to do what you're going to do, Vivi."

She didn't make it sound like a compliment.

XVII

The tightening was unmistakable. It was as if a rope were being twisted inside her chest. Vivi was hanging up her coat in the hall closet, and she told herself that maybe she had moved a little awkwardly. Maybe what she felt was just a muscle stretching.

Mrs. Minkus walked into the hallway. "Hi," she said brightly. "How did the shopping go?"

"I forgot to buy boots," Vivi replied, offering a scowl in return. She dropped the bags with her jeans and sweater on the floor.

Clearly deciding to ignore Vivi's crankiness, Mrs. Minkus said, "That's all right. Maybe we can do it tomorrow. Can I take a look at what you bought?"

Vivi shrugged. All she wanted to do was get to her bedroom and use her inhaler, just as a precaution, of course; but there stood her mother, with an expectant smile on her face, and the last thing Vivi wanted to do was raise suspicions.

"You didn't get much," Mrs. Minkus said as she peeked in the bag.

"Nothing looked good on me."

Her mother pulled the red sweater out of the bag. "Is this the right size? It looks so big."

"It covers me," Vivi replied flatly.

"And jeans." Mrs. Minkus didn't bother taking them out. "Well," she said with a sigh, "we can look for some other things when we shop for the boots."

"Sure." There was a wheeze with her answer. Hoping her mother hadn't noticed, Vivi took back the sweater and the bag and headed off to her room. As soon as she was out of her mother's sight, she rummaged around in her purse for her inhaler and uncapped it. There was no doubt now. The familiar constriction, the difficulty of taking a breath was beginning. Like a thirsty person needing a drink, Vivi shakily took a hit from her inhaler. Then she lay down on her bed.

There were so many bad things about asthma. Foremost, naturally, was the awful, scary uncertainty about taking the next breath. But Vivi also hated the way it made her second-guess herself. Should she have used the stronger inhaler? Taken a pill at lunch? Maybe she should tell her mother she was having problems? No. Mrs. Minkus would try to stay calm, with little success. *I'll be fine,* Vivi told herself, and tried to ignore the panicky voice inside that was saying, *But what if you're not?*

It was getting harder to breathe. Vivi stood up and walked around a little. Moving to her bedroom window, she pulled back the curtain and looked out at the lake, now a dusky gray in the late winter light. Vivi's room didn't have the expansive view of the living room; an apartment building blocked much of the water, and a sliver of Lake Michigan was all she got. It was enough because Vivi always thought of that slice of water as her own, a private piece of ever-changing nature that only she could see.

As it almost always did, looking at the lake calmed her, and for a few moments, Vivi thought she was out of the woods. She heaved a sigh of relief, but then, the sigh got caught about halfway down her chest, and when she tried to grab the next breath, it didn't come.

The other inhaler, Vivi thought to herself. It was a stronger formulation, and she was supposed to take it only when she was sure the other one hadn't worked. She wasn't sure. Her dad would probably be home soon, but should she wait to ask him? Maybe she'd be wasting valuable time.

It struck Vivi, how in her old life, making decisions was never a problem for her. Andy was the one who would dither around trying to choose what to eat in a restaurant or which movie to go to while she rolled her eyes. Now she couldn't decide whether to use her extra-strength medication, and was so frightened by the thought of having to go to the emergency room—always the next step when her breathing was uncontrolled.

The wheezing was getting worse. There was no doubt about that now. Vivi hated, hated that hissing sound. It was like a snake inside her. She fumbled around in her purse. Where was that inhaler?

"Hey," Andy said, sticking his head in the room. "Mom wants to know if you had something to eat."

Not trusting her voice, Vivi just nodded.

Andy looked at his sister quizzically. "Are you okay?"

She tried to keep her breathing steady. "Sure."

"Oh. Okay. Well, Mom's going to make cocoa. Wanna come out and have some?"

"No. Thanks."

Andy stood there for a moment, searching her face. Then he just nodded and left.

Vivi would have breathed a sigh of relief. If she could breathe. She went back to her purse and found the stronger inhaler, but before she could use it, there was a knock at her door. Putting it behind her, Vivi managed to say, "Come in."

"Darling," Mrs. Minkus said, "Andy said you didn't want any cocoa, but why don't you come out and join us anyway? I got some of those delicious cupcakes that you like so much from the patisserie."

"Mom . . ." Vivi hoped her mother didn't notice it was more of a gasp than a word.

"I'm not going to take no for an answer. Your father will be here any minute, and then we're going out for dinner later, so let's just take a break. How about a cup of tea instead? That will warm you up."

Mrs. Minkus just stood there, waiting. When she got into family mode, there was usually no stopping her, so Vivi stuffed her inhaler in her sweater pocket and followed her mother into the dining room.

One lovely thing about her mother was that she could make even the smallest event seem like an occasion. Today, she had set the table with her good china, because Mrs. Minkus said you should use your best things, not save them. When she was in the right mood, Vivi liked that celebratory feeling that her mom could evoke. Right now, she wasn't in the mood.

"Oh good, your dad's here," Mrs. Minkus said, hearing, as Vivi did, his key in the door. "Andy," she called toward her son's bedroom. "We're just about ready to sit down."

Damn, thought Vivi. She had wanted to sneak into the bathroom and take a hit of medicine before her father got home. He could be a little opaque sometimes, but if she was wheezing, his doctor's ear would hear it.

Andy wandered into the kitchen, and Dr. Minkus came in from the hallway, still wearing his overcoat.

"Judd, we're having a high tea, just like the British do. Take off your coat and stay a while." Mrs. Minkus smiled.

"I'm cold," her husband replied, giving her a kiss on the cheek. "I'll hang it up in a second. This looks nice," he said approvingly, looking at the festive table. "Does it really have to be tea? Can I get a cup of coffee?"

Mrs. Minkus laughed. "I've got a pot in the kitchen."

"Great." Dr. Minkus turned toward his children. Vivi, trying desperately to keep her breathing even, was already sitting down. Andy was looking at his sister with concern. Dr. Minkus followed his gaze. "Vivian," he said sharply. "Are you all right?"

Surrender. She was in trouble and if it wasn't obvious this minute, it would be soon. She shook her head.

"Have you used your meter?" Dr. Minkus asked.

Vivi shook her head again. She hated her meter. She was supposed to use it to monitor her breathing, but she avoided the machine whenever possible. "The readings don't lie," her doctors and of course her parents always told her. "You can't think you're fine if the meter shows otherwise."

Which was why she didn't use the meter.

"Andy, go get it," Dr. Minkus directed.

Vivi took the extra-strength inhaler from her pocket and showed it to her dad.

"Wait until we take the meter reading."

As soon as Andy rushed back in with the peak-flow meter, Vivi breathed into it. Without looking at the number, she could read the result on her father's frowning face.

"All right, Vivi, take two hits on your strongest inhaler, then get your coat. We're going to the hospital."

"No," she managed to gasp.

"Yes," he replied crisply. "Jill, I'm going to take Vivi in a cab. It will be faster than getting the car out of the garage."

"I'm coming, too," Mrs. Minkus said, her face twisted with worry.

"You can follow us."

Andy had already gotten her coat and hat from the closet. As he gave them to her, he also shoved something in her hand.

Vivi looked down at the angel coin. As she struggled into her coat, Andy said, "It was on your dresser, next to your meter. Take it with you, okay?"

Nodding, Vivi tried to smile at Andy. As soon as she was ready, Dr. Minkus hustled her out downstairs where the doorman quickly hailed them a cab.

Once they were on their way, Dr. Minkus asked, "Do you feel the inhaler working? Just nod or shake your head."

Instead, Vivi shrugged. She wasn't sure.

Dr. Minkus put his arm around Vivi. With his other hand, he reached into his pocket and pulled out his cell phone. Vivi barely listened as he called ahead to the hospital and told the ER he was bringing his daughter in. She was too busy concentrating on breathing.

The hospital wasn't very far. The cab dropped them off at the emergency room, and Dr. Minkus hustled Vivi into the brightly lit room. It wasn't the first time Vivi had been there since her asthma had gotten so severe, and going to the hospital brought up two very different feelings in her. Hate was one. Hating having to be here, worried and scared, looking at other worried and scared people, sitting in uncomfortable chairs, waiting for someone to take care of them. The other feeling was relief, a wash of relief, that she was somewhere safe, that although she wasn't out of the woods yet, at least someone would be coming soon to lead her through.

Dr. Minkus had barely registered her at the front desk, when a nurse holding a clipboard called her name. Vivi could feel the stares of the people who had been waiting much longer, and she turned to her father with a questioning look and managed to squeak, "Me first?"

"You can't breathe. That takes precedence over some of their ailments," Dr. Minkus responded.

Vivi just nodded, but she wondered if the elderly Asian man clutching his stomach would have agreed.

The nurse ushered Vivi into a curtained cubical. Dr. Minkus cleared his throat and said, "I'll be right outside. "Will you let me know after you've done the initial tests?"

"Yes, Dr. Minkus," the nurse said, whose name tag read Mrs. Reich. She handed Vivi a thin cotton gown, the embarrassing kind that barely closed in the back. Once her father was out of sight, Vivi changed with the nurse's help, and then the usual tests began, blood pressure, blood tests, and a more sophisticated metering of her breath. In a matter of moments, an ER doc, an intern or a resident who didn't look that much older than she was, appeared to listen to her chest with his stethoscope. Fortunately, he wasn't very good-looking, otherwise her humiliation would have been complete.

"So . . . Vivian . . . ," he said after consulting his chart. "I'm Dr. Trace. Do you have your inhaler with you?"

It was still hard for Vivi to talk, so she gestured to her coat. The nurse got the inhaler from her pocket and gave it to Dr. Trace. While he was examining it and typing something into a computer on the counter, Mrs. Reich walked over to Vivi and handed her the angel coin. "This was in your pocket, too. Would you like it?"

Vivi nodded. It was probably silly, but Andy had given it to her so hopefully, it seemed rude to exile it back to her coat.

Dr. Trace turned back to Vivi. "It says here you've taken

two dosages. Let's have you take another one now. And we'll get you some oxygen. Then we'll see where we're at."

Later, what Vivi remembered about the next hour or so was that she alternated between being frightened and bored. During the moments when she could breathe calmly, there was nothing to do but look at the cracked ceiling and try to make recognizable shapes from the water stains. Then her chest would tighten again, the wheezing would start, and Vivi could feel herself start to panic. By then, her parents had been allowed in to see her briefly, but Dr. Trace had asked them to go back to the waiting room. Probably, Vivi figured, because her father made the younger doctor nervous. Dr. Minkus could have that effect on people.

The other thing was that she was cold. Freezing cold. It might be the dead of winter outside, but outside had nothing on her cubical. Mrs. Reich brought her a blanket when Vivi had rubbed her shoulders, but it was almost as threadbare as her gown. "Turn up the heat, people," she wanted to yell, but it wouldn't do any good. It was better to save her breath.

Dr. Trace reappeared with her parents right behind him. "Okay, we're going to start you on an IV of steroids and get you up to a room."

Vivi looked at her parents. "I have to stay?" she asked, upset.

"Calm down, Vivi," Dr. Minkus said. "You can't go home with an IV in your arm."

"It will probably just be overnight," Mrs. Minkus said, but there was an uncertainty in her voice that Vivi picked up on immediately.

"Sure?" Vivi whispered.

Dr. Trace cleared his throat. "We'll see tomorrow," he said, clearly trying to assert himself as the person in charge.

"Now let's get you upstairs before registration gives the room away to someone else."

Her father stayed with her while the IV bag full of liquid medicine was hooked up, in a short but painful process. The bag was attached to a tube, which was attached to a large needle that stayed in Vivi's arm; when the medicine was finished, the bag would be changed. Dr. Minkus frowned as Mrs. Reich poked and prodded, trying to find a vein that would accept the needle. Vivi tried hard not to squeal or squirm, figuring it would only extend the process. Once she was hooked up, an orderly appeared and wheeled her upstairs. In the elevator, he smiled at her and asked, "How you doin'?" but Vivi just turned her head and didn't say anything, even though her more regulated breathing made it easier to talk. It would have been rude to reply, "I feel terrible, I look worse, I've got a tube attached to a bag stuck in my arm, and now I have to stay here for God knows how long. How do you think I'm doin'?"

Her room was small, but at least it was private. During Vivi's previous hospital stays, she had always shared a room, once with an elderly woman who thought Vivi was her grand-daughter. So even though the yellow on the walls was a mustard color and the window looked out on the parking garage, Vivi was relieved to be alone.

Not that you were ever really alone in a hospital. As soon as she was settled, a floor nurse came in to take her pulse and check her temperature with an ear thermometer. A few moments later, a cheerful cafeteria worker brought in a tray of food. On her way out, she almost bumped into Vivi's family.

Mrs. Minkus was carrying a small vase of flowers. "The gift shop was closing and I got the last one."

Looks like it, Vivi thought, glancing at the tired mums, but all she said was, "Thanks."

"How are you feeling?" Andy asked.

Instead of answering, she opened her hand, which was still clutching her angel coin, and smiled. Andy smiled back.

The room was so small that three Minkuses made it feel crowded. Dr. Minkus had taken the room's only chair and was flipping through the pages of her chart. "I'm sure they have you on the right treatment." Then, putting it back in its holder, attached to her bed, he said, "I called a new colleague of mine, Dr. Raphael. She's a pulmonary specialist, and she has a fantastic reputation. I asked her to come take a look at you, but she's out to dinner. She said she'd stop by on her way home."

Vivi shrugged. The last thing she wanted to see was another doctor. But she was stuck in bed, and if this Dr. Raphael decided to visit, Vivi didn't suppose she was in any position to stop her.

"Is your breathing easier?" Dr. Minkus asked.

"Yes," Vivi said, taking a deeper breath than she had all day.

"Well, that's wonderful, darling," Mrs. Minkus said, running her hand through her daughter's hair.

After that, things became awkward. There was nothing for the family to do but look at one another and urge Vivi to eat, which was the last thing she was interested in, especially since everything on the tray seemed to be the same color. The meat was brown, the gravy that sloshed over the mashed potatoes and carrots had turned them brown, and her cola was a bubbly brown. Only the red gelatin cubes added a spot of color, albeit one that was not particularly appetizing.

Finally, her family seemed as ready to leave as Vivi was to have them go.

Mrs. Minkus adjusted Vivi's pillow. "We'll be back first thing in the morning."

Oh, joy, Vivi thought.

Then Mrs. Minkus had a thought. "Or, maybe I should have them bring in a cot and stay with you since you have a private room."

"No, Mom, really, it's fine." *It's fine!*

"All right," her mother conceded. "Your father will have the nurses check on you regularly."

"They'll do that anyway," Dr. Minkus said, giving Vivi a kiss on her forehead. "I think you'll come home tomorrow."

"Hope so," Vivi replied.

"We'll call you later," her mother said.

"She's probably going to be asleep," Andy told his mother, accepting Vivi's grateful look with a nod.

"We'll just check with the nurse's station," Dr. Minkus said.

Now that her breathing was easier, her body less tense, Vivi realized how exhausted she was. "Yeah, I think I'm going to try to go to sleep now."

Her family was barely out of sight when Vivi felt her eyes closing. She had had a vague thought about watching TV, but before she could even look around for the remote control, she was asleep.

Later, she wasn't sure which of her senses prodded her awake. Was it the insistent smell of gardenias that seemed to pervade the room or the tinkle of bells? Maybe it was the glow. When Vivi opened her eyes, it looked like the glow was surrounding the woman beside her bed, but as she became more fully awake, she realized the door was open and the light was coming from the hallway outside.

"Hello," Vivi said.

The woman smiled. "Hello. I'm Dr. Raphael."

Vivi didn't say anything for a moment, as she took in Dr. Raphael. Tall, with skin a warm cocoa color, and a shock of silver-gray hair that was cut short, almost in a crewcut, Dr. Raphael radiated a calm that relaxed Vivi immediately. She could see now that the sound of bells was really the tinkling of the several charm bracelets on Dr. Raphael's wrist. The smell of flowers must have been her perfume.

"How are you feeling, Vivian?" Dr. Raphael asked.

Vivi sat up a little. She took a breath, testing. "Much better, thank you."

"I'm so glad," Dr. Raphael said with a smile that was dazzling. "Do you mind if I sit down for a moment."

"Please do." There was something about the doctor that made her want to be as polite as her mother always urged her to be.

Dr. Raphael shrugged off her velvety coat and pulled the chair closer to Vivi's bed. "Can you switch on your lamp?" There was a slight lilt to her speech.

"Of course." With the light came a Dr. Raphael who did not seem quite as ethereal as the woman in the darkened room, but still impressive. Very impressive.

"So, your father called me, Vivian, and asked if I could see you. Happily, my dinner wasn't far, so here I am."

"What time is it?" Vivi asked.

"It's about ten, not so late, but I'm glad you got a chance to nap. I'm sure you had an exhausting day."

Vivi looked up at her bag of medicine. It was almost empty. "Yes, it was. And scary." She didn't know why she had added that. Being scared was the last thing she liked admitting about herself.

"So how did this happen?"

"Well, I went shopping today, because I have to start going to school again . . ."

"You haven't been going to school?" Dr. Raphael raised her eyebrows slightly.

"I've been homeschooled for a while, since I got sicker."

Dr. Raphael just nodded and motioned for Vivi to go on. So Vivi told her about the shopping trip and coming home and having her symptoms hit full force.

"You stopped taking your medication, didn't you?" The way she said it was a statement, not a question.

Vivi was shocked. She had half expected her father to figure out that she had cut down on her medication, but she certainly didn't expect that insight from someone who had met her less than ten minutes ago. "How did you know?"

"I'm not a mind reader," Dr. Raphael said, but the way she was observing Vivi so intently, Vivi wasn't sure she believed that. "It's unlikely you would have gotten so sick so fast unless your medication wasn't working, and the medication almost always works. So, I assume you weren't taking it."

Well, she was caught, but Vivi tried to pretty up what she had done. "I didn't really stop. I just cut down my dosage. I was feeling better, so I didn't think I needed as much."

"Oh, you didn't." Dr. Raphael seemed almost amused, but then she grew serious. "I'm sure, Vivian, you've been told the consequences of not taking your medicine properly. Actually"—she gestured around the hospital room—"these are the consequences."

It was just a simple statement of fact, but it made Vivi feel bad and, worse, stupid. What had she been thinking?

"What *were* you thinking?"

For someone who claimed not to be a mind reader, Dr.

Raphael certainly seemed able to climb inside her head. But since the question seemed more like inquiry than accusation, Vivi answered, "When I found out I had to go back to school, I wanted to look better."

"It's better to look good than to feel good?"

Vivi didn't reply to that because she thought Dr. Raphael would think her answer was stupid, but, yeah, in some ways it was more important to her to look good than to feel good. Dr. Raphael didn't seem surprised by her silence. Actually, she didn't seem like the type who would be surprised by anything, so Vivi finally said, "I'm tired of being ugly."

"You think you're the opposite of that Ugly Duckling story, huh? You started out beautiful."

Tears filled Vivi's eyes.

"I won't tell you that you are still beautiful. You wouldn't believe me. Like in so many of those other fairy tales you'll have to find that out for yourself. What I can do for you is adjust your medicines and talk to you about ways you can help yourself get your asthma under control."

The advice was nothing that Vivi hadn't heard before, but there was some matter-of-factness, almost a certainty in the way Dr. Raphael spoke, that made Vivi hopeful. She almost didn't recognize the feeling.

Dr. Raphael rose and gracefully wrapped her coat over her shoulders. "I perhaps made that sound easy. It may not be. So much of what happens depends on you, not me." She looked at Vivi keenly. "It would be a pity, however, if all that happens is you look a bit better and your breathing improves." With one last jangle of her bracelets and a fleeting smile, Dr. Raphael left her room.

What did she mean by that? Vivi thought to herself. Well,

she was too tired to think about it now. As Vivi snuggled under her cover once more, she noticed the scent of gardenias still lingered. As she fell asleep, something curious about the doctor's visit floated through her mind. Dr. Raphael had never even opened her chart.

XVIII

Vivi supposed that an overnight stay in the hospital would buy her at least a week's reprieve from returning to school. She supposed wrong. On Sunday morning, she was released from the hospital, her breathing normal. Monday, her parents agreed, was a day to rest. Then, in consultation with Dr. Raphael (consultation in which Vivi was not consulted), it was decided that she could make her school debut on Tuesday.

When given the news by her mother late Monday morning, Vivi was shocked. She had merely wandered into the kitchen to get a glass of orange juice; her biggest decision of the day so far had been whether or not to get dressed. Then her mother, in a no-nonsense voice, told her school was on.

"After what I've been through?" Vivi asked, plunking her glass on the counter.

"What you've been through was of your own making," Mrs. Minkus replied tartly.

Vivi winced. Dr. Raphael hadn't ratted her out. After examining her test results before he took her home on Sunday and noting her improvement with the IV medicine, her father had quickly figured it out all by himself. In contrast to Dr. Rapahel's matter-of-fact reaction, her parents had gone ballistic. They were "angry," "disappointed," and "shocked at her irresponsibility." Lying in her hospital bed, Vivi tried to look weak and defenseless, but neither of her parents seemed inclined to cut her much slack. Once at home, she spent much of the day sleeping, which cut down on the recriminations. But late Sunday afternoon, her mother came into her bedroom, an unusual look of steely resolve on her face.

"Here's your medicine," Mrs. Minkus said, handing Vivi the pills and a glass of water, and standing ready to make sure she took it.

Vivi felt like she was about five years old, but she guessed she deserved it and held out her hand without comment.

"I'm going to have to keep watching you, you know," her mother continued. "I'm going to ask Andy to make sure you take it at lunch."

"I'm not going to screw up like that again," Vivi said. "I don't want to go back to the hospital."

"Hmmm" was Mrs. Minkus's only comment. From that, Vivi assumed she hadn't been won over by her daughter's logic, even though Vivi meant every word of what she said.

As Vivi had swallowed her pills, her father came into the room. "I spoke to Dr. Raphael. She's going to see you on Thursday."

"I liked her," Vivi said spontaneously, surprised that the words just seemed to pop out.

Finally, her father smiled at her. "Then I hope you'll pay attention to what she says and cooperate."

Cooperating was about all she could do. She brooded about returning to school the rest of the day on Monday, mostly trying to figure out what to wear. She wished now that she had put a little more effort into her shopping trip. By the time Andy got home, Vivi was in a really bad mood. As soon as he walked in, she bombarded him with protests about being pushed back to school.

He just shrugged and said, "Resistance is futile," and Vivi realized this was the first complete sentence he had said to her since she had returned home. Other than coming into her room a couple of times to say, "You okay?" there had been a lot of nothing.

Following Andy into his bedroom, Vivi continued, "Maybe you could say something to Mom? I'm still exhausted."

"I don't have much sympathy for you," Andy said, his gaze cool.

A shocked Vivi looked back at him. Andy was turning on her, too? Andy, her compliant womb mate, who was always the most supportive of brothers?

"You scared us," he said bluntly. "You scared me."

Was there a little wobble in his voice, there at the end? Vivi wasn't quite sure, but even the thought of it made her feel terrible. She had been so wrapped up in herself, she hadn't considered all the things that had changed in Andy's life because of her illness. For one thing, the bar mitzvah (well, bat mitzvah for her) was supposed to be a joint affair, but it had to be postponed because she had dropped out of Hebrew school, and her mother was too stressed out to plan a party. And their parents barely paid any attention to him, so busy were they worrying about her. "I'm sorry," she said in a small, soft voice.

"Yeah, you should be. Not taking your medicine." Andy just shook his head at her stupidity.

"But it was making me look so ugly."

"Vivi, I've told you a million times you could never really look ugly."

Vivi sat down on the edge of his bed. "You just don't get it. You're a boy. You don't care how you look."

Andy folded his arms and looked down at her. "Why shouldn't I care how I look? Am I so weird looking, I shouldn't care?"

For the first time in a very long time, Vivi stared at her brother, really took him in. She was jolted to see the image she had in her mind of Andy, small, a little twitchy, was actually very different from reality. How it had happened, she wasn't sure, but Andy had grown. She had heard the phrase that someone had "shot up overnight," but Andy really had. In April, they would turn thirteen, and suddenly Andy looked like a teenager and not a kid. There was something else about him as well, that Vivi couldn't quite put her finger on. If she had been paying attention, maybe she would have noticed when Andy started looking more sure of himself, more confident. Something must have happened to her brother for this change to take place, and maybe once he would have told her what it was, but he hadn't, and now she was too embarrassed to ask.

"No, of course you should care," Vivi answered quickly. "You . . . actually look really good."

A smile he couldn't help. "Really?"

"Yeah, really." Vivi smiled, too.

"I'm still mad at you," Andy told her.

"That's okay. I'm kind of mad at myself." Vivi got up to leave, but she had a hunch. "You like someone, right?"

Andy reddened. "What do you mean?"

"You know . . . oh, never mind."

Andy looked like he was about to confide in her, but then started busying himself with his books on his desk.

"We'll go to school tomorrow together, right?" Vivi asked.

"Sure. I'll be right there with you. Like always."

And he was. Their mother insisted on driving them to Odom, and Andy walked with her toward the school, but they hadn't gotten very far when Bette came running up to her and threw her arms around Vivi.

"How are you?" Bette asked. "Andy called me and told me what happened. I wanted to call you, or at least text you, but your mother wanted you to rest, and I didn't want to bug you."

"I'm fine. Did Andy tell you . . ."

"Yeah, I did," Andy interrupted. "I told her everything."

"How could you do something so dumb?" Bette asked.

This was embarrassing. Vivi definitely didn't want to get into it. "I'll tell you all about it later," she said. *Much much later, like hopefully never.*

Bette didn't look very happy with her answer, but she didn't press it. And then, before Vivi knew it, she was back in school. There was an air of unreality about it that lasted most of the day. She reported in at the office, went to her morning classes, and was relieved to see that she wasn't far behind in her class work. Her teachers had sent home assignments that her tutor had dutifully used as part of his lesson plan. Lunch was a bit of a surprise. Joe Garcia was among a larger lunch group, and he seemed eager to talk to her.

"How are you feeling?" he asked, plunking down next to her with milk and a homemade peanut butter sandwich.

She had barely said a word to anyone in her classes. A shyness she had never felt before seemed to envelope her, and for the first time in their lives, she had an inkling what Andy's timidity must have felt like. All morning, she had snuck looks at the other kids to see if they were talking about her, making remarks about how different she looked, but she hadn't caught anyone staring.

"How you feeling?" Joe asked, a little louder, as if her lack of response was because she hadn't heard him. Andy turned to him and frowned.

Taking a bite of her salad, her head practically in her lettuce, Vivi said, "Okay."

"But better, right?"

"Well, I'm here." Why was Joe so interested in her health?

"Yeah, I thought so," Joe replied.

There was something about his confidence that really annoyed her. What did he know about anything? "As a matter of fact, I was in the hospital over the weekend." Now, why had she said that?

Joe looked at her with shock. "What happened?"

"An asthma attack. Why are you so surprised? I have asthma, sometimes I have to go to the hospital."

"I just didn't expect to hear that."

He didn't expect it?

"My mom has some problems with her lungs," Joe continued.

"Like when your cat was lost," Vivi said. Joe nodded.

"But she's been pretty good lately since she got a new doctor. Dr. Raphael put her on some medicine that's really helping her."

"Dr. Raphael?" asked Vivi, finally looking directly at Joe. "She's my new doctor. I have an appointment with her on Thursday."

Joe's face cleared. He looked almost happy. "Dr. Raphael. Well, she'll help you out. My mom says she's never had a doctor like her. Dr. Raphael, huh? That's great."

After that, talk turned to *Big River,* and Vivi felt like she had stepped into an ongoing conversation, one that had been continuing for a long time. Fred was bemoaning the fact that the director was thinking about cutting one of the songs, which was just stupid, and Lane, whose spiky hair looked like it must contain a half a jar of gel, was upset that the parents who had volunteered to make the costumes weren't working fast enough. All the while, Bette was humming one of her songs under her breath, which seemed to be a habit of hers that drove everyone crazy, because Ollie, who couldn't be nicer, finally said to Bette, "How many times have we asked you, Bette? Enough with the humming."

Bette looked around the table with surprise. "I was doing it again?"

"Yeah," Andy said gently.

"I guess it's just a nervous habit. And the closer we get to the play, the more nervous I get."

If Vivi had felt shy before, now she just felt alone. *Big River,* she could see, was going to be the topic of the day, every day until showtime. The school's collective mind was somewhere else, and Vivi didn't know how to get herself there and wasn't even sure she wanted to.

As the *Big River* conversation swirled around her, Vivi put her hand in her pocket and felt around for her angel coin. She had made sure it was there before she left for school. Holding it, rubbing her finger over the angel she couldn't see, she didn't even mind when Andy leaned across the table and whispered, "Did you take your medicine?"

Instead of getting mad, she just smiled at him and said, "Just about to. You can watch." And he did watch as she pulled the two pills out of a baggie in her backpack and washed it down with her milk.

The rest of the day went on uneventfully until almost the

end of last period when Mrs. Wu stuck her head in the door of English class and asked if she could see Vivi.

Embarrassed, because this time the kids were really looking at her, she gathered her books and followed Mrs. Wu to her office.

"How are you feeling, dear?" Mrs. Wu asked as she settled herself behind her desk and indicated that Vivi should take a seat.

"Fine," Vivi replied automatically.

"It must be a bit overwhelming to be back."

What was the right answer to that? "No, it's fine."

"Fine and fine, well that's fine," the principal said, but Vivi could see Mrs. Wu wasn't entirely convinced. "You'll let me know if that changes, won't you?"

"Of course." *Not,* Vivi added silently.

"What I wanted to see you about, Vivian, is *Big River.* I'm sure Andy must have told you all about it."

"Oh, yes. I'm up to speed on *Big River.*"

"So you've heard him practicing."

"I've been helping him. He brought home the sheet music so I could accompany him."

Mrs. Wu's face lit up. "You have? That's wonderful."

Vivi wouldn't have called it wonderful. It had been more of an obligation than anything, but she had to admit, there was something about the music, bouncy at times, at others, soulful, that could raise her spirits.

"You see, I was wondering how you could be involved in the play at this late date."

"Oh, that's all right," Vivi responded quickly. "I don't have to be involved."

"No, all of the seventh and eighth graders are taking part in one way or another. Obviously, most of the jobs are taken, but now that I know you're familiar with the music, I think I have the perfect thing for you."

Vivi wasn't sure she liked where this was going.

"You see, this play is getting a lot of attention. There have already been write-ups about the project in the newspaper, and now one of the local TV channels has called me to say they are interested in doing a story on it, perhaps even taping it for broadcast."

Vivi had never seen Mrs. Wu look happier.

"I'm sure you know that Flora is our pianist for the show, but she's running into a conflict. Has Andy told you with all the interest we've scheduled one more performance?"

He had. His *Big River* chatter had gone up several excited notches at the news, and that was saying a lot. Vivi nodded warily.

"Well," Mrs. Wu continued, "Flora, unfortunately, she has to be out of town for the final Sunday performance. Her grandmother is having a seventy-fifth-birthday party, and we've been scrambling to find a way that she could be with us, and it's just not working out. To complicate things, Sunday is the last day Maple Tree can let us use their theater because they're mounting their own production."

"Mrs. Wu . . ." Vivi wanted to head this off as quickly as possible, but she wasn't as fast as Mrs. Wu.

"So, Vivian, I'm sure you can see why I'm so delighted to hear you know the score."

Oh, she knew the score all right.

"You can play the last performance, Flora can go to her grandmother's party with a clear conscience, and we don't have to finagle the dates for either Maple Tree or Channel Two."

If Mrs. Wu got any higher, Vivi was going to have to

scrape her off the ceiling. Time to bring her down. Immediately. "I'm sorry, Mrs. Wu. I don't think I can do it," she said quickly.

Mrs. Wu was surprised. "Why not?"

"I just don't think I'm up to it." *Physically, mentally, emotionally,* she added to herself.

"Oh, dear," a deflated Mrs. Wu said. "Are you sure?"

"You said to tell you if I wasn't fine, well, really . . ." She let the rest of the sentence hang there, and the principal did the rest.

"I did. And I do understand, but, Vivian, this is only your first day back. Perhaps I sprang this on you too early. When I spoke with your mother, she said she wanted you to participate fully, so naturally I thought . . ."

"I had an asthma attack this Saturday," Vivi informed Mrs. Wu. "I was in the hospital overnight." She lowered her eyes to her lap.

"I didn't know." Mrs. Wu's voice was—finally—full of concern. "Obviously, it was too soon to bring up *Big River.* Perhaps later . . ."

Vivi said nothing. She wanted to squash this plan like a mosquito, so that Mrs. Wu would forget about it forever, but the appropriate phrase didn't come to mind, and "No, no, never, never, uh-uh-uh," which she and Andy had used to great effect when they were six, wouldn't cut it.

"You may feel stronger in a couple of weeks," Mrs. Wu said optimistically. "We still have some time to settle this."

"Yes, ma'am."

Mrs. Wu checked her delicate diamond watch. "The rehearsals have started. Why don't you go backstage and watch."

Vivi grabbed her books and nodded. "Yes. I'm going to do that." She didn't have a choice, since her mother had made it clear that she wouldn't make more than two trips a day to Odom, and when Andy had rehearsals, Vivi would have to wait until he was finished.

"I can take the bus home," Vivi had told Mrs. Minkus, but her mother said, "No, I'll pick you up," and since it didn't seem worth fighting over, Vivi agreed.

By the time Vivi left Mrs. Wu's office and headed to her locker, the school had an eerie, empty quality. Not so the auditorium. It was as if Vivi had left a black-and-white movie and suddenly arrived into a world of Technicolor. Kansas to Oz. Onstage, five guys, including Fred, were singing "The Boys." Vivi knew the tune well; it was one of the tunes that featured an Andy Minkus violin solo.

Settling herself into an aisle seat toward the back, Vivi watched Fred, now transformed into Huck Finn, and the rest of the boys as they cavorted onstage. They were good, really good, and the number was lots of fun. Then the director called for a rehearsal of the scene in which Huck and Jim head down the Mississippi on a raft. Together they harmonized on a rousing, joyful song of escape that made Vivi smile just listening to it. She finally understood why Andy and Bette were so excited about *Big River*. If this rehearsal was any indication, the Odom students were in the midst of putting on a show that looked and sounded professional, and everyone involved seemed to know it.

"The sets are over at Maple Tree," said a voice behind her, but close to her ear.

She turned around with a frown. Joe again. "Sets?" she whispered.

"I worked on the sets. Me and this guy, Mike, from Maple Tree. We're moving them 'cause pretty soon the rehearsals are going to start over there."

"That's nice," Vivi said turning back toward the stage.

Joe got up and slid into the seat next to her. "How are you feeling?"

"You asked me that at lunch," Vivi replied sharply. This guy was getting annoying.

Looking embarrassed, Joe said, "Yeah, I . . . I just wanted to know how you got through the day. It being your first and all."

Vivi softened. A little. "Everything went okay. Just a regular day at school."

"Yeah, and probably no one made fun of you, right?"

Now Vivi frowned, but Joe continued on, "Because you don't look all that bad. Like that time when I said your face was fat, well, it's not really. 'Puffy.' That would be a better word."

It took just a few seconds of Vivi staring at Joe with shock before he realized he had said the wrong thing once again. "I mean you look okay."

Seeing the stricken expression on Joe's face, Vivi almost felt a little sorry for him. He wasn't trying to be mean, that was clear, he was telling the truth. Someone must have told him that honesty was the best policy.

Someone was wrong.

XIX

"A couple of days back, and it will be like you've never been away." That's what Mrs. Minkus had said in the car on the way to school on Tuesday. Vivi didn't know her mother's definition of "a couple," but if she meant two, then she was wrong. Because Thursday was over and school felt just as odd and uncomfortable as it did the day before yesterday. As she grabbed her coat from her locker, Vivi wondered if school would ever feel normal again.

Shoving her hat down over her ears and pulling on her mittens, Vivi headed outdoors, on the lookout for her mother's car. The appointment with Dr. Raphael was at four, which technically should give them plenty of time, except you could never count on the traffic and you could usually count on Jill Minkus to be late. It drove Vivi's father wild, the one thing her mother did that actually made him angry. Sometimes Vivi wondered if it was her form of rebellion.

This time she was only about five minutes past her stated arrival time. Vivi hopped in the car and reveled in the heated passenger seat.

"Hi, sweetheart," her mom said. "How was school today?"

"It was okay."

"Are you feeling all right?"

"Yes, Mom," Vivi answered with an exaggerated sigh.

"And if I wasn't, we're on the way to a doctor's office, so there's nothing really to worry about."

Mrs. Minkus turned her eyes from the road. "I can't help worrying about you, Vivian, you're my daughter. And you don't make it easy to stop with some of the stunts you pull."

"Can we talk about something else?" Vivi asked sullenly.

"Yes. Let's talk about our Florida trip."

It was worth another try. "Can we talk about something else?"

"No," her mother said shortly without even a smile at Vivi's lame attempt at humor. "First of all, I'm sure you're aware that your thirteenth birthday is going to fall at the end of that week."

Vivi had noted that, but mostly as a date on the calendar. A year ago, she would have been excited about finally getting to a number with the word "teen" at the end of it. The bar/bat mitzvah would have meant a big party, but now, the last thing she wanted was to be the center of attention, and Andy's disappointment notwithstanding, she was glad it had been postponed. "Yes, I know."

"So my question is, do you want to do something special that day?"

Vivi shrugged. "Like what?"

"Well, we're not going to be that far from Disney World. We could drive up and spend the day there."

"Disney World?" Vivi almost snickered. "Mom, this is our thirteenth birthday, not our third."

"Disney World isn't only for kids. There's Epcot Center and a lot more," Mrs. Minkus said stiffly. "I mentioned this to Andy, and he thought it would be fine."

"I'll talk to him," Vivi said, trying for an accommodating tone. "Maybe he and I can come up with something."

Mrs. Minkus's frown softened. "All right. Let me know so we're not scrambling at the last minute."

As they pulled up to the medical building where her father also had his office, Vivi felt a buttery relief flow through her. She was actually looking forward to seeing Dr. Raphael, although she would never tell her mother that. The late-night meeting in her hospital room now seemed like something out of a dream. She wondered what it would be like to talk with Dr. Raphael in the daylight.

"Do you want me to come into the examination room with you?" Mrs. Minkus asked hopefully as they approached the doctor's office.

"No, Mom."

"All right," Mrs. Minkus said as they took a seat in the waiting room. "But I do want to talk to her afterward."

It took a while, but eventually a friendly nurse settled her in the examination room, took her blood pressure, checked her breath flow, and gave her a paper robe that was even more embarrassing than the cloth number she had worn in the hospital. Fortunately, she barely had time to leaf through the old copy of *People* she found in the room before Dr. Raphael came in.

In the daytime, she seemed even more, well, sparkly than she had when she appeared in Vivi's hospital room. It wasn't just her snapping brown eyes and disarming smile. She looked very, very happy, and very . . . Vivi tried to come up with just the right word, but the best she could come up with was "alive."

"So," Dr. Raphael said, looking her over, "I can see you're taking your medicine, Vivian."

"Because my face is all puffy again?"

"Because you're not flat on your back, struggling for breath," Dr. Raphael replied tartly. "How does that feel?"

"Pretty good," Vivi admitted.

Dr. Raphael pulled up a chair to the examining table. "Yes. As someone with asthma, you should know that to breathe is to live."

Vivi thought that was pretty obvious, but Dr. Raphael's next sentence was not. "You can't do what you were put on earth to do if you're not breathing," she continued conversationally.

"Put on earth to do?" a confused Vivi repeated.

Dr. Raphael laughed her vibrant laugh. "Do you think we're just here to buy things and take up space?"

"I haven't really thought about it."

Dr. Raphael patted her knee. "Well, you're young yet, but it's never too early to start thinking about why you're here."

This conversation was taking a very odd turn, like their talk in the hospital had. Interested in spite of herself, Vivi decided to play along. "You mean, like you're here to be a doctor and help people?"

"Oh, we're all here to help each other. So, are you back in school now?" Dr. Raphael asked, finally glancing at Vivi's considerable medical file.

"Yes."

"And how is that going?" She pulled her gaze back up to Vivi.

"Not great." She didn't want to say more, but Dr. Raphael just waited, watching her.

"I don't know what I'm doing there," Vivi spat out, with more emotion than she had intended or even knew she felt. "Everyone is involved in this musical *Big River*. It's all anyone talks about."

"And because you've been gone so long, you can't be involved?" Dr. Raphael raised one eyebrow, as if she knew the answer, so there was no excuse to lie.

"Uh, not exactly. Our principal, Mrs. Wu, she did ask if I wanted to play one of the shows. I know the music because I've been accompanying Andy. He's violin. I'm piano."

"So you *can* be involved. You don't want to."

"That's right," Vivi agreed. "I don't want to."

"Why not?"

"Why do you think?" she asked defiantly.

"I can't imagine that your appearance has anything to do with how you play," Dr. Raphael replied mildly.

"I don't want anyone looking at me," Vivi said, tearing a little hole in her paper gown.

Dr. Raphael leaned back in her chair. "What *do* you want, Vivi?" she asked quietly.

Vivi didn't hesitate on the answer. It was just saying out loud a mantra that had been going around and around in her head for months now. "I want things to be the way they were before I got really sick." She glared at the doctor, waiting for her to laugh.

But all Dr. Raphael did was pat her knee, and the look she gave her contained so much sympathy, Vivi could feel tears welling up unbidden behind her eyes.

"I think most people who have been ill would say that, but of course, that's not the way time works."

"So I'm stuck."

"You can't go back and you can't seem to go forward, so if you mean you are stuck right here in the present, that's true."

Now Vivi wiped away one of the tears that had the temerity to fall.

"However, there must be things in your present that you are happy about."

Vivi looked at Dr. Raphael in disbelief. "I don't think so."

"All right," she conceded, "not 'happy.' But perhaps there are things for which you are grateful?"

"Grateful?" Vivi repeated dubiously.

"Well, you woke up this morning, you could start with that. And the sun is shining."

Oh, whoop-de-dee, Vivi thought, although she didn't have the nerve to say it.

"Have you ever heard of a gratitude journal, Vivian?" At Vivi's shake of the head, Dr. Raphael explained, "You take some time every day to write down all the things for which you are grateful."

"It would be an extremely short book."

Dr. Raphael smiled and shrugged. "You might find you have more to be thankful for than you think. Why don't you get dressed now, and come into my office. I have some good news for you and your mother."

Vivi slowly put on her clothes. Although she was anxious to hear this so-called good news, she was thinking about Dr. Raphael and how discombobulated she made her feel. She never said what you expected her to say. And then there was that whole happy thing she radiated.

When she finally got to Dr. Raphael's office, piled with books and a vase of red roses on the desk, her mother was already there, deep in conversation with the doctor.

"What did I miss?" Vivi asked.

Mrs. Minkus smiled at Vivi. "The doctor thinks she has a new medicine that can help you."

"Really?" Vivi asked.

"It's medicine that's been very effective at calming the in-flammation in the lungs that can lead to an attack. It doesn't work for everyone," Dr. Raphael cautioned, "but you're a good candidate, and if it's effective, we can cut down on the steroids."

"Isn't that great?" Mrs. Minkus asked, the smile on her face replacing the frown of worry that was her usual expression when she was talking to her daughter.

Vivi didn't know what to say. A bit of hope was beginning to sprout, and she wasn't sure she wanted it to. What if this medicine didn't work? Once again, Dr. Raphael seemed to know exactly what was on her mind.

"This isn't the only trick in my bag, but it's a good place to start." She reached into her drawer and took out a packet of medicine. "Here's a week's sample. Take one pill a day and make sure you call me if you have any of the side effects that are listed on the piece of paper," she said, pointing to an insert in the box. "Ask your father to go over this with you. And call me when you have one pill left. Then we can evaluate."

Mrs. Minkus reached for the pills as if they were the Holy Grail. "Thank you, Doctor."

But instead of giving her the packet, Dr. Raphael handed them over to Vivi. "I think Vivian can be entrusted with them, eh?"

Vivi nodded as she took it and placed it carefully in a side pocket of her bag, right next to her angel coin.

"Modern medicine. Something to be grateful for, yes, Vivi?" Dr. Raphael said with a wink.

Vivi didn't know whether to smile or scowl, while Mrs. Minkus, sensing there was more going on than she was privy to, seemed a little peeved she wasn't fully in the loop.

On the way to the car, Mrs. Minkus commented, "You

seemed to have developed a good relationship with Dr. Raphael."

Vivi didn't answer right away because she wasn't sure that was true. The doctor was intriguing, and she certainly seemed to know her business, at least Vivi hoped she did, but she also felt like Dr. Raphael was pushing her somewhere she wasn't sure she wanted to go. "It's fine," Vivi said curtly. The medicine was safely in her bag, and that's all she wanted from Dr. Raphael right now.

By the time they got home, Vivi was tired. Yet, instead of going right to her room to lie down, she sat at the piano in the living room and ran her hands over the keys. The shiny black baby grand wasn't new. It had been in the house for as long as she could remember, and both her parents had taken enough lessons as children to be able to play decently. But since she had been old enough to take lessons, starting at around age five, everyone in the family knew that the piano really belonged to her.

She had had a funny relationship with the piano over the last eight or nine months. Once it was decided that she was going to be homeschooled, Vivi had expected she would spend even more time at the piano, but instead she had shunned it and tapered off her lessons, at least as much as her parents allowed. Why, she wasn't quite sure. All she knew was playing, as it always did, made her feel better, and there was a perverse part of her that didn't want to feel better.

But she hadn't quit playing altogether. Once it was clear that Andy and his violin were going to be an important part of *Big River,* her mother had insisted that Vivi accompany him as he practiced, and he practiced pretty much all the time. Vivi didn't mind playing with her brother because she could just pound out the songs without any real emotion behind them. It was just an exercise, she told herself, even though it hurt her a little because playing the songs of *Big River* reminded her that there was a whole world spinning merrily along without her. No, there was no pleasure in piano alongside Andy, and she had been glad about that.

Now she tentatively sat down on the piano bench and flexed her fingers. Although much of her training had been in classical music, and she could knock off a little Brahms or Beethoven with the best of them, for her own pleasure she liked to play old-time rock and roll: Beatles, Rolling Stones, even some folk music, which she would then improvise upon, the way jazz pianists did. As she ran the keys and began doing familiar warm-up exercises, she was hit with a flood of memories: her first piano recital, in her piano teacher's studio, playing Brahms's "Lullaby," and standing up afterward in her pretty purple velvet dress with the matching hair ribbons and curtsying to the applause. Going up to music camp in Wisconsin, where practicing with the camp band took precedence over doing arts and crafts or going swimming. Starting Odom in the third grade and being delighted that music and singing and acting were something that people did at school.

For the first time in a very, very long time, Vivi allowed herself to just play. There was a lovely relief in not having to follow any written music, as she did when accompanying her brother; this was pure playing, feeling like she was simply a follower on the road music was taking her.

Later, she couldn't recall any particular piece of music that she played. She was vaguely aware that Andy had come out of his room to listen, and she saw her mother out of the corner of her eye standing in the kitchen doorway. She also could not have said how long she sat at the piano, though she heard her father's key opening the front door as she was winding down.

"Vivi, we'll be eating soon," her mother almost whispered as she walked from the kitchen to her bedroom.

"I'm tired, Mom." She felt as if she had played herself half-way around the world.

"Why don't you lie down for a while. You can have your dinner when you feel like getting up."

That was a first. If there was anything Mrs. Minkus was a stickler for, it was the family sitting down to dinner together. "Thanks," Vivi said gratefully. "I think I'll do that."

She had barely flung herself down on the bed, pulling over her a pink afghan her grandmother had crocheted for her when she was a little girl, when Andy knocked at the door. She knew his knock, slightly tentative, but at least he knocked at all. Plenty of brothers would just have barged in. She thought about saying, "Go away," but she was feeling mellower than that. "Come on in, Andy," she called instead.

Without waiting to be asked, he pulled the chair from her desk next to her bed. "Wow, Vivi. I mean, *wow*!"

"The piano?" When he nodded, she said, "I know. I haven't lost it."

"I didn't think I was ever going to hear you play like that again."

Vivi sat up and hugged her knees. "I didn't think so either." Then she remembered she hadn't had a chance to tell Andy about her conversation with Mrs. Wu, so she filled him in.

"So that's why you started playing again?"

That startled Vivi. "No, of course not. And besides, I told her that I don't want to do it."

"Why not? You know a lot of the songs, we've practiced them a million times."

Vivi didn't know how to explain that playing for herself in her living room seemed, oh, sweet, but getting in front of an audience who'd be watching her seemed almost impossible. So she settled for a simple "I just don't want to."

Andy, who always seemed to understand what Vivi thought and felt, sometimes before she thought or felt it, stared at her blankly. "But we're going to need you if Flora can't be at the last performance. And you're playing great, better than ever."

She wished he wouldn't look at her like that. It made her feel guilty, and Vivi hated feeling guilty. "I'll think about it, okay?" She said it to get him off her back, and from the relieved look on his face, she could tell she'd just about succeeded. Before he could press her further, though, she decided she'd better change the subject. "So Mom said she talked to you about our birthday."

"Yeah, she wants to know what we want to do."

"She said you wanted to go to Disney World," Vivi said, trying to get a rise out of him.

"I did not," Andy said indignantly.

"I'm only kidding." Vivi played with the crocheted holes in the blanket. "I mean, Mom said you thought Disney World would be okay, but I knew you weren't big on it."

"I don't see how we can pick something to do," he complained. "I don't even know what's down there. I did have one idea, though."

Vivi looked up from her blanket work. "Yeah?"

"It's not exactly an idea for our birthday, but it's something that might make the trip more fun. For you." Andy got a twitchy look on his face, and that meant he was both nervous and embarrassed.

"For me?" Vivi asked curiously.

"Well, you're always so stressed out, so I thought it might be good if we asked if Bette could come down with us. You seem more relaxed when Bette's around," he added hurriedly.

Vivi considered this. The trip would be more fun if Bette was with them. Bette's dad would probably be happy to pay her way down, and Vivi knew that her parents had reservations for a two-bedroom suite at the hotel. She and Bette could share the second room, and Andy could sleep on the living room couch. He probably wouldn't mind since it was his idea. His idea. The phrase clanged in Vivi's head. "Bette. Yeah, that would be great. How did you come up with an idea like that?"

Andy wouldn't look at Vivi. "I don't know. It just came to me. Thought you might like it."

Vivi almost burst out laughing. "*I* might like it."

Reddening, Andy said, "You do like it. You just said so."

"And I have a feeling that I'm not the only one who'd like Bette with me on my thirteenth birthday."

Finally, Andy grinned. "Okay, you got me. I guess it wasn't that hard to figure out."

"Well, it did take me a minute. A minute longer than it should have. I do think it's a great idea, though. And it shouldn't be that big a deal." She explained about the sleeping arrangements.

"Great," Andy said with a touch of relief. "I forgot about that. I figured we'd have two hotel rooms, and I wasn't sure where that put me."

"We'll tell the 'rents we've got it figured out, and if Bette's dad will spring for airfare, we should be good to go." They smiled at each other with satisfaction.

Vivi got out of bed. She wasn't as tired now, and dinner would be a good time to convince her parents another kid was exactly what they needed to make their vacation complete. As she went to her dresser to get her brush, she noticed Andy in the mirror. He looked like he had more to say.

"Spit it out," she said without preamble.

"We . . . don't have to tell Bette this was my idea, do we?"

Vivi turned away from the dresser. "Of course not," Vivi said with a burst of twin loyalty. "But does Bette know that you . . ."

"No! She might even like Joe. I'm pretty sure he likes her." Andy looked both glum and angry at the same time.

"Well, I don't think she likes him. She would have said something to me."

"Really?" Andy asked hopefully.

"She might find him . . . intriguing." Actually Vivi knew for a fact that Bette did find him intriguing. It was the very word she had used. "But intriguing is dangerously close to weird. She couldn't like him more than she likes you."

"Hope not," Andy muttered, "because he's a jerk."

"I didn't think you knew Joe all that well." Now Vivi's curiosity was piqued.

Andy's face closed. "I guess maybe he's better than he used to be," he finally said, "but . . . oh, never mind. Let's go ask Mom and Dad if Bette can come with us."

"Oh, Andy, that's not how we're going to do it. We have to make it seem like it's their idea."

"How are we supposed to do that?"

"Just follow my lead," Vivi said confidently. For the first time in a very long time, at least a small piece of herself felt like the old Vivian. She didn't write it down, but she knew it was something to be grateful for.

XX

Persuading their parents to let Bette join them on vacation turned out to be the easy part. Just seeing how their kids' feelings about the trip had changed from bored acceptance (Andy) and active antagonism (Vivi) to a modicum of enthusiasm made Dr. and Mrs. Minkus more than willing to agree to take Bette along.

So Vivi was shocked when the sticking point turned out to be Bette. Vivi had made the call right after dinner, proffered the invitation, while tactfully explaining that if Mr. Miller would pick up the airfare, her parents would cover everything else, and then waited expectantly for some verbal burst of enthusiasm from Bette. What she wasn't prepared for was silence.

"Bette? Are you there?" she asked, taking the phone into her bathroom and closing the door behind her. Vivi was getting the feeling this phone call might take longer than she had thought.

"Yes, I'm here. It's really nice of you to invite me, Vivi, but I'm not sure the timing is going to work."

"Why not?" Vivi said, slamming down the toilet seat. "It's spring break. It's been a long, cold, lonely winter, to quote the Beatles, and I'm asking you to fly to the sunshine. What could be bad about that?"

"Oh, I'm sure the trip would be great. But part of my

spring break is going to overlap with Barbra's, and I want to see her. And then *Big River* will be coming up just a couple of weeks after the break, so I've got to practice . . ."

"Bette, your sister is in Evanston, less than an hour from your house by subway. You can see her anytime. Does her break overlap the first or last part of ours?"

"Last."

"Well, there you go. We go away over the first part. So you'll still have time with Barbra. As for the songs, Bette, there are only two, and you know them by heart. I've heard you, you're great. What else have you got?" Vivi, feeling she had effectively diminished Bette's arguments, got up to examine her face in the bathroom mirror. She wanted to know exactly how fat her face was, so she could keep track of how it was shrinking once she cut down on her steroids. Thinking about how much better she was going to look made the mirror less of an enemy.

"Well, I'll probably want to hang out with Lane and, uh, maybe Joe . . ."

Now things were starting to come into focus. "You don't want to be away from Joe?" Vivi tried not to shriek.

"I didn't say that," Bette said defensively.

"Well, I hope not."

"I think he's kind of intriguing."

"There you go with the 'intriguing' again." Vivi couldn't help thinking about Andy. Her brother was lots of great things, but intriguing wasn't one of them. "Look, he can be intriguing during the last part of the break. Anyway, I think he's strange. He keeps asking me how I'm feeling."

"So that's a nice thing."

"I guess." Vivi opened the medicine cabinet to look for some acne cream. She had noticed the start of a pimple on her chin when she was examining her face. "But really, you can't give up a practically free trip to Florida for a boy." Vivi felt a slight twinge of guilt, trying to persuade her best friend to take a trip to Florida for a boy she didn't even know liked her.

There was another pause. Shorter this time. "I suppose it would be nice to go somewhere warm."

Wavering. A good sign. "Look," Vivi said, smearing a little of the ointment on the pimple, "ask your dad. If he says no, then, okay, but if he says yes, then you've got to think about it, right?"

"Right," Bette said in a resigned voice. Vivi couldn't deny she felt a small thrill of satisfaction. Here again was a little of the old Vivi, someone who could push people into doing what she wanted. The difference was the old Vivi would have taken Bette's folding as her due.

Once out the bathroom, she ran into Andy. "She's going to ask her dad," Vivi said.

Andy looked delighted and anxious at the same time. "So it might happen?"

"Keep your fingers crossed."

Whether it was Vivi's powers of persuasion or the crossed fingers, soon enough Bette was on board with the Florida trip. The vacation now became a small beacon of light in an otherwise exceedingly sleety, rainy, chilly end of winter. The weather matched her mood because despite Dr. Raphael's optimism, the new medicine still hadn't allowed her get off the steroids. At their last visit, Dr. Raphael had told her she was expecting too much too fast.

"Everything's working just as it should, and I can take you down two milligrams on your steroid medication."

"Two!" Vivi had practically shrieked. "That's nothing. Nothing."

For the first time, Dr. Raphael showed a flash of irritation with Vivi. "Dear girl, you know why it's difficult to get off the medication. Your body hasn't been producing steroids because the medicine is doing it for you. If you stopped the steroids suddenly, without giving yourself a chance to produce naturally, you could have a severe setback. So we take things slowly, and even so you might have a few symptoms as you cut back, a little achiness or joint pain. It should go away in a week or so. But on the whole, I'm pleased with your progress. And grateful for modern medicine," she added sternly.

Vivi was afraid that Dr. Raphael was going to ask her how that gratitude journal was going, which of course it wasn't. But although she wasn't writing anything down, at odd moments, when she was brushing her teeth or doodling her way through math class or before she fell asleep, reasons to be grateful did pop into her mind. Sometimes she ignored them; sometimes she considered them. Despite the way it might seem, she certainly was grateful for her new medicine, even though it might not be working as quickly as she would have liked, because it was working. One freezing day, she found herself grateful that her mother was home to drive her to school, and she was really happy about those heated seats. Vivi was also grateful that Mrs. Wu had backed off about her playing for *Big River*. She had given Vivi the role of prompter instead, which meant all she had to do was sit in the wings with the script and call out the correct line to anyone who forgot or stumbled. But it was so late in rehearsals that dropped lines almost never happened. That left Vivi to be mostly an observer, and she was comfortable with that.

Watching all the excitement that swirled around the play was interesting. The play almost took on a life of its own, and now that everything was falling into place, she could see why

Big River took up so much of the oxygen at school. In some ways, the production seemed like one big club, and although she wasn't a member, she admired the camaraderie the cast felt. Kids who otherwise probably would not even have talked to each other were, if not friends, cast mates, all working toward a common goal, and that seemed to count for a lot. Sometimes she wished she was more a part of things, but mostly she was glad to sit back and watch what was going on around her.

It struck Vivi that she had lost the art of participation. She noticed that she barely spoke up in class, and she didn't do much more in that regard at lunch. She had gone from someone who was always in the midst of things to someone who was on the periphery. In a strange way, it suited her. As when she sat in the wings watching the play, at the lunch table she also noticed things that before she would have missed. It was surprising what you could see when you weren't always talking.

Take Andy and Joe. Something was going on there that went way beyond whatever it was they felt for Bette. Andy wore a studied casualness, almost a disdain whenever Joe was around, which was totally unlike him. If Vivi knew anything about her brother, it was that he tried to make people feel included. Instead, it was Joe who was the one who was always reaching out. Clearly, niceness wasn't his default demeanor, and being friendly didn't come easily to him, that too was obvious. Lots of times, he seemed unsure of himself, and if the table talk turned to things money could buy, like vacations, Joe looked as if he was a couple of sentences away from getting mad. But Vivi watched as he took a breath and calmed himself down. She had to say she admired his effort. Joe also seemed to be trying to win Andy over, despite the cold shoulder Andy kept giving him. Now what was that all about, Vivi wondered as she watched.

Coming as close to invisibility as possible, if soothing, was also a little boring, Vivi found. It wasn't that long ago when she would have laughed at someone who chose the safest, most quiet path, and yet now she was that person. She wondered whether once the medicine kicked in and turned her back into the old Vivi if more than her looks would return, or if the confident, even daredevil, side of her was gone forever.

As much as she and Bette and Andy talked about the trip, and once Bette was in, she was the most excited of the three of them about going—for Vivi it almost seemed like a mirage, something that got farther away the closer you came. Then, a week before they were supposed to leave, reality slapped her in the face in the form of a bathing suit.

"I didn't think you'd want to go shopping for swimsuits," Mrs. Minkus said one Saturday, after being out most of the morning.

"You got that right," Vivi responded, barely looking up from her magazine.

"So I took the liberty of bringing home several for you to try on."

Now Vivi noticed the pink-and-white shopping bag hanging from her mother's wrist. She supposed that she could have argued, but what would be the point of that? In one week they'd be in Florida. According to the Weather Channel, it was going to be hot. Much of the time, they'd be at the beach or at the hotel pool. She needed a bathing suit.

"Sure," Vivi said, getting up from the couch. "I'll try them."

Mrs. Minkus looked relieved. "Good. Then come out and show me."

We'll see about that, Vivi thought to herself, as she took the bag from her mother. "Thanks for picking them up."

In her room, the door carefully closed behind her, Vivi

pulled the suits from the pink tissue paper in which they were wrapped and carefully laid them out on the bed.

"Not terrible," Vivi said. There was a staid yellow one-piece, a purple-dotted two-piece, and a tankini with a blue bottom and a red-and-blue-striped top. She rejected the two-piece without even trying it on. It was nice of her mother to think it might work, but, uh, no way. Cautiously, she picked up the yellow one-piece. If the color was meant to complement her blond hair, Vivi thought it was a bad choice, since the hue was more mustard than golden. Nevertheless, she was willing to give it a chance. Vivi resolutely pulled off her sweatshirt and jeans and shook out the suit and tried to pull it over her thighs and past her underpants. No go. Against her better judgment, she checked the size on the ticket. Yep, it was her regular size, which would now be known as the size she couldn't wear anymore. Quickly, she peeled off the bathing suit and threw it on the bed.

It was only through a sheer act of will and the knowledge that her mother would soon be knocking on her door that allowed Vivi to gather up her nerve and try on the tankini. With relief, she saw almost immediately this was going to be better. The boy-shorts bottom was forgiving and the top slid over her easily enough. She supposed that meant she had to look in the mirror.

With trepidation, Vivi closed her closet door, on the back of which a full-length mirror hung. Remembering the miserable experience of trying on jeans and knowing this was going to be much worse, she steeled herself for what was to come. For a second or two, she considered if she should even bother looking. She needed a suit, this one seemed to fit, what difference did it make how it looked? But whether it was to reassure herself or torture herself, Vivi decided she had to peek.

What she saw surprised her. The suit fit all right. She looked lumpy in it, but she had expected that. What she hadn't expected to see was the absolute mope staring her in the face. This wasn't just a puffy girl who was showing the results of months of strong medicine, this was someone who looked as if she hadn't given herself a thought in all that time.

Running her hands through hair so long and limp it lost most of its curls, Vivi tried to remember the last time she had had it cut. Her mother, who took a lot of pride in the way she looked, had urged Vivi to come with her every time she had gone to the salon for her own coloring and cutting, but to no avail. Why hadn't she gone? Vivi now wondered. It didn't seem worth the hassle, she supposed, because she didn't think a haircut would distract from the rest of her appearance. Still, she could see that looking like she was wearing a corn-colored mop on top of her head probably only called more attention to her appearance.

Glancing down her body, Vivi's displeasure deepened. She had never been an athlete—musicians usually weren't—but she did like to swim and bike. Those activities had stopped after a few of her more serious asthma attacks, even though her father had urged her to do as much as she could. He had even had her mother enroll her in a yoga class because he thought it would help her breathing, but since she went during the day, when all the other kids were in school, she was usually the youngest by at least ten years. Sure that everyone in the studio wondered why she wasn't in school, too, feeling uncomfortable and out of place, she had quit the class, even though she rather enjoyed yoga.

Smoothing her hands over her hips, now it was her fingers that caught Vivi's eye. Even they didn't seem like they belonged to her. So many years of practice had made her hands strong, her fingers flexible. Whenever there was a jar that was difficult to open, Vivi was always called upon to do the untwisting, with someone in the family usually cheering her steely grip. Now her fingers seemed more like pieces of spaghetti than strings of steel. Being Andy's accompanist didn't seem to be enough to keep her hands in condition.

Vivi slipped off the bathing suit and put her clothes back on. She wandered over to her window, so she could see her sliver of lake. Today, it was calm, with only the occasional ice floe to mar the water's gray smoothness. Putting her hand in her pocket, Vivi found her angel coin and took it out. It was the same silver-gray as the lake, but the angel on it seemed to have a shinier hue. It didn't really seem possible that the figure on a piece of metal could be more brilliant than the background, but even as Vivi looked more closely, that's what seemed to have happened. Maybe she had sort of polished the angel with her thumb; she did have a tendency to rub it when she had it out. That was the only explanation because otherwise metal didn't just change. Yet looking down at her lithe angel, it seemed to have changed for the better while she had become more dull.

Vivi's thoughts were interrupted by a tentative knock at the door. Turning away from the window, she called, "Come in, Mom."

"So how did the suits work out?" Mrs. Minkus asked nervously, so obviously ready for an assault that Vivi felt sorry for her.

"The tankini was good. Did they have another one in a different color? Maybe I should get two."

"Two! That's a good idea. I think they also had one in brown and gold. I can go back to the store tomorrow and pick it up." Just the thought of shopping for an item Vivi actually wanted brightened Mrs. Minkus's mood enormously.

"And, Mom . . ."

"Yes, sweetheart?"

"I was thinking I should get a haircut before we go."

"A haircut!"

Vivi was afraid her mother was about to swoon. "You'll call for an appointment?" she asked crisply. *Don't make too much of this* was implicit in her tone.

Mrs. Minkus pulled herself together. "Of course. I'll let you know when Carla can fit you in."

"Hey, Viv," Andy said, coming into the room. "Chase is coming over to practice a couple of our harmonica and violin numbers. Can you accompany us?"

Normally, Vivi would have hesitated and then followed that up with a regretful no. She thought Chase, an eighth grader, was great on the harmonica, and it was fun to listen to he and Andy try to one-up each other when they played the several duets they had in the play. But while having her accompaniment wouldn't hurt, it wasn't necessary for their practice either. In the past, she would have enjoyed just listening to them from the safety of her room. But now it seemed like it might be fun to play along with them. "Sure, I can," Vivi responded.

"Great!" Andy said. "Chase will be here in about an hour."

"I'll be ready," Vivi said. She looked down and flexed her fingers. They could use a little exercise.

XXI

"It's warm," Andy said, stepping out of the airport.

"It's hot," Bette corrected.

"It feels great," Vivi added. A sultry breeze ruffled her hair, and Vivi's immediate thought was how glad she was to have curls again. Carla had whipped her hair into a bob that brought back all its original bounce. Looking in the salon mirror, Vivi had been surprised, not just by how good her hair looked, but how much better a simple thing like a cut made her feel.

Following Dr. and Mrs. Minkus from the airport across the busy street to the car rental place, Bette, who had never been to Florida, was thrilled by the palm trees that lined the airport streets, while Vivi and Andy were equally delighted to shed the jackets that had been necessary to get them out of Chicago. The process of choosing a car was tinged by bickering between Vivi and Andy about color; however, the ride to the resort where they were staying was blessedly event free. This was mostly due to the car's excellent GPS system, and Mrs. Minkus's determination not to say anything when Dr. Minkus made a wrong turn anyway.

Vivi and Andy had stayed at a number of nice vacation spots with their parents over the years, but as soon as Dr. Minkus pulled into the spacious driveway of the Coconut Bay

Resort, the twins could see this place was going to rank right near the top. As the Minkuses checked in, the kids looked around the airy, field-size lobby that led out from several directions to a wraparound veranda. Huge vases of pink and white blossoms sitting on the marble floors, along with sunshine coming through open doorways and floor-to-ceiling windows, gave the impression of the outdoors being moved inside. Vivi squinted toward one of the doorways and said, "I think I can see water."

"The pool?" Andy asked.

"No. The ocean."

"I can't wait to get out there," Bette said, her eyes sparkling.

"Maybe we can take a walk along the beach later," Vivi said. A walk didn't imply bathing suits, and despite the satisfactory tankinis in her suitcase, she wasn't ready to don one quite yet. Putting together enough clothes for the trip had been a challenge in itself. Fortunately, her mother had purchased some capris, a peasant blouse, and a sundress at the end of last summer for her enlarged figure, and they still fit. Funnily enough, the one who had the most trouble coming up with a wardrobe was Andy. He seemed to be getting taller every day, and now he had a good two inches on Vivi. When, at his mother's insistence, Andy finally tried on his clothes from last summer, Vivi had practically fallen down on the floor laughing. Shorts that had been a respectable length were now short shorts, his summer pants looked like they were cropped, and he had filled out a little, too, because he seemed to be bursting out of his shirts. Since Andy had put off the trying-on until the last minute, Mrs. Minkus told him they'd have to do some shopping as soon as they got to Coconut Bay, which annoyed him to no end. But now, catching sight of a corridor of boutiques, he said to Vivi, "I hope they have something for me to wear in one of these shops. I'm broiling in these jeans."

Dr. Minkus, now holding the room keys, gathered his wife and the kids together and herded them to the elevator.

"What floor are we on?" Vivi asked.

"Eleven," he responded.

"Oh good," Mrs. Minkus said. "We'll have a view."

And what a view it was. A long balcony ran the span of the well-appointed living room, and it looked out at the calm bay dotted with boats. After everyone took a look, Vivi and Bette went to their room; with its two queen-size beds and flat-screen TV hanging on the wall, it was identical to the Minkuses' room. Bette flopped on the bed closest to the full-length window. "Can I have this one?"

Vivi would have preferred that bed, but feeling charitable, she just nodded. Andy came into the room with his suitcase. "I need to put this in here, okay? Mom doesn't want my stuff messing up the living room."

"No," Vivi answered decisively. "We don't want you coming in and out of here whenever you need something. There's a hall closet, put it in there."

"All right." Andy shrugged and left, pulling his small suitcase behind him.

"He's so agreeable," Bette said affectionately.

What kind of description was that? Vivi thought to herself. It was certainly nowhere near "intriguing." Vivi made a note to herself to talk Andy up to Bette. Because as brothers went, Andy was so much more than "agreeable."

Dr. Minkus called into the girls' room, "Vivi, Bette. Can you come out here a minute? We need to talk to you."

Bette got off the bed and said to Vivi, "We couldn't have

done anything wrong yet, could we?" Dr. Minkus always made Bette a little nervous.

"I don't think so," Vivi answered.

When they got to the living room, Vivi's parents were sitting on the couch, her mother already in her tennis outfit.

"Now, kids, we want you to have fun," Dr. Minkus began, "but we also want to know where you are and what you're doing. Unfortunately, I'm here to work more than play, and I have meetings and lectures I have to go to starting this afternoon. In fact, I'm due at one now."

"I'll be around," Mrs. Minkus said. "Mostly at the tennis court, I hope," she added with a smile. "You all have your cell phones with you?"

Andy, Vivi, and Bette nodded.

"So I want you to check in with me at least every hour."

"Every hour!" Vivi protested.

"All right, maybe every other hour. But if you're not together, I want calls or texts from everyone. You too, Bette."

Dr. Minkus pulled three plastic key cards out of his pocket. "You can use these to charge meals or snacks," he said, handing them out. "Don't go overboard."

"No, sir," Bette said.

"'Sir,'" Dr. Minkus repeated approvingly. "Music to my ears." He checked his watch. "Okay, you've got most of the afternoon. Your mom and I will probably have drinks with some of my colleagues, but we should be able to go out to dinner together, and if not, you guys can order room service."

"Andy, before I get down to the tennis court, let's go get you some clothes," Mrs. Minkus said.

"Great." Andy turned to the girls. "Will you wait?"

"Don't take too long," Vivi said.

"Oh, I'll be as fast as I can," Andy muttered.

"Vivi," Dr. Minkus said, turning his attention to her. "Make sure to take your medicine."

"Dad . . . ," Vivi protested.

"It's easy to forget about things like medicine when you're on vacation," Dr. Minkus said firmly.

"I won't forget."

"Well, that's good," Mrs. Minkus said, getting up. "Let's go, Andy."

Once her parents and Andy were out the door, Vivi said to Bette, "I can't wait to get out of these Chicago clothes. What about you?"

"Good idea. And I want to unpack. The stuff in my suitcase is getting more wrinkly by the second."

In the bedroom, each of the girls took a couple of drawers and started shoving their clothes inside. They were really only going to be in Florida for three and half days, but both of them had enough clothes for a week. Vivi took out a white blouse embroidered with tiny red hearts and last year's white capris. She really liked the blouse, she thought as she put it on. It covered a multitude of sins.

"You're kind of dressed up," Bette said as she slipped into a pink T-shirt and a pair of shorts, which, as predicted, were pretty wrinkled.

Vivi immediately became self-conscious. "I have to wear something I look decent in," she said defensively. "I can't just throw on anything."

"You mean like I do?" Bette's eyebrows shot up.

Vivi didn't want a fight her first hour in Florida. "You know it's harder for me to look good."

Bette brushed her brown bangs out of her eyes. "Vivi, it's

not that hard. Even when you didn't look the greatest, you still looked okay until . . ."

"Until what?" Vivi demanded.

"Until you stopped caring," Bette finished bluntly.

Vivi sat down heavily on the bed. For a moment she was quiet. Then she said softly, "I'm starting to care now. It's a little scary, actually."

Bette immediately sat down next to Vivi. "You're feeling better, looking better every day. You should be happy, not scared."

"Do you really think I look better?" Vivi asked, her blue eyes trying to read the truth in Bette's brown ones. "Sometimes I think that cutting down on the steroids is really helping—Dr. Raphael took me down another milligram before we left—but sometimes, I think I look the same."

"Vivi," Bette said impatiently, "it isn't all about how you look."

"Not anymore," Vivi agreed with an unconvincing little laugh. "So I guess I'll try to find that inner beauty everyone says is so important." She was being sarcastic. And yet . . . wouldn't it be, well, a relief not to cling to the idea that how she looked defined her?

Bette seemed as sick of the topic of Vivi's appearance as Vivi suddenly was.

"Let's get out of this bedroom and at least wait for Andy on the veranda," Bette said, getting up. "We're wasting eighty beautiful degrees. Did you bring any sunblock? I forgot mine."

By the time Vivi had found some sunblock in her mother's cosmetics case on her bathroom shelf, Andy was letting himself in the room.

"That was quick," she heard Bette say.

"I don't know why it takes girls so long to shop. I found

some shorts and shirts, Mom paid for them, done. I even wore stuff right out of the store so we could get going."

"What about the tags?" Vivi said, coming into the living room.

"The saleswoman cut them off. Now can we go? I'm hungry."

Dr. Minkus had bought everyone bagels at the airport while they waited for their bags, but Vivi knew it was now way past Andy's feeding time. Lately, he had a huge appetite, which was probably fueling all that growing.

"Mom told me there's a burger bar near the pool," he said as they gathered their things. "Let's try that."

The resort was so large, finding the burger bar proved a little difficult, since it turned out there were three swimming pools. One was a lap pool for the more serious swimmers; the second was slightly larger, surrounded by deck chairs and attached to a kiddie pool so it attracted mostly families. But the pool that entranced them, if you could even call it a pool, was the third. Really, it was more like a river that meandered through the resort, sculpted with tiny coves, some of which contained their own mini-waterfalls. Vivi was impressed. This pool might well be worth getting into a bathing suit for.

"Excellent," Andy said approvingly.

"I can hardly wait to get in," Bette agreed. "Shall we just go back to the room and change?"

Maybe she wasn't quite ready yet. "Why don't we eat first?" Vivi suggested. "The food place is right over there."

Since it was past lunchtime, the burger bar, designed to look like an open-air thatched hut, was almost empty. Before very long, Andy was digging into a burger and fries, while Vivi and Bette picked at salads.

"Can I have some of your fries?" Vivi asked.

"Why didn't you order some yourself?" Andy grumbled.

"Too many calories," Bette answered for her, "but I wouldn't mind a couple, myself."

Andy immediately shoved the plate toward Bette. The difference between a sister and a potential girlfriend, Vivi thought to herself as Andy reluctantly offered her his fries as well. But she waved the plate away when her attention was drawn to a boy walking slowly past the burger bar. He was older than she, but not by much, fourteen, fifteen at the most. Tall and looking as if he worked out. Vivi could only see him in profile, but what a profile it was, strong, attractive, and made more mysterious by the black sunglasses that hid some of his face. Yet it wasn't really his looks that had caught Vivi's attention. He reminded her of someone, but for the life of her, Vivi couldn't think who that might be.

Bette followed Vivi's gaze. "Nice," she said, nodding.

Andy glanced around, too, and when he saw who the girls were looking at, he said, "Oh, him."

Vivi immediately pounced. "You know him? How?"

"His father's a doctor and Dad knows him. They were in the elevator with us."

"What's his name?" Vivi asked. Perhaps, she thought, she had met him before, at some doctor thing, and that's why he seemed familiar.

"Something weird. I didn't catch it."

Bette and Vivi looked at each other. Typical. But maybe, Vivi thought, if he was here with the convention, she'd see him again.

Andy swallowed the final bite of his hamburger. "Can we go swimming now?"

When they finally got changed and settled in deck chairs, the late afternoon sun wasn't nearly as strong as earlier, but after the chill of the Midwest, it still felt delightful. They had picked spots by the largest pool, not far from where they had eaten lunch. Vivi, self-conscious in her swimsuit, had made sure she had her terry-cloth wrap, which, instead of taking off, she wrapped more tightly around her.

"Aren't you going in?" Bette asked as she pulled off the sleeveless T she had worn over her suit.

"Soon." Vivi noticed a little jealously that Bette, long and lean, looked really good in her purple two-piece.

Andy, who apparently got a new bathing suit along with everything else, shifted from foot to foot, clearly ready to get in the water. "Let's go, Bette."

Vivi put on her sunglasses and pulled a magazine out of the straw bag she had brought, which also carried her water bottle and sun lotion. Her angel coin, which she had clutched during the sometimes bumpy plane ride was there, too. Afraid she might lose it, she had carefully zipped it into a side pocket.

Vivi had just started reading an article called "The Hottest Fashion on the Planet" when she felt someone blocking the sun. Looking up, she saw the boy she had noticed before standing over her. Close up, she could tell that his face was not quite so perfect as it appeared from a distance. A thin scar curved from his ear to his chin and dominated the left side of his face. For some reason, it didn't really detract from his appearance. It made him look unique.

"Hi," he said.

"Um, hi."

"Can I sit down?" he asked, pointing to the empty lounger next to her.

"Oh, sure." Vivi told herself she absolutely must get past two syllables in her next answer.

"Is that your brother?" the boy asked, gesturing toward the pool.

"Yes, and my friend Bette." There, five at least.

"I met him in the elevator. My name is Uri."

"Ur-*e*?" Andy was right, the name was weird.

"It's a family name. What's yours?" He took off his black sunglasses, and Vivi could finally see his eyes. They were the color of the sky, which at the moment was a quite brilliant blue.

"Vivian."

"That's a little uncommon, too," he said. Vivi noted a hint of an accent, but she couldn't quite place it.

"Most people call me Vivi."

"Okay," he smiled. "But I like Vivian."

He likes Vivian! Swooning!

"Aren't you going swimming, too? I was in earlier, the water was great." Uri looked at her steadily, as if he expected something of her, though she couldn't imagine what.

Unconciously, Vivi fiddled with her robe. "I think I want to read for a while."

"Do you? Then I won't disturb you," he said, getting up.

Part of Vivi wanted to say, *No, wait, don't leave! I'd much rather find out about you than the gauzy skirts they're wearing in Brazil.* But the boy's unexpected presence had rattled her, and she let him go, first managing to call out, "See you later, maybe." He waved back in response.

Now that Uri was out of sight, the feeling of familiarity Vivi had experienced at the burger bar came flooding back. Who did he remind her of? The question was like an itch that wouldn't go away, but rather than keep scratching, Vivi suddenly decided that the thing to do was divert herself with a swim. Uri was right, the water did look inviting, and no matter how safe it was to sit poolside, broiling in her robe, she was sick of being sidelined. Feeling a rush of the old Vivi, she threw off the robe and marched to the edge of the pool, not even bothering to see if anyone was looking. Easing herself into the pool, Vivi held on to the ledge for a moment, then finally let the water take her.

When was the last time she had been swimming? Vivi couldn't remember, but oh, it felt good. Doing a lazy breast-stroke, Vivi frog-kicked her way down to one of the pool's small coves, where she ducked behind the falling water. It was like standing behind a tiny waterfall, in a space designed at the most for three people. Watching the other swimmers from her secure little vantage point was initially intriguing, but after a few moments of standing there alone, she was bored. Moving out from under the rush of water, Vivi swam a little and floated a little more, while the sun's hot, embracing rays made her duck under the water every once in a while. Surprised that the swimming wasn't exhausting her, Vivi nevertheless decided to get out of the pool before it did. Andy and Bette were already back, playing a card game.

"We texted Mom," Andy said, barely looking up.

"Gin," Bette said, laying down her cards on Andy's lounger.

"I didn't know you played gin," Vivi said to her brother, as she toweled off.

"Bette just taught me," he said, throwing down his de-feated hand.

"I can teach you, too," Bette said, "but we can only play two at a time."

Two at a time was how it went for the next day or so. Andy was taking full advantage of being with Bette, and to-gether they went swimming or played games in the arcade. Tomorrow, they were going to rent bikes and go for a ride along the beach. Vivi was always invited to come along, but she didn't. Bette remarked the next afternoon, while they were resting up before dinner, "I've barely seen you."

"Do you mind?" Vivi asked. Bette didn't. It was kind of fun watching Andy trying to figure out how to go from friend to boyfriend, and coming up with things for him and Bette to do together.

"Well, I want to spend time with you, too, not just Andy, but you've always got your nose in a book or you say, 'Maybe later.' What's up with that?"

"I don't know," Vivi answered honestly. "I just feel like taking it really easy."

"Are you feeling okay?" Bette asked, rolling over on her side.

"Yeah, I am." In fact, Vivi couldn't remember when she had felt better. The sun and water seemed to have a healing effect that was somehow magnified because she was alone. Of course, a part of her was hoping that Uri might appear and intrude on her solitude, but it hadn't happened yet, and she was okay with that, too.

Between conference stuff and tennis, she hadn't seen much of her parents either, but tonight they were all supposed to have dinner together at one of the resort's fancier restaurants. It was going to be the twins' birthday celebration since her parents had to go to a banquet tomorrow.

"What are you wearing for dinner?" Vivi asked Bette.

"I only brought one dress," Bette said, "and I think I should iron it."

"Iron it?" Vivi hooted. "Since when do you iron things?"

"I just want to look nice," Bette responded defensively. Was she blushing or was her redness just too much sun?

Deciding to get inquisitive, Vivi asked, "So, since you're spending a lot of time alone with Andy, how's that going?"

Bette got out of bed and went over to the closet. "I think I saw an iron and an ironing board in here."

"Yes, by all means, don't neglect the all-important ironing. But what else can you tell me?"

Bette said casually, "Andy and I are having fun."

"Yeah, I've been watching you."

"His birthday is tomorrow," Bette said, and then both girls started laughing. "I guess you know that."

"So are you guys going to do anything special?" Vivi asked.

Bette looked shocked. "We wouldn't do anything without you. And we really haven't talked about it."

"But you like him, right?" Vivi finally just spit it out. Enough with the tiptoeing.

Bette shook out her dress and put it on the ironing board, and then went into the bathroom to fill the iron. "What's not to like?"

Vivi barely heard her over the running water, but she smiled.

Although usually the last to be ready, tonight Vivi was the one done dressing first. Since Bette was wearing a dress, Vivi put on the black-and-white dress she had brought and grabbed a white shrug in case the air-conditioning was up too high in the dining room. Andy was on the living room couch, watching TV.

"You haven't even taken a shower, yet," Vivi said.

"Mom's hogging hers, Dad hasn't had his turn yet, and Bette's still getting dressed in your bedroom." He finally took his eyes off the screen. "Hey, you look nice."

"Thank you. I think I'm going to take a walk downstairs and just meet you at the restaurant. Will you tell Mom and Dad?"

"Sure," Andy said, his attention back on the movie he was watching.

Vivi took the elevator down to the lobby, and with no particular place to go, she wandered toward the wide entrance that led out to the water. Before she got outside, though, her attention was caught by an empty banquet room with a piano off in the corner. The room was dim and quiet, but there was still enough daylight for Vivi to make her way easily across the heavily carpeted floor to the piano. It seemed to be calling to her.

There was something magical about being alone in such a big room with such a beautiful grand piano, and after quickly looking around to make sure she was alone, Vivi put her fingers to the keys and began to play a song from *Big River* called "Worlds Apart." It had caught her attention one day while she was looking over the score. There was no violin part in it, so she had never practiced it with Andy. It was a song just for the piano and the voices of Huck Finn and Jim, singing about how though they looked at the same sky, the same stars, they saw them through very different eyes. Despite looking at life through separate prisms, they both took comfort in being together. So she played the song just because she liked it, and it seeped inside her, and maybe because it touched her in the place where it was all right to feel different from everyone else.

When she was done playing, Vivi was startled to hear soft clapping behind her. She whirled around, and there was Uri, smiling at her.

"How long have you been there?" she asked, trying not to show how embarrassed she was.

"I was walking by and heard the music, which was kind of

weird because the room seemed empty. So I followed it, and just came in and listened. You're very good, you know."

Vivi stood up and was about to brush off the compliment, in the same way she was smoothing the wrinkles out of her skirt. But that seemed such a false thing to do, and she instinctively knew Uri would think it was silly, too. So all she said was "thank you."

Uri ran his fingers over the piano keys.

"You play, too?" Vivi asked.

"Not like you," he said with a laugh. "My playing is like Little League. You're the World Series. That's a gift. Do you play in public or just in empty ballrooms?"

"I go to a school that focuses on the performing arts." Then she surprised herself by saying, "But I was away for a while. I was sick."

Uri peered at her. "Are you better now?"

"Getting there."

He looked at her with deep understanding. "I know what it's like to be sick." He touched his scar.

"What happened?" Vivi asked.

"Oh, I had to have something removed. Ruined my looks." He laughed ruefully.

"No, it didn't," Vivi said honestly.

Uri smiled, and at that moment, anyone would have agreed with Vivi's assessment. "Well, the important thing is I survived."

"It's good to remember what's important," Vivi told him, though she immediately realized she was talking to herself as well.

"Yes, it is," Uri replied, and once again, with the intensity of his look, came the strong sense of recognition Vivi had felt before. "Hey," he said, looking around, "it's getting dark. Do you want to go out and watch the sunset?"

That sounded romantic, if a little unusual. "I . . . I should call my parents and see if they're at the restaurant. They might be waiting for me." Pulling her cell phone from her pocket, where it was nestled next to her angel coin, she called her mother, who sounded harried when she answered. "No, we're not there yet. Andy's just dressing now, and your father is on the phone, one of his patients at home is in the hospital. We moved up the reservation time, so you don't have to meet us for at least twenty minutes. Are you getting bored?"

"No," said Vivi, glancing over at Uri. "So I'll just see you at the restaurant." She quickly hung up before her mother could come up with some alternative plan. "I've got time."

"Good, let's go then."

When they got out to the spacious terrace overlooking the ocean, Vivi was surprised to see how many people were there, and they seemed to be waiting for something.

Uri directed her to a spot at the railing where they could watch the sunset.

"Are all these people here for the sunset?" Vivi whispered.

Uri nodded. "It's a Florida thing."

Vivi shrugged and was glad when a woman moved in and took up a smidge of her limited space because it pushed her a little closer to Uri.

"So have you been playing the piano for a long time?" Uri asked.

"About six years."

"What is that, about half your life?"

"No," said Vivi, pretending indignation. "I turn thirteen tomorrow."

"Tomorrow?" He looked as if he was making a note of it. "I have to play golf with my father in the morning, but maybe we could celebrate when I'm done?"

"That would be nice," Vivi said. She wondered if "nice" was the wrong word, especially since inside she was yelping, *fabulous,* but Uri just smiled at her, and everything seemed okay. After that, they just stood there quietly and watched the sun almost plummet into the water as it got closer to the horizon, turning the sky first pink, then red, then violet as it finally disappeared. The viewers dispersed quickly, but Vivi and Uri lingered for a moment. Then, he walked her to the Italian restaurant where she was having dinner. She could see her parents, Bette, and Andy getting out of the elevator, heading down the corridor, and she wanted to say good-bye to Uri before they arrived.

"So, I'll be at the pool tomorrow afternoon, okay?" she said hurriedly.

"I'll be there." Uri nodded and casually walked away.

Food was eaten and conversation went on around her at dinner, but Vivi was only vaguely aware of all that. She was back in the darkened ballroom or out watching the sunset with Uri. After dinner, she and Bette and Andy went back to the room and watched movies, but if someone had asked what they were, she couldn't have come up with titles. The most she would have said was the first one was animated and was sort of scary. The second was about a dog.

As Bette and Vivi brushed their teeth before they went to bed, each with a sink of their own, Bette looked at Vivi's reflection in the bathroom mirror. After spitting out her toothpaste, she asked, "Where were you at dinner?"

"Huh?"

"You ate three pieces of garlic bread, and you hate garlic bread."

"No wonder I feel like I should brush my teeth again." Vivi wiped her lips with a washcloth. The girls got into their respective beds, and Vivi said, "I'm going to turn out my light, but you can read if you want to."

"No, I'm tired, too."

Lying there in the dark, Vivi said, "I watched the sun go down with Uri out on the terrace."

Bette didn't say anything for minute, and then answered with a yawn, "Then I would have had my mind on other things at dinner, too."

As soon as Vivi opened her eyes the next morning, her first thought was *birthday!* followed quickly by *Uri!* After that she didn't have much time to think about anything at all because her parents had arranged for a birthday cake to be delivered for breakfast—breakfast!—and she and Andy received some very satisfying presents, including new iPods for both of them. Then Dr. Minkus surprised everyone by announcing he was taking the morning off from his meetings for a boat ride, which Vivi found exhilarating, especially when they were so far from shore it seemed like water and sky was all there were. Back on land, she glanced at her watch and wondered if it was too soon to start looking for Uri.

With amazing speed, she changed into her bathing suit and, along with Andy and Bette, hit the pool area, but when Andy asked if she wanted to go in, she shook her head and said she would wait. And wait she did, putting down her magazine every few minutes to look around. Then she wondered if she could have misunderstood Uri about the time or maybe the place. After a while, Bette and Andy came back and sat with her.

"We're going to change and then rent bikes," Andy said. "Do you want to come?"

"No, I think I'll stay here for a while."

Andy looked hurt, so Vivi looked at Bette pleadingly. If Bette hadn't already guessed about Vivi meeting up with Uri, she seemed to understand now. "You'll see us later, though, Vivi, right?"

"Oh, sure," Vivi said brightly. About ten minutes after they were gone, though, Vivi was beginning to regret not joining them. What was she doing sitting alone on her birthday waiting for some guy she didn't even know? Gathering her things, Vivi decided to throw in the towel, literally, as she tossed the hotel's towel over the lounge chair and got up.

"Hey, Vivian!" Uri was slightly out of breath as he sprinted toward her.

Vivi wanted to be mad, or at least look nonchalant, as if she was indifferent to his arrival—at last—but she couldn't help smiling at Uri because he was smiling at her.

"I'm so sorry," he said apologetically. "We played eighteen holes, and then I had to make a stop . . ."

"It's all right," Vivi said. "It just gave me more time to work on my tan."

He touched her nose. "More pink than tan. Can you take a walk with me?"

"Sure," she said, slinging her bag over her shoulder.

He led her past the pool area toward the real beach and for a few moments neither of them spoke. Then Uri said, "I was hoping we'd have more time together."

"Well, you're here now."

"Not exactly." He answered Vivi's questioning look. "My father is a bit, well, quixotic. He's decided he's ready to drive home." Glancing at his watch, he added, "I've just got a few minutes."

"Oh, no." The words had slipped out involuntarily.

"I know, it's crummy. I tried to talk him into staying, but he's finished with everything he needs to do at the conference, and when he gets an idea in his head . . . he's checking out now."

Vivi kicked at the sand. "Thanks for coming to find me anyway. You didn't have to."

Uri pulled at her arm. "I said I would. I wanted to."

Looking at him intensely, Vivi asked, "Why?" *Why me?* was what she was thinking.

He seemed to hear the words anyway. "Anyone who heard you play would want to know you better, Vivi. You play like an angel."

Vivi flashed back to a time when she was a small girl and had been lost in a downtown department store. She and her mother probably hadn't been separated very long, but it seemed like forever, and when her mother found her, she had been flooded with relief and happiness. That's how she felt now. Like she had been found.

"Oh, I almost forgot," Uri said, fumbling around in his pocket. He pulled out a small paper bag from the hotel gift shop and handed it to her. "The selection wasn't great," he added ruefully.

She peeked in the bag and drew out a white leather notebook—well, vinyl probably—dotted with black musical notes and closed by a little gold lock, a tiny key dangling from it.

"It's perfect," she said, smiling up at him.

Uri leaned toward her and, as gently as the Florida breeze, kissed her on the forehead. "Happy birthday, Vivian."

They looked at each other for a long moment that was interrupted by a voice calling Uri's name. A man, high up on the terrace where they had watched the sun go down last night, was waving his arm.

"That's my dad," Uri said. "I've got to go." He loped off,

back toward the hotel, and she watched him climb the stone steps to the veranda. When he got to the top, he turned and waved. Then he was gone.

Vivi held the notebook in her hand and flipped through the clean, neatly lined pages before carefully putting it back in its paper bag. Well, she guessed she had gotten herself a gratitude journal after all.

And she knew exactly what the first entry would be.

XXII

Vivi's second huge disappointment came when she returned to school. It was as unexpected as the first.

That one, a big, bad surprise, had come in Florida. It was just moments after Uri disappeared that Vivi realized she had neither his e-mail address nor a phone number. Come to think of it, she didn't even know his last name.

As she walked slowly back toward the hotel, clutching her notebook, Vivi told herself she would just have to bite the bullet and ask her father for pertinent information. Once she knew more, she could see if Uri had a Facebook page or maybe she could track down his phone number and call him at home.

Dr. Minkus was alone in the suite when she got back, which made playing detective a little easier. He wouldn't delve into the hows and whys behind her questions the way her mother would.

"Hey, birthday girl," he called from the bedroom. "Come here for a minute." When Vivi appeared at the door, he asked, "Does my tie look all right with this jacket?" The convention ended tonight with a banquet, and apparently, the doctors were getting dressed up.

"Yes. You look great."

"Thanks," Dr. Minkus said. "I thought I brought two ties, but this is the only one I can find."

"Dad," Vivi began, a little nervously, "I have to ask you something."

"Go ahead, sweetie," he said as he tried to put on his cuff links. "But can you help me with these?"

"Sure," Vivi said. As she fiddled with the cuff link, she asked, "What was the name of the doctor you saw in the elevator the first day we were here?"

"In the elevator . . . ?"

"Yes, and he introduced you to his son Uri." Vivi tried to keep the impatience out of her voice.

"Oh, yeah, a good-looking kid."

"Mmm-hmm," she answered noncommitally as she fastened the second cuff link securely.

"Thanks, Vivi," he said, shaking out his sleeve. "I have no idea who he was."

"What? Andy said you knew him." Vivi tried to keep the panic out of her voice.

Dr. Minkus, picking up his comb and turning to the mirror, was oblivious to the crisis bubbling up in front of him. "You see a lot of the same doctors at these conferences. You meet them, and the next time you see them, they look familiar and you say hello, but you don't really know who they are."

"Dad, this is important. Can't you come up with his name?"

"Vivi, I probably never knew it. We were both in the elevator, he said hi, I said hi. He said, 'Is this your family?' and I think I said, 'This is my wife and my son, Andy, and his friend Bette,' and he said, 'This is my son . . .' What did you say his name was?"

"Uri."

"Okay, Uri. We all said hello, they got out at their floor, and that was it." Dr. Minkus looked at Vivi curiously. "Did you get friendly with this boy?"

She definitely did not want this conversation to veer into mother-question territory. "Not really, I just met him a couple of times. I forgot to get his e-mail address."

"Oh, that's too bad. I can't help you out, though. I have no idea how you'd get ahold of him."

Neither did Bette, after Vivi confided in her that night as they lay in their beds with the lights off. Vivi didn't tell her everything, of course. How could she say that Uri made her feel full of the possibilities of life, when she wasn't sure that was a feeling to even be trusted? The strong sense of familiarity. Well, that she couldn't have explained because she didn't understand it herself. Carefully, though, she told Bette about how they were supposed to meet and how he had to leave and how she had absolutely no way to find him.

"That's awful," Bette exclaimed. "You don't even know his last name?"

Vivi shook her head. "Maybe he can find me, but I don't think he knows any more than I do."

"I'm sorry, Vivi."

She decided to confide one more thing, just because she couldn't keep it to herself. "Bette," Vivi whispered. "He kissed me. Just on the forehead, but . . ." It was as if she could still feel the kiss there.

"Vivi, Andy kissed me, too. Not on the forehead."

For a second, the thought of Andy kissing Bette made her forget Uri. "Really! Wow!" *Way to go, Andy,* Vivi thought.

"It was pretty great," Bette said happily.

Vivi was happy about Bette being so happy, but she couldn't help but be the tiniest bit jealous that Bette and Andy would be able to see each other every day, and she'd see Uri, well, maybe never?

★   ★   ★

Since coming home from Florida, Vivi hadn't been able to come up with one workable idea that would put her in touch with Uri. And since she hadn't heard from him, she assumed he was running into the same roadblocks, that is if he was even trying to get in touch with her. She was almost relieved when school began on Monday, because she did have a plan for that.

As soon as she got to school on Monday, she stopped in the office and asked if she could make an appointment with Mrs. Wu. The secretary looked at her curiously, but said she could stop by at lunchtime. For the rest of the morning, Vivi carefully rehearsed what she was going to say, so she would look assured and prepared.

Bette raised her eyebrows when Vivi told her that she was going to miss lunch because she had an appointment with Mrs. Wu, but that's all Vivi told her.

Vivi felt only a few butterflies flitting in her stomach when she actually took a seat in the principal's office.

"Is everything all right, Vivian?" Mrs. Wu leaned across her desk. "Are you feeling okay?"

"Oh, yes, I'm much better. I'm on a new medication that's really helping."

"Excellent," Mrs. Wu said. "So how can I help you?"

Vivi took a breath. "When I first came back to school, you asked me if I could play one of the shows of *Big River,* and I told you I couldn't. But like I said, I'm feeling better now, so I'll be glad to play the last show." She was secretly glad that the last show was going to be the one that the television station wanted to tape, because a little bit of the limelight sounded fun. That wasn't the reason she had decided to take up Mrs. Wu's offer, though. Maybe it was her own growing realization how important music was to her, or perhaps she was just feeling like herself again. But either way, she was ready to embrace Uri's words about music being her gift.

Waiting expectantly for Mrs. Wu's surprised but happy reaction to her news, Vivi didn't quite realize at first that the expression on the principal's face was not exactly screaming, Oh, goody!

"Well, I'm glad that you think you're up to participating now," Mrs. Wu said carefully, "but things have changed. I just don't think that will be possible."

"I don't understand," a stunned Vivi replied.

"Opening night is just two weeks away. Flora will be playing the first and third shows. Over break, her family decided to move her grandmother's party to Chicago, so everyone can attend *Big River*. The party will fall on the night of the second show, and Mrs. Kepler will play that one."

"Oh," Vivi said, trying to gather her thoughts. "But I thought Mrs. Kepler was just sort of a backup for Flora. Wouldn't you rather have a student playing instead of a music teacher?"

"Vivi, if you had only come to me sooner, or when I first asked you," Mrs. Wu said with a sigh. "But at this late date, it's more than just playing the music. Flora and Mrs. Kepler have been practicing for months and the cast is used to them. Besides, the director has made changes in the music that you don't even know about. It would be too difficult to get you up to speed."

There didn't seem to be anything left to say. Vivi thanked Mrs. Wu and left her office. Once out in the hallway, she stood there and tried to figure out where she should go. She didn't want to return to the lunchroom and have to answer questions about her mysterious visit to the principal's office, which Vivi was in no mood to discuss. She decided to spend the rest of lunch period outside where she could be alone and, instead of eating, try to digest how her plan had gone so wrong.

It was nice out today, warm. Not Florida warm, but springtime-in-Chicago pleasant, and the heavy sweater she was wearing was enough to let her feel comfortable. Wandering over to a secluded stone bench, Vivi sat down. So, no show for her. What good was a gift for music if nobody heard her play?

Still, it was a little hard to be depressed when the sun was shining, a pleasant breeze was blowing, and everything around her was smelling so new and alive. She glanced at a nearby tree and saw that little green buds were appearing on its branches, which made the tree look as if it were covered with a shawl of lacy green. When she was a little girl, before she had been to school, she was fascinated by the way trees would be looking brown and dead one day and showing color the next. She asked her mother how it happened, and why she couldn't see the very moment things began to change.

"Well," her mother had told her. "It's nature. Trees and bushes and flowers go to sleep for the winter, and then when you're not looking, they wake up again."

"It's like magic," the young Vivi had responded.

"Yes, in a way, it is magical."

And even now, after a number of nature units, Vivi still thought it was magical. Okay, she told herself, maybe she couldn't participate in *Big River,* but there would be other musicals to take part in and other venues to play. She couldn't imagine not playing, sometime, somewhere, so, like the leaves, she'd just have to wait until the time was right.

But if making herself feel better had been possible when

Vivi was sitting out in the spring sunshine, it was much harder on Tuesday when she was backstage at the Maple Tree Theater with the old, worn promptbook in her hand.

This was the first day that the kids were getting to perform at Maple Tree, and in the bus coming over, there had been nothing but anticipation and excitement. Vivi had wondered if she could get out of her role as prompter, since the actors knew their lines by now anyway, but she thought she might look like a bad sport if she broached Mrs. Wu now after being turned down as a pianist. So while the cast and crew were trying to get themselves acclimated to their new venue, Vivi found a tall stool and carefully placed it in the wings.

Watching the flurry around her—the musicians tuning up, a couple of actors singing snatches of songs, even costumes being fitted on several reluctant kids—Vivi wished again that she was more a part of things, but she told herself that even if the extent of her participation was just sitting in the wings, waiting for actors to screw up so she could feed them their lines, she would at least try to have some of the fun everyone else seemed to be having.

"Vivian?" Mrs. Wu interrupted Vivi's thoughts. "Do you have a moment?"

"Of course, Mrs. Wu."

"I was thinking about our conversation yesterday. I might have been too hasty,"

Vivi felt her heart flutter a little. "You want me to take one of the shows?"

"Not exactly, no." Noting the disappointment on Vivi's face, Mrs. Wu quickly added, "But there's no reason you can't pick out one number, perhaps one you and Andy have particularly worked on, and perform it in the shows. You're so talented, it would be a shame if we didn't find a way to have you participate."

It was all Vivi could do not to jump off her stool and throw her arms around Mrs. Wu. The instant realization of how that would look to the rest of the assembled cast and crew kept her in place. She didn't try to keep the happiness out of her voice, however, as she replied, "That would be great. We could do 'Muddy Water.' That's mostly piano and violin."

"Wonderful," Mrs. Wu said, patting Vivi's shoulder. "I'll let the director know that you're going to take part, and we'll get you into rehearsal."

Vivi felt like she was in the middle of a happy dream, and over the course of the next two weeks, she didn't wake up. The song "Muddy Water" was the rousing highlight of the show, and Vivi loved being able to sit down at the piano, and, with Andy at her side, bring it to life. What was especially nice was that everyone seemed happy for her: Her friends, of course, and her parents were over the moon. But kids she didn't know very well told her she sounded great, and even Flora didn't seem to begrudge her a turn on the piano bench.

Her one wish was that Uri could be there to see her. She wrote in her journal almost every night, although it was more like a diary with a few nuggets of gratitude thrown in. She especially liked writing in it because holding the book in her hand reminded her of Uri, who now seemed liked a figment of her imagination.

"Vivi," Mrs. Minkus said, coming into her bedroom a few nights before the opening. "With all the excitement, don't forget you have an appointment after school with Dr. Raphael."

"Mom! I can't miss a rehearsal now," she said.

"I explained to Dr. Raphael about the show. She's very pleased you're playing in it, and she agreed to stay late to see you. So we'll go after rehearsal. She's a very special woman," Mrs. Minkus said, and even from her bed, Vivi could see her mother's eyes misting a little.

And that's when it hit her. The someone Uri reminded her of was Dr. Raphael.

After her mother closed the door, a confused Vivi tried to figure out how that could possibly be. What in the world did a teenage boy and a middle-age doctor have in common that would cause Vivi to recognize a similarity, literally at first glance. As she had so many times before, she pulled out her angel coin, this time from her drawer where she had left it for safekeeping. She would have to thank Andy again for this small talisman. There was just something about it that radiated courage and goodness. Come to think of it, wasn't that the same feeling she had gotten from both Uri and Dr. Raphael, right from the first?

Vivi fell asleep, clutching her angel coin, still trying to make sense of this very strange connection.

Then, in what seemed a blink of an eye, it was opening night. Everyone involved seemed aware that he or she was a cog in a moving machine. It was going to take all of them, working together, to make the shows everything they should be. Months of work distilled into three performances.

Opening-night jitters should be called the Oh-My-God-I'm-Freaking-Out Crazies, Vivi thought as she waited for the curtain to go up. The air of anticipation backstage was so thick, it seemed you could poke it with a stick. Then the musicians struck up the overture, the cast took their places, and it was time to go, go, go. There were six songs before she performed in the middle of the first act as Huck and Jim jump on their raft and start their trip down the Mississippi. In the meantime, she was still on prompter duty. To keep her mind off her solo, Vivi paid more attention to following the lines in the script than she probably ever had. Occasionally, she snuck looks at the audience, enjoying themselves and laughing in all the right places. When the time arrived for the "Muddy Water" duet, feeling lots of excitement and the tiniest bit of dread, she left the wings to take her place at the piano.

Smiling tremulously at Andy, who was right beside her with his violin, Vivi put her hands on the keys and began to play:

"Look out for me, oh muddy water / Your mysteries are deep and wide . . ."

About halfway through, Vivi was thrilled to hear the audience clapping along with the music. That made playing even more fun. She put all of herself into the music, humming along under her breath, but every song ends. When this one did, she quickly moved off the piano bench to let Flora reclaim her seat, enthusiastic applause following her back to the wings.

Heart pounding, Vivi took the promptbook back from Joe, who had been drafted into subbing for her. "Awesome job," he said.

"Thanks," she replied, giving him a brilliant smile. She found her place in the book, though if someone actually dropped a line, Vivi wasn't sure she would have known it. Her head was back at the piano, reliving how exhilarating her musical turn had been. The rest of the show was practically seamless, and the few mistakes made were nothing the audience would notice. When Vivi came out to take her bow with the rest of the cast, the feeling onstage was one of pride in the performance and relief that it was over.

The second show wasn't quite as perfect as the opener, perhaps because with one show under their collective belt, the cast felt like *Big River* pros. That bit of overconfidence led to a couple of missed cues and one accident. As Huck, Tom Sawyer, and their pals danced to "The Boys," two of those boys knocked into each other and tumbled over. Fortunately, one of the song lines was "dance them till they all fall down," so Vivi hoped the audience, despite the embarrassed giggles of the "boys," would think it was all part of the act.

When the third and final show rolled around, a late Sunday afternoon matinee, the excitement was up to opening–night level, maybe even higher because of the Channel Two cameramen roaming around filming the show.

"I was so nervous!" Bette whispered to Vivi after she came offstage after one of her solos. "All I could think about was being on TV."

"You were great," Vivi assured her.

"So were you. It was your best yet."

Vivi couldn't disagree. She was a pretty honest judge of her own performances, and even looking at her last solo as critically as she could, she had to say her final rendition of "Muddy Water" was just about perfect. She wished she could tell Uri about it. And even though she knew it was crazy, she felt like somehow he knew.

Then, the lights dimmed, and it was over. Everyone started hugging and laughing, students and teachers both. Gary, their director from Maple Tree, made a short speech about how much everyone had accomplished and how professional the Odom students were, and how she hoped they'd all work together again. There were cheers and more hugging and a little bit of crying. It would have been horrible to just go home after the show was over, but fortunately, they didn't have to. The father of the eighth grader who had played Huck Finn's pa owned an Italian restaurant just a block from the theater, and he had offered it to the school for a cast and crew pizza party.

Vivi walked over with Bette and Andy. When they arrived, they were ushered into a large banquet room that was decorated with a banner that said, "Congratulations Cast of *Big River*." The room filled up, and waiters brought out steaming pizzas of all varieties. Vivi suddenly realized that she was starving.

"Let's eat," Andy said, looking happily at the food. So along with a bunch of other chattering kids, they made their way to the long tables where the waiters had put out the pizza and grabbed a couple of slices each.

There were only a few places to sit, so Vivi, Bette, and Andy took their plates to a corner of the room near a large wastepaper basket. Vivi had just taken a huge bite of pizza when she noticed Joe standing in the middle of the room with his pizza, looking around. Bette waved him over. Vivi noticed that Andy made a face, but he didn't say anything.

Joe hesitated, but he joined them. "Hey, you all did great."

"Thanks," Bette and Vivi answered, almost in unison. "And the scenery was awesome, too," Bette added.

Joe ducked his head. "Yeah, I was kind of hoping Mike, the carpenter from Maple Tree, would be at one of the shows, but I didn't see him."

Vivi's phone, which she had stuffed in the pocket of her jacket, started ringing. "Must be Mom or Dad," she said as she tried to juggle her pizza with one hand and get the phone out of her pocket with the other. When she finally extricated the phone, something else popped out of the pocket. It took an instant for Vivi to realize it was her angel coin. She had kept it in the pocket of the new black velvet jacket she had worn to all three of the performances.

Ignoring the ringing phone, Vivi immediately got down on her knees to hunt for the coin.

"What did you drop?" Bette asked, as Vivi frantically looked for something shiny on the dark wooden floor.

"It's a little medallion thing with an angel on it. I can't lose it."

"What did you say?"

There was something in Bette's voice—was it disbelief or excitement—that made Vivi look up from her search. "An angel coin." Spotting something nestled behind the wastebasket, Vivi sighed with relief, and said, "There it is." She grabbed it from its hiding place and got up. "See," she said, opening her palm. "It doesn't look like much, but there's something special about it."

Bette looked at Vivi with wondering eyes. "Where did you get my angel coin?"

"*Your* angel coin?" a confused Vivi responded.

"I found it in a charity canister full of money that Barbra had collected. She told me I could have it. Then one day in school last fall it disappeared."

"I got it from Andy," Vivi said, "but that was after Christmas." Both girls turned and looked at Andy, who was looking at Joe, who was looking like he wished he were anywhere else.

Vivi and Bette waited impatiently for an explanation, but for a long moment Andy stayed quiet as he figured out just what it was he wanted to say. Finally, he shrugged and said, "Joe gave it to me. He told me to give it to Vivi."

The girls exchanged glances. Joe?

"So how did you get it?" Vivi asked.

There was a moment of silence. Then Joe took a deep breath. "I had it because I stole it from you, Bette."

"You stole it from me?" a shocked Bette repeated. "When, how?"

"It was on your desk. You left it there after a test. And I took it."

"I remember now," Bette said slowly. "I thought I'd left it on the desk, but I went right back, and it was gone. I figured maybe I'd lost it somewhere else. I was frantic to find it." She stared at him. "Why did you take it from me, Joe?"

With each word coming out more uncomfortably than the next, Joe answered, "It was dumb. I was mad at you."

Now it was Bette who was mad. "For what? What did I do?"

"You could sing. And because your life was so perfect, I guess."

Bette just shook her head.

"Like anybody's life is perfect," Andy said under his breath.

"I know, I know. I said it's dumb," Joe said, his voice loud and troubled. He threw his half-eaten pizza in the wastebasket. "You'd been playing with the coin before the audition, and it brought you luck. I guess I wanted some of that for myself because things weren't going so good for me. So when I saw the chance, I grabbed it." Rubbing his hand over his forehead, Joe continued, "You know, it did bring me luck though." He paused. "Sometimes I thought maybe it was more than luck."

This was beginning to sound familiar. Curiosity began to trump Bette's anger. "What do you mean?"

"This guy, Mike, he helped me out, made me think a little different about things, and then my mom, she started feeling better because of Dr. Raphael." He looked at Vivi a little pleadingly. "That's why I wanted Andy to give the coin to you. So you could feel better, too."

Vivi didn't know what to say to Joe. Instead, she turned to Andy. "I thought you bought it."

"No," Andy replied carefully. "Joe gave it to me."

Joe and Andy, who now stood almost eye to eye, looked at each other. The girls could see something—they didn't know what, maybe a current of understanding—pass between the two boys.

"What's going on?" Vivi asked sharply.

"Nothing," Andy said.

"Nothing," Joe agreed. "You found my cat. I wanted to do something nice for you."

Vivi softened. "Well, you did. It helped me out, too."

"Me three," Bette added. "You're right, Joe. Things started to change when I found my angel."

All four of them looked at the small angel coin, still in Vivi's outstretched hand.

"So what do we do with it now?" Andy asked.

"It should go back to Bette," Vivi said promptly. "It belongs to her."

Bette took the coin from Vivi and rubbed her thumb over the angel. "It's kind of great to be able to touch it one more time, but the truth is, I don't feel like I need it anymore."

No one said anything, each lost in his or her own thoughts.

Finally, Joe said, "I have one idea."

Three pairs of eyes shifted to his direction.

"When I came in, I was walking by the register, and I saw they had gum there, so I bought a pack . . ."

"Joe," Vivi interrupted impatiently, "what does a pack of gum . . ."

"I'm getting to it. See, they had a can for charity on the counter, too. After people pay their check, they can throw their change in the can."

Realization dawned on Bette, Andy, and Vivi, and they began to speak all at once.

"Charity can."

"Where it came from."

"Pass it on."

Agreement was reached without another word. As one, they moved through the crowd and made their way to the front of the restaurant, where a smiling woman with her red hair piled on top of her head sat by the cash register. "Can I help you?"

"Oh, we just want to put a donation into the charity can," Bette said.

"Well, isn't that nice. You just go ahead and do that."

"It's for a children's hospital," Vivi said, reading the words on the canister. "Perfect."

"Who should do the honors?" Bette asked.

"I think Joe ought to," Andy said. "It was his idea."

Joe gave Andy a grateful nod, and then asked, "How about we all hold it one more time?"

Even though the room was noisy, the air around their small circle seemed very quiet as they passed their angel from hand to hand. Each of them said a silent thank-you. Maybe one said a prayer. With the others watching, Joe carefully dropped the little angel into the can.

It was gone.

"What do you think will happen to it?" Bette whispered as they turned back toward the party.

Vivi frowned. "I hope it gets to the right place."

"I wouldn't worry about that," Andy said confidently.

"No?" Joe asked. "Why not?"

"It found us, didn't it?"

Thank you for reading this FEIWEL AND FRIENDS book.
The Friends who made

ANGEL IN MY POCKET

possible are:

Jean Feiwel
PUBLISHER

Liz Szabla
EDITOR-IN-CHIEF

Rich Deas
CREATIVE DIRECTOR

Elizabeth Fithian
MARKETING DIRECTOR

Holly West
ASSISTANT TO THE PUBLISHER

Dave Barrett
MANAGING EDITOR

Nicole Liebowitz Moulaison
PRODUCTION MANAGER

Ksenia Winnicki
PUBLISHING ASSOCIATE

Kathleen Breitenfeld
DESIGNER

Find out more about our authors and artists and our future
publishing at www.feiwelandfriends.com.

OUR BOOKS ARE FRIENDS FOR LIFE